Still the One
DEBRA COWAN

D0003496

Silhouette®

INTIMATE MOMENTS™

Published by Silhouette Books

America's Publisher of Contemporary Romance

SILHOUETTE BOOKS

ISBN 0-373-27197-2

STILL THE ONE

Printed in U.S.A.

"Do you really believe we can put the past behind us and work together?" Kit whispered. "Do you really believe we can be friends again?"

Rafe stared into her eyes for a long moment, then lifted a hand and stroked her hair, his palm brushing her cheek. "Yes, I believe it." But his body tensed, and his eyes darkened. Was she asking too much of him? Could she even do it herself?

"Friends..." he murmured, his gaze devouring her. His hand slipped around her nape, urging her toward him. He was going to kiss her....

But then he stopped, looking dazed. "Bad idea," he said in a choked voice.

"Yes." She nodded. "Bad."

Kit wanted to scream. *Friends?* Was she kidding herself? Attraction still simmered between them, an attraction she had to fight. She couldn't get involved with Rafe Blackstock again.

She'd never gotten over him the first time.

Dear Reader,

Happy New Year! And happy reading, too—starting with the wonderful Ruth Langan and *Return of the Prodigal Son,* the latest in her newest miniseries, THE LASSITER LAW. When this burned-out ex-agent comes home looking for some R and R, what he finds instead is a beautiful widow with irresistible children and a heart ready for love. *His* love.

This is also the month when we set out on a twelve-book adventure called ROMANCING THE CROWN. Linda Turner starts things off with *The Man Who Would Be King.* Return with her to the island kingdom of Montebello, where lives—and hearts—are about to be changed forever.

The rest of the month is terrific, too. Kylie Brant's CHARMED AND DANGEROUS concludes with *Hard To Tame,* Carla Cassidy continues THE DELANEY HEIRS with *To Wed and Protect,* Debra Cowan offers a hero who knows the heroine is *Still the One,* and Monica McLean tells us *The Nanny's Secret.* And, of course, we'll be back next month with six more of the best and most exciting romances around.

Enjoy!

Leslie J. Wainger

Leslie J. Wainger
Executive Senior Editor

Please address questions and book requests to:
Silhouette Reader Service
U.S.: 3010 Walden Ave., P.O. Box 1325, Buffalo, NY 14269
Canadian: P.O. Box 609, Fort Erie, Ont. L2A 5X3

Books by Debra Cowan

Silhouette Intimate Moments

Dare To Remember #774
The Rescue of Jenna West #858
One Silent Night #899
Special Report #1045
"Cover Me!"
Still the One #1127

DEBRA COWAN

Like many writers, Debra made up stories in her head as a child. Her B.A. in English was obtained with the intention of following family tradition and becoming a schoolteacher, but after she wrote her first novel, there was no looking back. After years of working another job in addition to writing, she now devotes her full time to penning both historical and contemporary romances. An avid history buff, Debra enjoys traveling. She has visited places as diverse as Europe and Honduras, where she and her husband served as part of a medical mission team. Born in the foothills of the Kiamichi Mountains, Debra still lives in her native Oklahoma with her husband and their two beagles, Maggie and Domino.

Debra invites her readers to contact her at P.O. Box 30123, Coffee Creek Station, Edmund, OK 73003-0003 or via e-mail at her Web site at http://www.oklahoma.net/~debcowan.

ACKNOWLEDGMENTS

My deepest thanks to the following:
Ken and Lisa Gonzales for their help
with Colorado detail; Dr. Lee Warren, M.D.,
Chief Resident, Department of Neurosurgery
(thanks, cuz!); Vickie Taylor for hooking me up
with her brother, a great source of information;
and Captain Scott Spears, USAF.

Chapter 1

"What the—" Rafe Blackstock stopped cold in the doorway of his private investigations office. "Kit?"

The slender woman turned. Though her thick mink-dark hair was short now, her eyes were still the same unusual slate blue he remembered and deep with the same wariness, the same uncertainty as the last time he'd seen her. "In the flesh."

"I'll say." On this perfect June Sunday, he'd walked right in on his past, and his past looked darn good. Her faint musky scent squeezed his lungs.

His breath jammed somewhere under his ribs, but Rafe walked in and shut the door as if he hadn't just had the wind knocked out of him. He was disoriented, his head swam, and he had to remind himself where he was. Oklahoma City, not Norman. Not standing ten years deep in yesterdays.

He didn't know whether to shake her hand or hug her, so he simply stood there, arms hanging limply at his sides.

She gave him an uncertain smile. "Hello."

"Hey."

Kit Foley, who'd been his first love, who'd broken his heart and walked away. Kit, whom he'd thought he would never forget. She was here. Ten years older, beautiful in the way a woman becomes when she grows into her skin, her identity. It hurt his chest to look at her.

This case—her case—was the reason his office manager, Nita Howard, had paged him on Lake Arcadia about a missing persons case, why he'd put down that brand-new fiberglass rod.

Kit's dark-rimmed eyes paused hungrily on his features. Her voice went soft and shy, the way it did when she was in an uncertain situation. "It's been a long time."

No kidding. And Rafe suddenly felt every day of those long years in the wary pull of his muscles, the way her smoke-and-honey voice still stroked up his spine like warm fingers. Resentment, disbelief, unwelcome pleasure fused inside.

Kit. He couldn't stop his gaze from sliding down her body, the way his hands had done numerous times. "Lookin' good."

She blushed. "You, too."

Her coltish figure had rounded out, the angular edges of her hips now soft, her waist nipped in tightly. Her breasts were fuller, curving beneath the short-sleeved, cotton floral dress she wore. The wavy dark brown hair that had once reached the middle of her back was a shiny wedge that came just below her delicate ears. The style sharpened her cheekbones, highlighted her perfectly straight nose.

She was stunning. Her wide, dark-lashed eyes were bright with unshed tears, he realized, as her troubled gaze sought his.

"I need you—your help."

I need you. His muscles clenched against those words.

In the end, she hadn't wanted to need him, had wanted to stand on her own. She'd proven that by walking away.

He thought he'd forgotten how shattered he'd been when she refused to marry him the day before his college graduation. Thought he'd forgotten how pain had closed over him with brittle frigidity when she'd stammered that she couldn't leave her family responsibilities. Couldn't live with the way he took total control. She wanted a partner, not someone who made decisions without her.

Feeling as off balance as the day the Air Force had permanently grounded him from flying, Rafe walked around her to his desk. He felt a foolish urge to ask Nita to come in, but his office manager had left as soon as he arrived.

Kit's voice trembled, edgy and staccato. "I'm sure I'm the last person you want to see.... I didn't know where else to turn."

She was certainly the last person he'd *expected* to see. That old familiar awareness throbbed to stilted life. "How did you find me?"

"Um, this." She pulled a black pocketbook from her purse and slid out a neatly folded piece of newspaper. She handed it to him. "I saw this about three years ago."

Rafe skimmed it, his gaze going to hers as he realized it was the article the Associated Press had picked up on him. Two weeks after Rafe had left the Air Force, a child belonging to a major in Rafe's old Air Force detail had been kidnapped by the major's estranged wife. Rafe had set out on a one-man mission to find the child and succeeded. He'd also testified in the subsequent custody trial. The local paper had done a story, which had been picked up by AP.

Kit had seen the article. And kept it. Not knowing what to think about that, not wanting to think anything, Rafe handed it back to her.

She smiled uncertainly, slid the clipping in her pocketbook. "I called Kevin to see where you were and he told me. I found your phone number in the book."

He'd spoken to Kevin Strong just yesterday, and his college roommate hadn't mentioned a thing about Kit. Rafe made a mental note to tell his friend not to be so free with information.

Still not believing she was here, he cleared his throat. "How are you?"

"Fine." She shoved a thick lock of hair off her forehead, giving a sharp laugh. "Well, not really. That's why I'm here."

Rafe tried to dodge the images that crashed over him— the throatiness of her laugh, the sleek feel of her body against his, the tight perfection of his inside her. She'd been his first love. Even if he told himself he'd forgotten her, he hadn't.

Whatever had happened, he couldn't take this case. Right now that was the only clear thing in his mind, but still he couldn't deny a burning curiosity to find out what she'd been doing the last ten years, where she'd been.

"I can pay. Or…I guess I should ask about your fee."

"We'll work that out." Was she married? Divorced? Children?

He didn't want to ask or even acknowledge the questions ricocheting through his mind, didn't want to admit to the heat that squeezed his chest at the thought of her with another man. He'd moved on.

He knew their relationship on her side had never been as committed as it had on his. After so long, it shouldn't make him wince that it had taken him an entire year to get rid of her engagement ring. "What's happened?"

"It's Liz." She hesitated then said, "She's missing."

"Again?"

"Don't start, Rafe. This is serious."

"With *your* sister?" He arched a brow. "Since when?"

She gave him a flat stare.

"You're sure she didn't hook up with some guy at a bar?"

"I'm sure," she said tightly. "She's not like that anymore."

Rafe couldn't even imagine such a transformation, but neither could he ignore the panic in Kit's eyes.

Indicating the straight-backed chair in front of his desk, he eased himself down into his own overstuffed gray leather chair, grateful for the support at his back. "Tell me what happened."

Instead of sitting, she began to pace. Her soft cotton dress curled around her calves and clung to her lithe body, molding her perfect breasts. Rafe forced his gaze to her face, picked up a pen and pulled a legal-size notepad over to him.

"Can I get you something? Water, a Coke?" He was amazed at how calm he sounded, especially when he wanted to ask a million questions. *Do you still live in Tulsa? What have you been doing? Do you ever regret turning me down?*

She flashed him a tremulous smile, but her worry was tangible. "No, thanks."

He'd smelled this same raw desperation before in each of the twenty missing persons cases he'd solved.

"I'm a flight attendant for TransAmerica. Yesterday morning, I returned from a layover in Miami. I had a message, only thirty minutes old, from the hospital on my answering machine. The nurse said Liz had been in a car wreck." Kit dragged an unsteady hand through her hair. Fatigue and worry drew her features taut, flattened the sweet curve of her full lips. "I raced over, but when I got there, Liz was gone."

"Did you check at the nurses' station? Maybe she—"

Kit shot him a look. "Of course. They told me they

wanted to keep her overnight for observation, but she'd left with her husband, Tony Valentine.''

"Liz is married?"

"No. Yes. Supposed to be getting a divorce."

"Ah."

Kit's dark glare skewered him.

"And you?"

She blinked. "Me?"

"Married?"

"No." The word practically exploded from her.

Yes, that sounded like the Kit he knew. His mouth twisted, despite the satisfaction curling through him.

She shoved a hand through her hair again, then clasped her hands together. "Anyway, Liz just up and left with Tony."

Which was just like Dizzy Lizzy Foley, Rafe reminded himself. "Maybe she got back together with her ex."

"She lives with me. I would've known."

"Maybe she didn't want to tell you. She *used* to take off with one man or another a lot."

"Something's happened," Kit said stiffly. "Liz wouldn't just go off like this."

"What about that time she ran off with the high school quarterback? Stephen Hankins?" Rafe reminded her. "They were in Mexico, plastered on margaritas and begging a priest to marry them when you found her."

That had been right after the death of Rafe's grandfather. Kit had come home with him for the funeral, then left before it even started to chase after her sister. *Again.* Resentment curled through him. He thought he'd forgotten about that. Apparently not.

"So you won't help me?" Kit stopped in front of his desk, anger snapping in her eyes.

He kept his gaze on her, refusing to dwell on the protective urge that shot through him. "She *is* an adult and there doesn't seem to be any sign of foul play."

"She called me this morning, terrified."

He tapped a finger on his desk. "What did she say? Did she go with Tony willingly?"

"She said she couldn't talk long because the call could be traced. She told me she was all right, that she'd be calling me later to wire some money."

"To where?"

"She's going to let me know. In the meantime, I can get some money together."

Rafe bit off the sharp comment that rose to his lips and said gently, "It doesn't sound as if she's in trouble, Kit."

She inhaled deeply, her eyes fluttering shut briefly. "She is."

Whether Liz was in trouble or not, he could see Kit believed she was. Using his most soothing tone, he put himself on automatic pilot, which he should've done from the beginning. "Talk to me."

Her hands, on top of his desk, fisted. Then unfisted, fisted. "Tony, her husband, was in prison for a computer scam and he was released about two weeks ago."

Rafe held up a hand. "Wait a minute. Liz married a *computer* guy?"

"Yes."

"She doesn't go for computer guys."

"She did."

"He's not into sports at all? Doesn't play basketball or drive race cars or something?"

"No." Kit tucked a piece of hair behind her ear. "I told you she's changed."

Evidently not enough, Rafe thought.

Walking to the opposite wall, Kit halted in front of a vintage black-and-white photograph of turn-of-the-century Oklahoma City. She wrapped both slender arms around her waist. "Tony got a job, was really trying to get his life straightened out."

Her tongue darted out to moisten her rose lips.

Rafe's belly drew up at the sight of that tongue, and he glanced down, scrawling some notes.

"I'm not sure I understand it all myself," she said. "When Liz called, I told her to put Tony on so he could tell me what was happening. Evidently he was sent to prison for manipulating stock prices on the New York Stock Exchange, making some money for a friend in serious financial trouble. Tony told me that while he was in prison, a man contacted him, a man with ties to organized crime."

"Did he give you a name?"

"Alexander."

"First or last name?" Rafe's gaze tracked Kit's agitated movements across his plush burgundy carpet.

"He didn't say." She surreptitiously swiped at a tear, and Rafe's heart squeezed. She hated crying, hated even more for people to see it. Pulling a piece of paper from the side pocket of her purse, she passed it to Rafe. "Liz left this for me at the hospital."

Rafe took the note, read the curvy scrawl. *The mob's after us. I'll call.*

He resisted the urge to roll his eyes at Liz's dramatics.

Kit went on, "This man wanted Tony to pull the same scam for him on the prison computer, but Tony said he refused. Alexander threatened to hurt Liz if Tony didn't do what he wanted. Tony said that man—" She halted, her shoulders sagging.

Concern had Rafe's fingers curling into the arms of his chair. During that intense year they'd dated, he'd seen Kit cry only once, and it hadn't been the day they'd broken up. It had been the day she'd heard that her sister had eloped with the local hockey team's goalie. That had been marriage number one. He wasn't sure what number Tony, the computer guy, was.

Rafe knew he shouldn't touch Kit, but he rose, walked around his desk and settled his hand on her shoulder anyway, trying to discount the way she leaned slightly into his touch, the way her body heat shot straight up his arm.

She kept her head averted. Her musky scent slid into his lungs, knotting him up with regret and awareness. His hand was mere inches from the creamy flesh of her throat, the warm cleft where her neck and shoulder met, where he used to—

Get a grip. "Are you sure I can't get you something to drink?"

"No, thanks." She dragged in a deep breath, then went on in a wobbly voice that mangled his insides. "Tony said Alexander was responsible for Liz's accident, that he made it happen."

"Where was it?"

"Just north of One Fiftieth Street on Western. There's a hard curve there."

He nodded. "On the edge of Edmond city limits. I'm familiar with it."

Just two weeks ago, a man had made the local news for taking that curve too fast and flipping his car forty feet into the ravine below. Liz could've done the same thing.

"So," Kit said, "Tony did what Alexander wanted while he was in prison."

"Using the prison's computer? How long did it take the warden to catch him?"

"Never."

Rafe's eyes widened.

She glanced over. "He's that good, Rafe. A computer guru."

He nodded, prompting her. "But when he got out, Tony refused to help Alexander?"

"Yes."

"So you think Liz's accident was deliberate. And now she's disappeared with Tony. I can see why you're concerned," Rafe said gently. With some surprise, he recognized a flare of anger. Liz was always pulling stunts, putting Kit through all kinds of hell and expecting her to ride to the rescue. "Doesn't Tony think Alexander will look for him?"

"I really don't know what he thinks." She stepped away from Rafe and pulled a tissue from her purse.

Rafe's hand fell to his side, and he moved back to his chair. Jaw tight, he shrugged off the insidious thought that she'd once again rejected him.

"I begged Liz to meet me somewhere, but Tony said those men might be following me, too. I haven't seen anyone, though."

If someone from the mob was really tailing her and they knew what they were doing, Rafe knew she *wouldn't* see them. "She could be with Tony on a lark, Kit. Look at her track record."

"I know her track record!" Her gaze shot to his. "Would I be here asking for *your* help if I thought this was a joyride?"

Ouch. "You have to admit she's done this before."

"This is different, Rafe. I can tell. I heard how frightened she was."

"Of Tony?"

She frowned. "I don't think so."

"Did anyone at the hospital hear or see a struggle? Did Liz scream?"

"No, nothing." Worry carved deep lines beside her mouth.

"She probably went with him voluntarily, Kit."

"I don't know. I guess."

He hated the torture in her soft blue eyes. "So why would she do that?"

"She believes him, I guess."

"About Alexander?"

"And Tony's claim that he's turning his life around. He's called her every night since he got out, trying to mend fences. I thought she'd stand firm this time."

Kit said this last half under her breath, causing Rafe to narrow his gaze. She'd never said anything less than supportive about Liz before.

"He knows he made a stupid mistake and he's trying to fix it. He was doing well in his new job."

"If Liz went willingly, and it sounds like she did, there's really nothing you can do."

"I've got to find her."

"She'll come home. She always does."

She stared at him, her eyes huge in a face gone pale as chalk. "Tony said he could disappear, invent whole new identities for both of them. He can do it, Rafe. The FBI said it was a fluke they ever traced him to that computer scam in the first place. But running isn't the answer. Tony should confront the problem, not spend his life looking over his shoulder. Or forcing Liz to do the same."

Anger blunted her words. "I don't know if I should believe Tony or not, but can I afford not to? I've got to find Liz and help her, in case Tony *is* telling the truth about the mob being after him. I can't just turn my back on her."

She never had been able to, and Rafe knew she probably never would. Due to the death of their mother when Kit was fourteen and Liz eleven, Kit had taken on the role of mother rather than sister.

"I went to the police," she said. "They said there was nothing they could do. But I remembered that your uncle Wayne was with the FBI and he worked organized crime."

Her gaze, pleading and somber, locked with his. "That's why I came here."

Besides his uncle, Rafe had other contacts in the FBI. Which was why he knew the mob *was* moving into Oklahoma. "Why doesn't Tony just go to the FBI himself?"

"He doesn't have any evidence yet."

"Kit—"

"He told me he snatched Alexander's computer on the way out of town, that he's going to get the evidence off of there, but right now he doesn't have it."

"Tony's parole officer can go after him. Have you contacted that person?"

"Not yet."

"We'll do that." Rafe made another note. "The more people looking, the more pressure, the better chance of finding them."

"So you'll help me?" The hope in her voice, her face, latched on to his conscience.

He knew he should pass this case off, but he couldn't.

She'd been his first love. That connection would always be there, always mean something.

Bottom line—Rafe had never been able to turn his back on her.

"Please say you'll help me." Kit's voice rasped. "You know how to find people. I don't. Please, Rafe."

Her whispered plea raked up memories of another whisper.

I can't marry you. I want a partner, not a master.

She had always equated his proposal to giving up her independence. Ten years ago, Rafe had been exactly what she didn't need. Or want. Resentment burned through him as he ran a hand over his face. And yet... Kit needed his help. Their past shouldn't matter. He wouldn't let it. "Yes, I'll help you."

Chapter 2

Relief washed through her, and Kit let out the breath she'd been holding. "Thank you. Where do we start?"

Something sharp flickered in Rafe's eyes, and she was painfully reminded of their ending, the last time they'd seen each other. Regret flared, but she squelched it. Breaking things off with him had been best for both of them. She refused, as she had for the last ten years, to second-guess that decision.

"Start by telling me where Tony might go."

"I don't know. His parents in Davis, maybe." She could still feel Rafe's touch on her shoulder, a gentle comfort, yet it branded her skin. She began to pace again, thrusting a hand through her hair.

He spared her a glance, scribbling notes on a yellow legal pad. "Any place he and Liz might go together?"

"His apartment, but I already checked it out. No one was there."

She couldn't help staring as Rafe continued jotting notes.

The lush eyelashes, the too-straight patrician nose he'd inherited from his white mother. The high cheekbones, dark slash of brows and burnished skin testified to his Choctaw father. Rafe's blatantly male features were leather dark, lined by confidences she'd never shared, smiles she'd never seen.

While waiting for him in his office, she'd steeled herself against the old attraction, but she hadn't been prepared for the actual sight of him. The sleek black hair trimmed military short. The sculpted lips that had once turned her bones to water. Corded neck and biceps bared by the khaki T-shirt that loosely covered his hard, rangy chest. Lean runner's legs gloved in worn, starched denim. And scuffed tennis shoes.

"Where's his apartment?"

She dragged her gaze from Rafe, resumed her pacing. The movement helped dispel the warmth that had started to creep into her blood.

She gave him the name and address of a complex on the north edge of Oklahoma City, only a mile from her own house. The warmth of spring clung to him, as well as a mysterious scent that belonged solely to him. Not musky, not woodsy, but something in between.

Kit's pulse throbbed heavily, and her throat grew tight. He was still the most beautiful man she'd ever seen. For a moment, her worry over Liz was pushed aside in a sudden surge of emotion—regret, sharp and bitter. Affection, uncertainty.

Questions tumbled through her mind. What had brought Rafe back to Oklahoma City? Why had he left the Air Force?

The shock in his face upon seeing her had unnerved her, but not nearly as much as that instantaneous sultry heat in his eyes. Those black, smoldering eyes were now obsidian hard, remote.

Kit squared her shoulders, trying to push away everything except thoughts of her sister. She became aware that Rafe watched her impersonally, waiting for her to continue.

"Liz lives with me. She has for the last couple of years, since Tony went to prison."

He nodded, making another note.

Her heart squeezed at his distance. What did she expect? That he would greet her as if she were an old friend? Kit had ruined that when she'd refused to marry him. Rafe's matter-of-fact announcement that they would marry hadn't been the first unilateral decision he'd made, but it had been the one to unleash a long-buried panic.

Since her mom's death, Kit had made all the decisions in her family with the exception of a few financial ones. Her dad's work schedule prohibited him from spending much time at home, and Kit had stepped into the void left after her mom's death, taking care of the house and her sister. At first, she'd thrilled to Rafe's take-charge attitude, to the fact that she'd found someone willing to shoulder her burden. But when he'd expected her to move east with him so he could attend Navy flight school, just up and leave her father and sister, she'd realized she couldn't marry someone who made those decisions alone. She wanted to be his partner, not his insignificant other. So she'd said no to him.

The years had made a noticeable difference in him. He had always been lean, but now there was a whipcord strength in that leanness. A soberness in his eyes and face. A sense of…unpredictability that had Kit's pulse kicking up a beat. She shoved an unsteady hand through her hair again.

His cool black gaze urged her on.

So Rafe was gorgeous. And as remote as a stranger. So what? He was going to help her find Liz. That was what mattered.

A memory clouded his eyes. For an instant, some of the tension in his face melted away. "You said you were a flight attendant for TransAmerica?"

"Yes." On one of their first dates, they'd discussed the fact that Rafe wanted to be a pilot and Kit wanted to be a flight attendant. High with the exhilaration of new love, they'd declared it fate that they'd met and become involved.

Kit swallowed the sudden lump that rose in her throat.

His face closed again. "Where did Tony work?"

"For a major computer manufacturer." She gave the name. "He developed software for them."

"This was his most recent job? The one he started just out of prison?"

"Yes. I called there yesterday and left a message with the answering service for a friend of his, Mike."

"I'll check that out tomorrow."

"I also went down to Davis and spoke with Tony's parents. They haven't heard from or seen him."

"Could they be lying? Maybe hiding him?"

"Maybe, but I don't think so." Kit realized her hand was in her hair again and lowered her arm. Inhaling deeply, she took in the slight tang of Rafe's scent. Though quiet and often reserved, there was a steadiness, an intensity about him that filled a room. "They were very upset when I told them what was going on. They haven't seen Tony since he went to prison—they were too embarrassed and angered by what he did."

His gaze narrowed on her long enough to make her skin prickle with an unwelcome heat. Apprehension and a hint of anticipation swirled inside her, emotions that had nothing to do with her sister and everything to do with the man across from her.

"What if they're off in Las Vegas or some place like that?"

"I still need to find her."

"Would Tony hurt her?"

"I don't think so. I think he really did take Liz with him out of concern for her safety. I mean, we can't discount that, right?"

"I won't discount anything. I'll look at every angle. I'll start by going to his apartment, checking things out."

"I went there and couldn't find anything."

"I might know other things to look for."

"Of course." Kit couldn't help the stiffness of her tone. His silent scrutiny, the stoic face all combined to make her want to squirm. Through the years, she'd learned to handle some fairly intimidating men, and she didn't appreciate the way just one measuring look from Rafe could make her feel as if she were in his way.

"I'll also check with his parole officer."

"I didn't think to do that." She shook her head. "This whole thing has knocked me for a loop. I'm so upset I probably did miss something at Tony's apartment." She forced a smile, her chest tight and aching.

"That's what I'm here for. I'll look for anything that might give a hint to where Tony could've gone. Check with the airlines and the bus depot, see if he bought a ticket using a credit card, though I doubt it."

"I can do that." Kit pulled a scrap of paper and a pen from her purse.

"No."

Hand poised over her purse, her gaze snapped to his. "What?"

"*I'll* do all the checking and call you when I've found something."

She stiffened, crumpling the paper in her fist. "I want to help."

"I know what I'm looking for. You don't."

His voice was gentle, but steel rimmed the words and

sent a shaft of irritation through her. She'd hoped the years might've mellowed his insistent control. "I'm coming with you."

"None of my other clients—"

"I'm coming." The old anger swept in along with a flash of panic. Telling herself Rafe simply didn't understand how important this was to her, she took a deep breath. "I need to be there when you find her."

"I don't know anything about this Alexander character. If he actually is connected to the mob, he could be dangerous. Besides, you need to be safe and sound so Liz has someone to come home to when I do find her."

"She's supposed to call me. Wouldn't you rather be around to hear it?"

"You'll let me know."

She hesitated, then blurted, "Do you not want me along because of the past? Because of what I...what happened?"

His lips flattened. "No."

"I wouldn't blame you."

"I said no." Rafe bit out the words.

Kit took in the steel jaw, the piercing, narrowed eyes. Had he ever forgiven her for refusing him? "I won't get in your way."

She couldn't tell if she was reaching him or not. The Rafe she'd known—loved—hadn't had those black eyes that hardened to marble. Hadn't been able to disappear beneath a stoic mask of indifference. She couldn't tell what he was thinking or feeling. Panic sawed at her.

"I can't just sit around and do nothing."

"I don't like working with anyone," Rafe said bluntly.

"Well, I didn't *love* coming in here, but I did it." She clenched her fists, stepping toward him. "Liz is in danger. I have to find her. You don't know what it's like to feel helpless, to feel—"

"I do know." His voice lashed the air as he pushed out of his chair, tension coiling in his broad shoulders.

Kit took a reflexive step back, frowning at the harsh emotion beneath his words.

"I know helplessness, second-guessing, uncertainty—" He broke off, anger vibrating from him. "Don't tell me I don't."

She shook her head. "I didn't mean—I'm sorry."

"Don't presume to know anything about my life, Kit. Don't make assumptions about me."

What had happened? She swallowed the question. She had no right to know anything about him, no right to care. She'd given that up long ago.

He leaned across the desk toward her, eyes blazing, a muscle flexing in his jaw. "Just because we were involved once doesn't mean you know me *now*. Doesn't mean you know anything about me."

"I could say the same to you."

The air snapped tight, hummed with old anger, past hurts.

Fury tautened his carved features; his throat worked. "Let's agree to stick to this case," he said hoarsely. "And facts about this case *only*."

She nodded, her mouth dry, her heart hammering with the same wildness it had the first time she'd ever noticed him. He'd been running to class, up the hill past her. Long, lean legs bared by denim shorts, moving with a muscular fluidity that slowed her steps. The wispy image of his burnished flesh sliding against her pale skin floated through her mind.

She slammed the door on those thoughts. She wasn't going to let her hormones—or her memories—get in the way of finding Liz.

"It's not a good idea for you to come along," he said, pinching the bridge of his nose.

"Still think you ought to be calling all the shots, don't you, Blackstock?"

Surprise widened his eyes a fraction. "This is how I do business."

"This is why we didn't work out ten years ago."

Says you. His hands fisted as he studied the opposite wall. "I can move faster if I'm alone. And there will be situations where people might not talk to me if you're around. This really is best, Kit. Take it or leave it."

Ten years ago, she'd walked away from this very thing, but she didn't have that luxury now. "Maybe my sitting around doing nothing is not best for me. Or for Liz."

"Let me do my job. I'll check in with you as often as you like, every step if you want, but it's best if I'm solo."

She set her jaw, her gaze burning into his. "I'm paying your fee. I should get to call the shots."

"Not with me."

Frustration hardened her voice. "How did you get in this line of work, anyway? It's got nothing to do with flying jets."

His face closed. "Long story."

One he plainly wasn't going to tell *her*. Swallowing against a sharpness in her throat, she said, "Fine."

He tapped a finger on the desk, his gaze scouring her face. "No more talk about the past."

"Fine." She knew *that* was for the best, but the old wound inside her cracked open.

He irritated her, but even so, he was the one man she regretted walking away from. The one man who could reach places in her no one else ever could.

She couldn't ignore the knot in her belly that was part anger, part anticipation. Not affected by him? Who was she kidding?

She wanted him to reassure her, tell her he'd find Liz quickly, that she would be able to handle all this. But she squared her shoulders against the maverick wish. She needed Rafe to find her sister. That was all.

She couldn't let herself start needing him for anything else.

The sun sank to the horizon in a smear of gold and purple, edging the clouds with shimmering light. As Rafe drove north on May Avenue behind Kit's car, following her from her brother-in-law's apartment to her house, he rolled his shoulders against an edginess that worked through him, made him feel cornered. What he wanted right now was distance, but he'd needed Kit's access to Tony Valentine's apartment and her house.

She hadn't been shy about letting him know she didn't appreciate the way he did business. Even now, his blood charged at the thought. That sassy, sharp-tongued woman was not the Kit he'd known. No, sir. And he liked this new Kit. Which was why it would be better for both of them if he worked alone. Hell, it would be better for *him*. He needed to stay on this side of the past. Letting her tag along on this case would make that difficult, if not impossible.

He didn't like the idea of spending a lot of time with her. Hell, *any* time with her. Rafe's lips twisted.

The scent of fresh-cut grass and car exhaust drifted through the window of his '67 Stingray. Golden light shimmered across the Corvette's sleek black hood. He was making a big deal out of nothing. It was the shock of seeing her—his first love—after all these years, that was all. Plus the fact that he didn't like working with anyone, especially the client who'd hired him. But with Kit there was another layer.

Calling in to report once or twice a day he could handle. Breathing the same air, smelling her provocative scent, having her in his space—no, thanks.

He rubbed his chest against the ache that had settled

there upon first seeing her. The focus, the action of working the case would enable him to treat her like any other client. Eventually.

So far, so good. They hadn't discussed the old days while Rafe had searched Tony's place for scraps of paper, plane or bus ticket stubs, anything that might give a clue as to where Valentine had gone.

On the assumption that Valentine really was being watched by the mob as he'd told Kit, Rafe had swept the guy's place for bugs and surveillance equipment. And found nothing. As a precaution, he needed to sweep Kit's place, too. If he didn't find anything there, he'd be free to start working the case. *Alone.*

As he swung his 'Vette behind her late-model four-door compact in the drive of a small brick house, his stomach clenched. He'd never seen Kit's home, never known she lived in this popular older neighborhood. After college, she'd gone to work for a major airline in Tulsa. How long had she been in Oklahoma City? Longer than the three years since his own return?

Those questions had nothing to do with her supposedly missing sister. Rafe pushed them aside as he got out of the car, grabbing his device for detecting transmitters and his cell phone. Sergeant Kent Porter, a buddy from the Oklahoma City Police Department, had promised to call Rafe back after reviewing the report of the traffic accident that had sent Liz to the hospital. Porter had also said he would see what he could find out about any do-wrongs named Alexander.

Rafe followed Kit up the neatly swept concrete porch steps, flanked by terra-cotta pots brimming with yellow and white petunias. There were no memories for him here, nothing to distract him from the case.

Except the woman whose hips swayed so compellingly as she moved across the porch.

From the corner of his eye, he caught a flash of silver. He turned in time to see the tail end of a sedan cross the intersection at the end of the block. It looked like the same car he'd seen a few minutes ago on May Avenue, right before Kit had turned into her neighborhood. Which could mean that they lived nearby. Or that someone was tailing her.

The little pinch in his gut told Rafe it was the latter, but he'd check again for the car before he left to speak to Valentine's parents. He turned his attention to her home as she opened the front door and stepped inside.

He put a finger to his lips, then walked in, motioning for her to stay in the entry hall as he activated his bug detector. The late-model CPM-7307 had been modified by a buddy to also pick up the presence of hidden cameras. In addition to locating commonly used transmitters, the tool allowed Rafe to test AC outlets and phone lines. The small metal box, no wider than his wallet, included an output so he could listen for any phone modifications such as resistors or infinity bugs, anything placed on the wire itself.

Kit shook her head, wearing the same expression of amazement and disbelief she'd worn when he performed a search at her brother-in-law's apartment.

Rafe bit back a grin. Making a quick sweep, he moved through the living room, peripherally aware of the honey-colored walls and ivory woodwork, the bold punctuation of color around the room. One wall of built-in bookcases boasted two shelves devoted to titles regarding functional family relationships. *Interesting.*

The scent of Kit's light perfume trailed him, but he kept his focus narrowed. He found no bugs or cameras in the kitchen, no bugs in the phones or outlets there or in the living room. Moving down the short hallway off the foyer, he checked two bedrooms and the bath, then the ceiling fan in the living room and one in Kit's bedroom. He felt along the undersides of her fluffy, distinctly feminine bed, keeping a firm lock on his imagination.

He returned to the front part of the house to test the phone. The dial tones hummed normally, and he removed the earpiece, snapped off his machine and tucked the device into his back pocket of his jeans.

"All clear." He turned to where she still stood in the doorway. Red-gold sunlight pooled around her legs and shimmered through the light fabric of her dress, outlining her slender calves.

"This thing only scans one room at a time, but it's thorough. One tone sounds for bugs, another for video equipment."

She gave a short laugh and closed the door. "Where did you learn to do that?"

"I've picked up some things."

A shadow passed through her eyes and she nodded tightly, wrapping her arms around her waist.

"Think you'll find anything on that computer?" She referred to the desktop unit Rafe had confiscated from Tony's, along with some disks.

"If there's anything to be found on it. I've got a guy who's a whiz with that stuff."

"I hope so," she said doubtfully. At his raised eyebrows, she explained, "Tony's a computer genius. If he wants to hide or erase anything, he can probably do it."

As she moved from the wood floor of the foyer into the carpeted living area, Rafe was careful to stay in the center of the room. When she flipped on an overhead light, he took a closer look at the living room and the visible part of the kitchen. The soft neutrality of the walls, woodwork and carpet was offset by jewel tones of ruby, emerald and sapphire in pillows, candles, an area rug beneath the dark pecan oval coffee table and frames scattered on the walls.

Kit watched him intently. So still, so quiet. Waiting.

Awareness prickled his skin. As his gaze scanned the living room, he tuned in the soft snick of the undulating ceiling fan, the faint barking of a dog down the street. Something was off. Something—

Pictures. The realization hit him like a one-two punch. Rafe stepped closer to the wall, his gaze narrowing on the framed photograph there.

It was of Kit and her sister, brunette heads together, laughing. The distant sound of Kit's laughter filled his mind, and he shoved away the phantom sound, his gaze skimming the wall.

More pictures. Some of Kit and Liz. One of Kit with her father.

One of Liz and a nice-looking man. Tony?

Kit walked over and removed the photograph from the wall. "This is Tony, just before he went to prison."

Rafe nodded, taking the picture, studying the man's intelligent pale gray eyes, the shaggy, medium brown hair. Though Rafe tried to concentrate on the image in front of him, his thoughts skipped back. In college, Kit had never wanted her picture taken. She'd been almost fanatical about that. Rafe had come to learn that was due to her innate shyness.

The only photograph Rafe had ever had of him and Kit had been taken at his fraternity's spring formal. His mother probably still had it in his box of college stuff in the attic. Judging from the amount of pictures in this room, Kit seemed to have gotten over her aversion, he thought ruefully. Such a small thing, but not for her.

The Kit he'd known *then,* he reminded himself forcefully. Dragging his attention to the face of Tony Valentine, he struggled to bring to life something besides regret and a resentment that should have cooled long ago.

Kit walked to the mantel and took down another framed

photograph. "This one of Tony was just taken about a week ago. He sent it to Liz."

Rafe nodded, careful not to touch her as he took the frame. Valentine had cut his hair, almost a buzz cut. He'd grown a mustache and wore glasses. "I'll want to make some copies of this."

"Sure. Let me take it out of the frame." Her fingers brushed his as she took the picture.

Casually, he turned away, squelching the jolt of electricity that jumped up his arm.

"Tony had some pictures of Liz. When we checked his place earlier, I noticed they weren't on his refrigerator, where she told me he usually kept them."

Could've been a smart move by Valentine to keep Alexander from getting a good look at Liz. Or it could've just been Valentine's way of disappearing.

The photo Rafe had requested appeared over his shoulder, sans frame, and he took it, too conscious of the way Kit's breath tickled his neck. His gaze scanned the entertainment center, the collection of CDs that ranged from the Eagles to Elvis Presley. Before it could fully form, Rafe aborted the reminder of his and Kit's mutual pleasure in Elvis's "Can't Help Falling in Love."

More pictures lined the curved-leg table behind the sofa, and Rafe moved toward it. This case was all that mattered. There was a picture of Kit and her sister. Another of Kit in a pale pink satin gown that hugged every curve, bared her gorgeous shoulders. She stood next to Liz, who wore an ivory tea-length wedding gown, her hand on the tuxedo-clad arm of a man whose face was cropped off. Their father? Tony or another groom? Kit's lover?

That last thought ambushed him, and before he could stop, Rafe wondered how many men Kit had seen since their college days. Had she ever come close to marriage or had she pushed them all away before they could get too close? Was she involved with someone?

Rafe knew he should leave those questions alone, but there was one he had to ask. "Are you seeing anyone now?"

She blinked. "What?"

"Dating anyone?"

A frown snapped her dark brows together. "I thought we weren't going to talk about anything except this case."

"That's the reason I'm asking." Even while his chest tightened in anticipation of her answer, he managed to sound detached. "I need to speak with anyone who's had recent contact with your sister. They might know something without being aware of it."

"Or they might have something to do with her disappearance?"

"Right."

"I'm not seeing anyone," she said stiffly, avoiding his eyes. "Haven't for…a while."

He nodded, silently cursing the bubble of pleasure that bloomed inside him. "I'd like to take a closer look at Liz's room."

"This way." She walked past him and down the hall.

His gaze slid down the slender line of her back to the taut curve of her butt, the lean line of her thighs. She still had a class-A butt. And beautiful dewy skin. Rafe's gaze lingered on the soft magnolia flesh of her neck.

He forced himself to look away and rejected the awareness that had started a dim, persistent throb in his pulse after the initial shock of seeing her in his office.

As he'd asked—or rather ordered—she'd kept her conversation limited to answering his questions, nothing about the past. He could do the same.

Stepping into Liz's bedroom, Rafe took in the unmade

full-size bed. Kit walked over and began pulling the leopard print sheet taut, straightening the matching comforter.

A black bra strap hung out of the top of one dresser drawer; three pairs of stiletto heels cluttered the space between the dresser and the wall.

"Are any of her clothes missing?"

Kit stepped over to take a quick look in the closet. "No, I don't think so. And her suitcase is here."

He nodded. "Who did Tony work for before he went to prison?"

"Another computer manufacturer. He worked with hardware back then, rather than software."

"Any friends who kept in touch after he was put away?"

"Not that I know of." Nervous energy poured off her. Her voice grew quieter with each answer.

Rafe could see that she was trying to stay out of his way. Regret stabbed at that, but he didn't try to put her at ease. The more distance, the better. "Did Liz go see him?"

"Yes, at first. I don't think she's been in the last couple of months."

In here, it was easier to pretend Kit was just another client. In here, there was no danger of running into the past they shared.

He followed her into the hallway, paused when she halted in front of an open closet that housed a washer and dryer. A laundry basket full of clothes jutted out, and Kit reached to move it out of the door's path.

"Where does Liz work?"

"At a day-care center. It's by the airport. We drive to work together sometimes."

Rafe nodded, not sure how to define the strange heat that pushed under his ribs. Kit had become a woman he didn't know; she had a life he knew nothing about.

"She's had this job for more than two years, and I think she's really getting her life together."

Liz didn't sound much different to him than she had when he'd known her ten years ago, but he said nothing. "What number was Tony? Which husband?"

Kit half-turned, eyeing him flatly.

"Number two, three, four?"

"Number three." She flipped the tail of a shirt into the basket, then suddenly made a strangled sound. Her gaze shot to his.

"Kit?" He stepped toward her, concern spiraling through him. His gaze dropped to the basket then the shirt she fingered. At first he scanned for blood, something to explain why she'd gone so pale. Then he froze as he recognized the crimson-and-white basketball jersey.

His gaze locked on hers. Panic, disbelief, memory rippled across her features. Two bright spots of red crested her cheeks. His stomach flipped like it had the first time he'd taken up a fighter jet.

His thoughts wheeled back to the day after the Oklahoma University basketball team had made the NCAA playoffs. His college team hadn't had practice that day; he had hoofed it back to the frat house, intending to shower and pick up Kit for supper. But she'd been waiting in his room, wearing his jersey—*this* jersey—and nothing else. Number twelve.

He swallowed hard, his gaze sliding over her before he could stop himself. Memories burst in his head like popping flashbulbs. The full curve of her breast peeking out from the deep-cut armhole of his jersey, the hem skimming the center of her smooth, bare thighs, the flush of shyness she'd never lost even though they'd been lovers for months.

That fast, he went hard. He could taste the sweet musk of her skin, smell his scent on her. His body quivered like a newly strung bow.

He sucked in a ragged breath, and his gaze went to hers. He saw the way her eyes darkened to purple, the pink that climbed her neck, the frantic tap of her pulse in the hollow of her throat. She remembered, too.

Every touch, every kiss, every whispered forever.

Her reaction only hollowed his gut, sheared the edge off any control he thought he possessed. Involuntarily, he stepped toward her. For one hellacious, gut-twisting instant he wanted to drag her to him, kiss her and prove to both of them that there was nothing left.

As if coming out of a trance, Kit jerked into motion. She shoved the basket against the washer face and shut the door.

"Is that—"

"No." She flashed a brilliant smile, so brilliant it cut him to the core. "Looks like yours. Not yours."

Bull. He was tempted to call her on it, but he resisted.

Where would that get them? Why had he thought he could ignore the past? Kit *was* his past. And he was good and pissed over her slingshotting back into his life. Hell.

Rafe clenched his teeth against the razor-edged desire that slashed through him.

Remember, he ordered, trying to escape the grasping hands of memory, of *want,* pulling at him. Ruthlessly he dredged up the rejection he'd felt when Kit had refused his marriage proposal. When he'd said forever, he'd meant it; she hadn't.

"What about friends? Tony's friends?" he asked quickly, his voice rough, the words scraping his throat. "Can you think of anyone who might let Tony and Liz stay with them? Anyone who might hide them or know where they've gone?"

"No," she whispered, then cleared her throat. "Maybe you can ask his parents—"

His cell phone jangled, and Rafe grabbed at it like a drowning man going for a rescue line. "Yeah," he said, almost ashamed at the enormous relief that rolled through him.

It was Porter, and as the cop spoke, Rafe's jaw clenched tighter. The ambivalence he'd tried to shake off seconds ago surged back. Displeasure merged with concern. And his protective instinct, always deeper and stronger with Kit, roared to irritating life.

"Thanks, Kent." He disconnected, his hand curling over the phone. "We'd better get going if we want to make it back from Davis before midnight."

She started, taking a step toward him. Her soft scent curled around him. "What? You want me to go? Hel-lo! Just two hours ago you flat out told me you didn't want me along on this case."

Rafe exhaled and turned to fully face her. "That was before I talked to my buddy at the OCPD."

She frowned.

"He says the officer investigating Liz's accident believed she wasn't paying attention to her driving. That her accident wasn't deliberate."

"But—"

"I've dealt with this officer before, and I don't trust his judgement," Rafe said baldly. "Neither does Kent."

"Are you saying you believe what Liz told me? That someone ran her off the road?"

"I'm saying…" He gentled his voice. "I don't like the odds, Kit."

"So Tony was right," she murmured.

"Maybe. Kent said he also might have an idea about this Alexander person. And…"

"And what?" Anxiety pulled at her features.

He hated dumping all this on her at once, but she deserved to know what they might be up against. "I noticed a car behind me on the way over here. The same car, three different times."

She shook her head. "What—"

"It's possible you're being tailed. I'll know better when we leave here."

"Tony was right about that, too?" She sagged against the wall, her features wan and suddenly ravaged by fatigue.

Compassion and protectiveness swept through him. His first impulse was to put an arm around her, but he stayed where he was, giving her time to absorb it.

She stood quietly for a few moments, her fingers thrusting repeatedly through her hair. Fear, uncertainty skipped across her features then resignation. She straightened, her voice shaky. "I guess we'd better get going."

"You all right?"

"Yes." She wouldn't meet his eyes, and Rafe couldn't stop the hard squeeze in his chest.

Fighting the vortex of memories, the emotion sucking at him, he pivoted and walked out of the room. "On our way out of town, I'll drop off these photos and have some copies made."

He didn't like the concern for her that chewed at him. He wanted space, needed it; instead he was spending the next three to four hours with her.

"Tomorrow I'll take Tony's computer to the office, see if my contact can salvage anything useful off there. I'll also check out Tony's current employer and his parole officer."

She nodded and followed him into the hallway, still looking shell-shocked.

"Could you write down the name of anyone else who might've been implicated in the scam he pulled, anyone who testified against him?"

"Sure," she said faintly.

His body humming with frustration and remembered passion, Rafe waited on the lawn while she locked the front door, then walked toward his car. She halted uncertainly at the edge of the driveway.

His gaze shot between her car and his. It would be dark

soon, but he'd made the drive south between Oklahoma City and Davis many times. The Department of Public Safety was more tolerant of his night blindness than the United States Air Force had been. Besides, he needed something to occupy his hands and his mind. Needed a release for the energy seething inside him, needed to feel the raw power of the 'Vette beneath him. "We'll take mine," he said gruffly.

She moved to the passenger side and opened the door before he could. Once inside, she shut her door with a loud click.

Gripping his keys so tightly they bit into his palm, Rafe walked to the driver's side. Maybe he didn't need to take her to Davis. Maybe she'd be safe here. But could he risk it?

No. He slid behind the wheel and started the car, leashing the resentment churning inside him. He could tell himself he might feel the same caution for any client who was possibly being tailed by the mob, but this wasn't just any client. This was Kit.

And as much as he wanted to, he couldn't deny that seeing his old jersey had hit him hard. Or why.

The connection he and Kit had shared had been deeper than any he'd ever had. An ember had ignited in the secret part of him only ever occupied by Kit. A part he'd thought erased by years and resentment.

Inches away from her, webbed by her faint scent and the torturous images that had seared his brain moments before, Rafe knew she still owned that tiny place inside him. He hated that little revelation, but he couldn't ignore the fact that she might also be in danger. So much for avoiding his past.

Chapter 3

Arousal fired little points along her nerves. Rafe had nearly kissed her. Even now, hours later on the return trip to Oklahoma City from Davis, that thought hammered through Kit's mind. With every pulsing sense in her, she wished he had.

Thank goodness he hadn't.

Smoky midnight swirled around them. Phil Collins crooned on Rafe's state-of-the-art car stereo. Kit ran a hand over the Corvette's buttery soft tan leather seat, not surprised that Rafe drove such a speedster. He'd always said he had a need for speed. As they traveled north on I-35, leaving behind the south side of Oklahoma City, lights from the highway and roadside businesses flashed by in a blur. For the late hour, there was still a fair amount of traffic.

She glanced over her shoulder, as she had every couple of minutes since they'd lost the tail outside her neighborhood a few hours ago.

It wasn't the dread of seeing another car following them

that had her nerves feeling raw and exposed. It wasn't the compact space and tight lines of the Corvette's interior that made her feel…cornered. Or the fact that Rafe had barely spoken since they'd left Tony's parents. It was the way Rafe's body heat formed a wall against her arm, the way his dark, rich scent stroked her senses.

It was the fact that she couldn't stop thinking about that split second in the hallway when memories had crashed over both of them, when naked hunger had tautened Rafe's features.

Only he had ever looked at her that way. Other men had said they wanted her, but none of them had ever looked at her as if they *had* to have her. For that one heartbeat of time, she'd wanted to fall into his arms, call back what they'd shared. And that was dangerous.

She was no more willing to give up her independence now than she had been in college. At fourteen, she'd been handling responsibilities most women didn't handle until they were twenty-one, and she wasn't going to give that up. Couldn't, really.

The truth was she'd never gotten close to any man, until Rafe. Or *since* Rafe, she thought ruefully, staring over her shoulder again.

Her gaze shifted to his chiseled profile then dropped to his mouth. During their trip to Davis and the visit with Tony's parents, she'd managed to dodge thoughts of that near kiss. But now…

Her nerves were shot, and she'd been in Rafe's company less than twelve hours. Again she turned, searching the play of shadow and streetlights for a car that might have been behind them too long.

"I can't believe I was really being followed," she murmured, wishing she weren't so aware of his lean fingers on the steering wheel, the broad hand that rested on his jeans-clad thigh.

He changed lanes, a smile in his voice. "If you're going to look for a tail, it's best if you aren't too obvious."

"Oh." She faced front.

"Keep an eye out either by looking in your rearview or your side mirror."

Her gaze sliced to the right. Illuminated by the high-powered roadside lighting, the side mirror showed a beat-up pickup pulling a horse trailer and following some distance behind. A sporty red car passed them on the left. "Maybe you could teach me some things. I mean, about how to spot a tail and how to lose one."

"Sure." Was it her imagination or did his voice tighten?

He'd been reserved since they'd left her house, answering questions when she asked, but not making conversation. She should probably follow his lead.

The effortless way he'd lost the men who followed them reassured Kit. And grated on her at the same time.

As long as she was with him, she didn't have to worry that she would lead Alexander's men anywhere, but she wouldn't, *couldn't* be with Rafe all the time.

Her body thrummed with awareness of his rich, earthy scent. She fixed her gaze on the side mirror, glad when they exited onto I-235 North in the center of the city.

Seeing his old basketball jersey had affected her like a kick to the stomach. Brought back the memory of the look on his face when he'd found her in that shirt so long ago. Surprise, then a slow-curling, wicked smile as he'd tumbled her onto his rumpled bed. That had been the first, and only, time she'd initiated their lovemaking.

At the memory, her cheeks heated and she shifted against the smooth leather at her back. "So, did you believe Tony's parents? You really think they don't know where he is?"

"Yes. If Valentine's parents had seen him, I think they would've been nervous, evaded my questions. Plus I checked around outside while you stayed inside with them.

There were no signs that anyone had been there. And I don't think they faked the concern they feel for Tony and Liz. Or their anger at Tony.''

"I was really hoping we'd learn something down there." She blew out a frustrated breath. "Now what do we do?"

"Like I said, I'll check on the computer we found at Tony's place. I'll talk to his employer and parole officer tomorrow."

"I want to come along." She half-turned to face him in the car, lacing her fingers together against the urge to touch him. Thank goodness, they were nearly at her house. "I know I can help, if you'll just let me."

Regardless of his answer, she didn't plan to sit around waiting on him to learn something and call her with a daily report.

"We've already been over this."

"What if you don't find them? I will have done nothing to help Liz and I can't live with that. I stayed out of your way at the Valentines and you *are* the one who wanted me to go."

He sighed, running a hand over his face. "That was for your safety."

"And what if I'm still being followed?"

"We'll deal with it."

"I really need to do *something*." Then grudgingly, "Please?"

His jaw set as he exited the highway and headed west on Wilshire toward May Avenue. Heavier traffic zoomed along these streets than had been on the highway. At one point, he swerved sharply, reminding Kit that he'd done the same thing about an hour ago. He must've been trying to miss an animal or a pothole.

"What about your work schedule? Are you flying out anywhere in the next couple of days?"

"No. I called in yesterday." Had it really been only a

day and a half since Liz had disappeared with Tony? "I've
built up a few weeks of vacation and my boss said I should
take some time."

"At least I won't have to worry about where you are
and I can concentrate solely on finding your sister."

So glad I could help. Kit bit back the sarcastic words.

How had he gone from flying for the Air Force to this
job? She didn't ask. It was better not to know about the
life he'd made without her.

Her mind and body ached from trying to deny how much
she'd wanted him earlier. If Rafe sensed she couldn't get
past that, he'd be out of here so fast she wouldn't know
what happened.

He swung into her driveway and killed the engine. "I
want to check your house again for bugs."

"You didn't find anything before." She paused with her
hand on the door handle.

"Don't you wonder where those guys went after I shook
their tail?"

She should have. She hadn't.

"It's possible they came back here, installed a little
something to make sure they could keep track of you."

"All right." After getting out of the car, she moved up
the sidewalk and onto the porch in front of him. He stayed
close, close enough that she could feel him at her back. She
swallowed against the way her nape prickled. She unlocked
the door and waited for him to enter first.

She felt so out of her league with all this stuff, and Rafe
acted as though it were second nature. When—how—had
he learned to do investigative work? Obviously he needed
to know these things for his current job. She knew he probably wouldn't welcome her questions so she kept her mouth
shut, walked in behind him and closed the door.

He motioned for her to turn on the light then the stereo,
so she did, keeping the volume at a moderate level. The

deep voice of a local DJ boomed out of the receiver before whiskey-voiced Chris Isaak began to sing about doing a bad, bad thing.

Inserting the earpiece into his left ear, Rafe headed down the hallway. His gaze was narrowed and his nostrils flared in a way that Kit had never seen.

He looked like a...predator, dangerous, unfamiliar. Kit couldn't stop the spike of excitement in her blood pressure.

From what he'd told her at Tony's, she knew that this time he would start at the back of her house and work his way to where they'd come in. He moved first to her bedroom, then Liz's, turning in a slow circle in each room. Kit followed slowly, trying to ignore the slow roll of his hips, the ripple of muscle beneath the khaki T-shirt.

He made quick work of the bathroom and gave her a thumbs-up. She let out a sigh of relief. She could not handle knowing someone was watching her in the bath.

Her gaze locked on his hands. Strong, gentle hands sprinkled with a faint dusting of dark hair. Surrounded by the seductive bass of Chris Isaak, Kit found herself swamped by memories of those hands on her body, stroking, teasing, pleasing.

She wrapped her arms around her middle and forced herself to watch Rafe, to pay closer attention to the pictures on the walls, to the light switches, the blades of the ceiling fan, just as he did.

When he walked through the living room toward the kitchen, he halted abruptly. Pressing the earpiece close to his ear, he listened intently. He prowled the perimeter of her kitchen, returned to the living room. She moved to the sofa, feeling along the cushions, inside the lampshade, her gaze going questioningly to his. He nodded, those lean fingers edging around the casing of the wall phone as he glanced at the bug detector he held.

He reached up to slide a hand along the blades of the

ceiling fan, and his T-shirt rode up to expose sleek brown skin. When he stretched, muscle flexed across his flat belly, drawing her eye to the waistband of his snug jeans.

She straightened, pulling her gaze away to scan the room, telling herself to keep searching for audio or video equipment, though she hardly knew what to look for. Rafe moved to the wall, studied the air-conditioner return where the wall met the ceiling. He ran a finger along each pleated opening of the vent, then moved away, seemingly satisfied.

Once again his gaze traveled the room, pausing on the sofa.

He went from relaxed alertness to rigid readiness. Her gaze followed his as he looked down at the tool he carried and she saw a green LED flash. Rafe slipped the bug detector into the back pocket of his jeans. With a few silent strides, he passed in front of her and stopped at the sofa, close enough that she could feel the warmth from his body.

Dread pinched at her.

He turned, wrapping his fingers around her elbow. The heat that shot up her arm barely registered as he drew her gaze to the sofa.

He pointed, and she stared for a moment without realizing what she looked at. Then…instead of the dark plaid-covered sofa button she expected to see, she saw a flat black button. Not a button, a bug. *A listening device.*

She turned, shock rippling through her. "Can they hear—"

He hauled her to him, his mouth crashing down on hers.

Kit stiffened, her eyes going wide. Hot, hard lips moved over hers as a shock wave jolted her body. Then she sagged against him. Just a little.

Half-formed thoughts tumbled around in her head. She might've imagined it, but for an instant she thought his lips softened, coaxing the strength out of her the way they used to. He lifted his head, his dark gaze smoldering on her lips then lifting to her eyes.

She blinked, swaying. A breathy sound escaped her, and a flush darkened Rafe's skin.

He leaned toward her, and she couldn't form one rational thought. Just... *Oh, yes*.

Then his breath burned her ear, sent a shiver down her spine. ''Don't talk.''

Talk? She couldn't *breathe*. Her hands curled into fists, nails biting into her palms.

He skimmed his lips up her temple, back down to her ear. She began to tremble. And reason kicked in. She pushed at his chest; his hands tightened on her upper arms.

Again he whispered, barely audible, ''That's a bug. Play along.''

Aloud, he said, ''Ten years and you can still do this to me.''

His voice spilled over her like heated oil, torching a desire she'd buried too long. She knew it wasn't real, knew he didn't mean anything by it. Still her fingers curled into his T-shirt; she needed something to steady her legs.

His lips skimmed hers again. His hands smoothed down her back, flexed at her waist. Kit fought the urge to push away. She understood that he was playing for their unseen audience, but she shuddered anyway.

His lips came back to her ear, heat inching under her skin. ''I found the camera, too. On the wall, four o'clock.''

Why was he talking about the time? Oh, he meant somewhere on the wall. A deep breath sawing out of her, she turned her head to the right.

Long fingers captured her jaw, gently forced her head to his. Black eyes seared hers, and he whispered against her lips, ''Sorry, *my* four o'clock.''

She nodded dumbly, her body pulsing almost painfully.

His hands curved over her hips, and his voice rumbled out. "I am so ready for you."

It was all an act for whoever was watching and listening, but it didn't feel like acting to Kit. Still, she struggled to catch up, to be as cool as he was.

His eyes might be distant, but there was a flush beneath his skin. His breathing was slightly uneven.

He curled one knuckle under her chin, tilting her face toward his. "It's been a long time," he groaned. "Too long."

To whoever watched, it probably appeared that they were kissing again. Kit lifted her head, her lips brushing his. Needles of heat slid under her skin. She forced herself to follow his gaze to the left, searching for the camera.

Rafe kissed her cheek, her temple. Her heart ached with a strange combination of sadness and anger as she struggled to pretend, the way he was.

This close there was no way he could miss the way her nipples had hardened and heat—of embarrassment, of arousal—flushed her body.

He breathed in her ear again. "The camera's in the light knob."

Her hands flexed involuntarily, bunching his shirt as her gaze shifted to the round knob on the wall that controlled the overhead light and ceiling fan. She tried to focus on what he said, but all she could think was she wanted him to kiss her again. For real, this time.

No, no, she desperately corrected. Where was her pride?

What pride? her conscience taunted. To even be here with him, she had to pretend she had none.

She could feel the power of his thighs bracketing hers, the flat, hard muscle of his belly, the lingering taste of his mint gum on her lips.

Tears stung her eyes, and Kit stiffened her spine. He felt it, trailed those wicked fingers up her back. His touch only fanned a languorous heat, and her irritation spiked. She didn't like how he sent her pulse skyrocketing, didn't like the way she ached to arch into him, wrap her body around his.

Resentment flared. Did he know how he was affecting her? Was he enjoying it? His voice was cool; his eyes weren't. In a perverse need to find out if she could still affect him the way he did her, Kit slid her hands up his chest, around his neck and pressed full against him. She took a reckless satisfaction in seeing his eyes widen, feeling the sudden flex of his body against hers.

Going up on tiptoe, she whispered in his ear, "Now what?"

The satisfaction she felt was quickly squashed when he hauled her to him, one thigh insinuated between hers and pressing against the damp heat between her legs. Her hands clamped on to his shoulders for the sole purpose of support.

His gaze lasered into hers. He kissed her again, his mouth covering hers with ruthless purpose. Controlled deliberation. A warning to back off. *Now.*

It triggered something wild and angry inside her. Reacting on pure instinct, she slid one hand into his thick dark hair, curled the other around his strong, warm nape.

For a moment, he stiffened. Then his restraint snapped. His hands tunneled into her hair, gripping her head as he deepened the kiss, his tongue sweeping into her mouth, claiming every part of her. She couldn't think, didn't want to.

It had been so long. He felt so good. Hard, hot male against her, his kiss seducing the strength from her legs. Her hands splayed across his back, pressing closer.

He pulled away, his breathing ragged, the muscles in his neck taut and straining. Surprise flickered in his eyes, then disappeared. "Get your things," he rasped. "Let's finish this at my place."

She nodded, barely aware of moving down the hallway and into her room. With sweat-slicked palms, she dragged an overnight bag from the top of her closet and threw in a change of clothes, underwear. Heartbeat thundering against her ribs, she managed to remember her toothbrush and makeup.

Away from him, she could think. Yes, she needed to be away from him, she thought desperately as she dragged the back of her hand across her lips, still burning from his.

That kiss hadn't felt like playacting to her. It had felt vividly, painfully real. Reminded her of what she'd thrown away.

When she returned to the front room, he reached for her, planting another kiss on her lips. But she felt the difference this time. This kiss was constrained, like the first one. Studied.

She tried to corral the sensations raging through her body. With one hot hand at her waist, Rafe guided her outside. She turned to lock the door, and he pressed close.

His chest felt like tempered steel against her shoulder blades. His body heat seared through the fabric of her dress. Throat tight, breasts tingling, she shut her eyes.

Only when she turned did she see that he wasn't paying attention to her at all. He was checking out her porch light, studying the doorbell for signs of other bugs or another camera. Resentment shot through her, and she squashed the urge to knock him flat on his butt. He was doing a job, she ruthlessly reminded herself. He was here for Liz, not her. Not *them*. There was no *them*.

Still, how could he be so calm? She felt shaky, ready to shatter, and he looked fully in control. He was no longer flushed. His pulse beat slow and steady at the side of his neck whereas hers fluttered so rapidly she felt it in her throat.

He walked down the sidewalk and turned, waiting for

her. Looking as unaffected as if he didn't even know her, as if she hadn't felt the hard swell of his arousal against her belly moments ago. It had meant nothing. It had been only for the people listening in on them.

Kit reminded herself of that at least twenty times on her way to his car. Trying to steady her thundering pulse, she walked to the opposite side of the Corvette. Across the car's top, their eyes met.

"Sorry about that. The kiss, I mean." He gestured toward the house with irritating nonchalance. "It was the quickest way I could think to stop you from announcing we'd found their bug and tipping them off about the camera."

What was she supposed to say? *Oh, it's all right that you kissed the breath out of me.* It wasn't. She wondered if it was going to be.

"Sure. No problem." Her voice caught, and she fought the urge to hide her face in her hands. "What do we do now?"

"You're coming home with me."

"But…" Panic clawed at her. "Is that a good idea?"

"You have a better one?"

"How about anywhere but there?" she drawled.

The glint of male satisfaction in his eyes had her clenching her jaw. "Wouldn't it be better, *safer* if we—I went to a hotel?"

He slid her a look. "We can, but I can't guarantee the security of a place like that the way I can my own house."

"Of course." The only thing she understood was that she needed to be away from him, and that wasn't going to happen tonight.

His house. A dull throb built at the back of her head.

"Like it or not," he said brusquely, "we're stuck together."

He obviously didn't like it.

"And we both might as well get used to it. I'm not letting you out of my sight until we find that ditzy sister of yours."

"You never did understand Liz," she snapped. "Well, you don't have to. You just have to find her."

"That's the plan," he said through clenched teeth.

"Fine."

"Fine."

Her glare went unremarked. Panic closed across her chest as she got into the Corvette. She told herself that finding Liz would be worth risking her heart again. Worth *anything,* but after that staged seduction scene, she wasn't sure she was up for even five more minutes with Rafe Blackstock.

Chapter 4

Want clawed through him. As Kit ducked into the passenger side of his car, Rafe went down on all fours, then slid under the 'Vette. If there was a bug in her house, there was possibly something on his car or hers. At first glance, he saw nothing so he stretched his arm up and felt the undercarriage.

Blast her, she'd gotten him all hot and bothered in there, plastering her lush bod against his and issuing that silent but unmistakable challenge—I can make you want me, too.

That had never been the damn issue between them, just as it hadn't been his real intent to fire her engines in there a minute ago. It had been instinct that had fueled the way he'd hauled her to him and silenced her with a kiss, instinct to keep her from announcing to their unseen audience that they'd found the bug and camera. Now he was paying the price because it had been pure want that exploded in his veins when she'd retaliated. Pure desire that had him pulling her to him, wanting to wrap both those long legs around his waist and say to hell with caution.

That was stupid, and he wouldn't do it. Not just because he needed a clear mind in order to ascertain the danger Kit faced, if indeed there was danger, but also because he wasn't giving her another chance to stomp all over his heart.

His mouth twisting, he tried to forget how she felt against him, how she'd surrendered to his kiss for just that one beat of time. There had never been any question of the sexual chemistry between them. Their problem—her problem—had been that she couldn't commit. Her accusation that he was too controlling had been true at the time, but that hadn't been the whole issue.

Sliding his hands along the lip of the car's frame, he cursed the way his gut jumped at the remembered feel of her full breasts pressed against him, the wicked slide of her tongue against his, the deep wine *taste* of her.

More memories crowded through his mind, memories of their days together at OU, their nights, that time in the car on the way back from his parents' place. Rafe slammed a mental door on those thoughts, ruthlessly turned his mind to the task at hand. Around one side of the car, then to the back and around the passenger side. His fingers grazed something. Aha.

He lay on his back and scooted under the car as far as he could. There it was, a little black box with a flashing red light. The bastards. Well, this proved someone was following her. Not that he needed more convincing after finding that bug and camera in her house. How serious these bad guys were had yet to be determined.

Rafe moved out from under the car and stood, walking up to Kit's car. Her house was relatively old and didn't have a garage. He'd probably find a tracking device on hers, too. Sure enough, he did.

She rolled down the window. "What are you doing?"

"Looking for tracking devices."

"And?"

"There's one on my car." He knelt, felt around the wheel well, up along the lip of her frame, then moved around to the front of her car. "And there's one on yours."

He stood, dusting his hands. He'd been right to insist she come to his house tonight. Now all he had to do was keep his hands off her.

After easing into the driver's seat, he took the tissue Kit offered and cleaned his hands as best he could.

"What do we do now?"

"Leave the device on your car. You won't be using it."

"What about the one on yours?" In the fading sunlight, she looked wan and worried.

He grinned. "We'll dump it somewhere."

She nodded, her blue-gray eyes searching his.

"It'll be all right," he said, compelled to reassure her.

"I hope Liz is, too."

Rafe had no answer for that so he started the engine and backed the 'Vette out of Kit's drive. He turned north on May Avenue and headed toward his house in Quail Creek. Amazing how close they lived to each other. Amazing they'd steered clear of each other until now.

She sat on her side of the car, arms crossed tightly. He figured she was probably still mad about his comments concerning Dizzy Lizzy. That was for the best. The more distance between them, the better.

Still, as he slid a look at her pale golden skin, the finely sculpted profile, his whole body tightened. In all fairness, their breakup hadn't been entirely her fault. He'd blamed her all these years for not speaking up, but back then he *had* been too controlling, too insistent on his own way.

Even when he'd proposed, he hadn't *asked* her to marry him; he'd simply told her she would and how they would live. The realization jolted him, and he jerked his gaze to the road. That had been a valid reason to turn him down.

Besides her keen sense of family responsibility, had his control played a part in why she couldn't commit to him? The only excuse he had for his domineering behavior was that he'd been young and stupid.

As she looked out the window at passing scenery, holding herself away from him, he realized it didn't matter now. They'd gone their separate ways.

Spying a police cruiser up ahead, he changed lanes and pulled into the small parking lot of an all-night doughnut shop. She sent him a questioning look and he grinned, slid out of the car and moved around to remove the tracking device from the belly of the 'Vette.

He walked to the black and white, slapped it on the underside of the bumper and got back in his car.

Kit laughed. "That was good."

"It'll keep them busy for a while."

"Until we get to your house?"

"Yeah."

Her smile faded, and he recognized the shadows in her eyes as memories from the past. Memories she was fighting as much as he was. The silence stretched between them, stilted and unfinished. Regret pricked at him. He was swept with a sudden urge to touch her, reassure her, but about what? The past was past. Best to leave it alone.

He put the car in gear, reversed and pulled onto May Avenue. They drove in silence to his house. His life was markedly different from what he'd planned, even aside from Kit. She, on the other hand, still appeared to be her sister's self-appointed rescuer.

Despite the years that had passed, Rafe wasn't willing to play second fiddle to Dizzy Lizzy. Yes, the more distance the better. And that meant keeping his hands to himself. After that kiss, which even now rattled him, he knew she could still affect him like a neutron bomb. He couldn't allow himself to get close to her again, not physically, not emotionally.

He'd have to protect her, find her sister without letting it become personal. *They* were over. They couldn't go back; he *wouldn't* go back.

For the fourth time in the last half hour, Kit rose from the supple, navy leather sofa in Rafe's living room and walked toward the sliding patio doors. He had grilled chicken and vegetables for dinner; she'd cleaned up afterward. And thirty minutes ago, he'd invited her outside, but she'd thought it would be more prudent to stay inside. Away from him.

She hadn't been able to stop thinking about that kiss at her house. It had completely ambushed her senses. And unleashed the curiosity that had been hammering at her since seeing him this morning.

Rafe's finding that tracking device had convinced Kit that her sister *was* in danger, no matter what he said. She'd gotten a chuckle out of his putting it on the police cruiser. He was still so darn cute. Which she didn't need to be thinking about, either.

Still, if they were going to be stuck together, she wanted to know how he'd gotten back to Oklahoma City. It had unsettled her to learn that they lived within five miles of each other and she hadn't known it.

Finally, prodded by the curiosity she'd been trying all day to deny, she stepped through the sliding glass doors onto the patio and closed the door behind her.

Flagstone tile in variegated shades of cream and terracotta formed a far-reaching patio and framed a small rectangular pool. Potted plants in oversize ceramic planters guarded each corner. Bunches of petunias, begonias and other annuals spilled against a tall wooden privacy fence. A six-foot-wide border of grass edged the fence and butted up against the tile. The pool, covered with a blue tarp, waited to be filled with the first water of summer. Last week's Memorial Day had surely been hot enough for swimmers.

Light from inside the house washed across the tile, shimmered off the cushioned lounge chairs around the pool. It was a perfect early summer night, growing cooler as the darkness swallowed the last of the sun. The stars burned bright in a velvet sky. Moonlight skittered across the patio, danced with the darkness. Kit squinted into the shadows.

"Over here."

Rafe's smoothly dark voice came from behind her and sent a shiver over her skin. She turned, rubbing her arms. She attributed the tightening of her belly to a sudden breeze, not the delicious timbre of his voice.

About ten feet to her right, she saw the silhouette of his upper body. The muted glow of house lights behind him played against his raven hair. Broad shoulders, seemingly carved from the night, rose from the water of a hot tub. Steam curled around him, and as her eyes adjusted, she saw he had leaned back against the wall of the hot tub, arms spread on either side, waiting, watching. Aggressive, male, primally appealing. He was familiar, and yet not. Her knowledge of the boy bumped into the mystery of the man.

She swallowed against the purely feminine flutter in her stomach and squashed the urge to scurry back into the house.

"If you want to join me, there's an extra suit over there." He inclined his head toward a storage closet partially visible in the shadowed alcove behind him, which also housed a grill and a picnic table. His teeth flashed white in the darkness. "Or you can go without. I won't be offended."

To cover the sudden dip in her stomach, she retorted,

"Yeah, that's why I came out here. To get naked with you."

He chuckled, and she found herself smiling. He was over there; she was over here. She was safe.

Still, that kiss from this afternoon was fresh in her mind, and the feel of that lean hard body against hers had opened the floodgate on memories that were better ignored.

"You sure you don't want to join me?"

"Yes," she murmured, wondering what he would do if she actually climbed in there with him.

"Pull up a chair or scoot over and dip your feet in. Feels pretty good." He swirled a hand through the water invitingly, stirring moonlight and shadows around his bare, glistening chest.

She hoped he had something on beneath that water. He'd done his share of skinny-dipping in college.

"You've got a real bachelor setup here. The hot tub, the pool, the extra suit." She couldn't keep the bite out of her voice.

"People leave things," he said with a shrug.

Which answered nothing. She itched to slip off her shoes and stick her feet in the warm water, but she knew it would be safer to stay dressed, keep some distance between them. Rafe, even without the seductive softness of night, had always been able to make her do things she regretted later. Like kissing him back there at her house.

Forcing the words past her tight throat, she asked, "So, where do we start tomorrow?"

She glanced over as he ran a wet hand through his dark hair, muscles flexing in his biceps with the movement. "We'll stop at Tony's parole officer first, see if he's heard from him at all. Then we'll pay a visit to Tony's employer."

Kit nodded.

"Was that what you really wanted to know, Kit?"

She jerked her head toward him. "What?"

"You've got curiosity written all over you. Just ask me."

She ground her teeth. How could he still read her so easily, after all these years?

Water bubbled gently around him. His black eyes glittered at her.

"Now you believe me about Liz, right? After finding that tracking device."

"I believe someone's after *you* and I believe that's tied to your sister. I don't know how dangerous they are."

She knew he didn't believe her that Liz had changed. That was all right. It didn't matter what he thought. He only needed to find her sister.

Kit walked to the edge of the pool, her hands clasped behind her back. "How did you get to Oklahoma City, Rafe? What happened to the Air Force? The fighter jets?"

He went abruptly still. She could feel it even from this distance. She glanced over, noted the rigid set of his wide shoulders, the way even the water seemed to stop moving.

He tilted his head back, stared at the star-studded sky. Moonlight slid down the column of his long throat. "I developed night blindness. Botched a landing, and the requisite exam showed a pretty severe case."

"Night blindness?" She stepped toward him. That explained his sudden swerving on the way to Davis and again on the way back. "Are you okay? How severe?"

"Not so severe I can't drive," he said dryly. "But I can't fly jets, that's for sure. At least not for the Air Force."

"I had no idea." She found herself at the edge of the hot tub, looking at his face, half hidden in shadows. "I know how much you wanted that."

"I had six years, and they were great." He reached for the towel behind him and stood, water sluicing down his body. His hard-muscled, *naked* body.

Her eyes widened and she whirled around. "You could give a girl some warning."

"I suppose. You know I don't generally wear a suit." There was a tightness in his voice that made Kit ache deep inside.

She'd forgotten that he liked to do things in the nude. He'd never been as concerned about his nakedness as she had been about hers. She remembered the time they'd gone skinny-dipping at the university pool after hours. How their splashing and teasing had turned to stroking, their water-slicked bodies sliding hotly against each other.

Her throat dried up. She wanted to touch him, and laced her fingers together against the urge.

"You're safe," he said wryly. "It's not like you haven't seen all of me before."

She turned, relieved to see that he had wrapped the towel low on his hips. His chest was fuller, more defined than it had been when they were lovers, but still sleek and devoid of hair. All the way to the towel hanging low on his hips.

"After I was discharged, I came back to Oklahoma, to be near my folks."

She remembered his parents as very loving, their family close. Rafe was their only child, something she'd wished for herself during some of Liz's more moronic moments. Willa and Dale Blackstock had been extremely accepting of her, but Kit wondered how they'd feel about her now. She hadn't seen them since rejecting Rafe's marriage proposal, hadn't talked to them at all.

She had sensed no regret in Rafe's voice that he could no longer fly fighters, but surely he felt it. He had dreamed of flying fighter jets his entire life. His whole college career had been planned around that. And to have to give it up? It had to be frustrating, at the very least.

"I'm sorry," she said.

His head came up; those black eyes lasered into hers. "For what?"

"The night blindness."

"I dealt with it."

"Still, it couldn't have been easy."

"It wasn't. What do you want, Kit? To see a little blood?"

"No," she gasped, lifting her chin against the stab of hurt his words caused. "No."

"Sorry." He moved around the hot tub, stopped a few feet away from her. Close enough that she could feel the heat from his body pulse against hers. After a long look at her, he faced the night, studying the sky. "That wasn't fair."

"It's all right." Was this what they'd come to? She really thought she'd moved past the regret, the resentment. Evidently not. And neither had Rafe. Or had he?

Her curiosity had driven her out here. Maybe she should just let things be and go back inside. She turned to go.

"You're right." His words stalled her movement. "It wasn't easy. At first I was pissed all the time. Felt sorry for myself for quite a while."

"Which was probably one reason you went after that missing child," she suggested quietly.

He looked at her, thoughtful, his Choctaw features noble and proud in the moonlight. "Probably."

A faint smile curved his lips, and Kit couldn't keep her gaze from moving down the corded column of his neck, the sleek breadth of his chest. Her gaze rose to his, and she realized he'd seen her watching him. A flush heated her cheeks and she looked away.

"So you took up private investigations. Lucky for me."

He moved behind her, heat and shadow against her back as he edged around and walked slowly to the end of the pool. "Right. I like what I'm doing now. I'm good at it. It offers me the chance to help people, sometimes in desperate situations. And my night blindness doesn't hold me back. I can't fly jets for the Air Force, but I can still fly sometimes. And I have a job that matters.''

"It does matter." She met his gaze across the few feet that separated them, wishing she understood this strange mix of regret and exhilaration. He still got to her, she admitted, but now she knew what was different about him.

He had assumed, but not ordered, that she would stay at his house. And he'd asked if she had a better idea. In college, he wouldn't have given a thought to any idea different from his own. He was still confident, probably more than most men, but no longer arrogant. His confidence had always held high appeal for her, and without the sharp edge of his youth it sent a shaft of warmth through her. Made her want to stay out on the patio and talk about nothing with him all night long. Which was dangerous.

"You seem to love investigation. You certainly seem to know what you're doing."

"I try." He glanced at her. "And what about you, Kit? Do you still love flying? Working in the air?"

"Yes." She smiled, her stomach jumping as he walked toward her. The towel parted to reveal a glimpse of ropy muscles in his thighs. Dark eyes glittered at her, and her nerves fluttered. "I was transferred over here almost four years ago. Liz moved in with me two years ago."

"After Tony went to prison."

"Right."

"And do you have any regrets in your past?" His tone gave nothing away, but in that moment she was hit with a muscle-clenching sting of regret.

She had never allowed herself to wonder if things might have worked out between them. The possibility that she could have made a mistake had been too much for her to deal with, in addition to the pain of walking away from him. But she wondered now. Staring into his deep black eyes, she wondered if he ever thought about it. How long had it taken *him* to get over the rejection?

She didn't kid herself that he had remained uninvolved all these years. He was too gorgeous, too gentlemanly, too darling to have remained unattached, and celibate, for the past ten years. But for one brief moment, she wished he had. She wished it with everything in her. Still, that was none of her business.

His gaze probed hers, and she felt as if he could sense the regret rolling through her, see right through her as he'd always been able to. "I'm sorry, you know." Her voice cracked, but she kept her gaze locked on his. "I never meant to hurt you."

He closed the distance between them, his gaze sharp as steel. "I know that. Now."

She blinked back an unwelcome burn of tears. "Do you understand why? Did you ever?"

"You said it was because I was too controlling." His gaze roamed over her face, lingered on her mouth before returning to her eyes. "Now I see that I did railroad you. Do you know I only realized today that I never asked you to marry me? I just told you we were getting married."

"I should've said something long before that day, but I found I couldn't. I liked so much about you and I liked having someone to make decisions for me."

"At first," he reminded wryly.

"Yes, at first." She shoved an unsteady hand through her hair. "Have you…were you able to forgive me?"

A long pause. The air between them ached with regret, unspoken words. "Yes."

"Really?" Her heart leaping, she moved another step closer, trying to read his eyes, full of secrets she'd never share. She read a hesitancy in him, couldn't tell if resentment lurked beneath it or not.

"I have, Kit."

"I hope so. I honestly never meant to hurt you. I was stupid—"

"We were both *young*," he corrected firmly.

She nodded.

"Hey, I'm okay. Things happened the way they should have."

"Do you believe that?" she whispered.

He stared into her eyes for a long moment, then lifted a hand and stroked her hair, his palm brushing her cheek. She resisted the urge to turn her face into his hand.

"Yes, I believe it."

"Then we can work together? Put the past behind us?"

His body tensed; his eyes darkened. Was she asking too much? Could she even ask it of herself? "Be friends again?"

"Friends," he murmured. His hand slid around her nape, warm and strong against her flesh. The slight pressure of his touch urged her toward him.

Staring into the midnight darkness of his eyes, Kit's mind froze for a moment. Her body pulsed with the clean, male scent of him, the brush of his hard body against hers, the all-too-familiar feel of his hand in her hair. He was going to kiss her, and though Kit told herself that was a bad idea, she didn't pull away.

She waited, wondering, hoping he wouldn't follow through, then wishing he would.

His gaze devoured her, and Kit felt her belly pull tight in anticipation. Her lips parted as his head lowered. His breath washed against her lips, and her pulse shot into orbit.

Lost in the swirl of cool air and body heat, the scent of him filling her, she raised her arms, but before she could embrace him, he stopped. Dragged his gaze from her lips and met her gaze looking dazed.

"Bad idea," he said in a choked voice.

"Yes." She nodded. "Bad."

He dropped his hand and stepped away from her, leaving her feeling exposed, alone. "I think we can manage that."

Manage what? Kit wanted to scream. Just like at her house, her mind was foggy with the want that had roared back to life when she'd gotten within a foot of Rafe.

"We were friends once, right? We can do that again." His voice sounded rough, almost hoarse. He flashed a quick smile and turned for the house. "Better hit the sack. We've got an early morning."

She gritted her teeth in frustration that she'd let herself be seduced, even for a minute. For some reason, his words unleashed a deeply buried resentment in her. "Still issuing orders, I see."

"And you're still dropping everything to rescue your sister." His features hardened; that generous mouth flattened.

"Which you could never deal with."

His jaw tightened; he turned for the doors. "I just wanted you to have your own life."

"You wanted me to have *your* life."

He halted, shoulders stiff and forbidding. Then he looked over his shoulder at her. "Touché."

Regret bit deep; Kit wished she hadn't said that.

They stared at each other for a long moment. "Now we've both got our own lives," he said flatly.

"Yes." It was what they'd both wanted, why they'd split up in the first place. So why did that feel so hollow to Kit?

He opened the doors and waited this time, looking at her questioningly. Recognizing the truce he offered, she moved toward him.

Kit bit back a groan. Her sister was not worth this! When she found Liz, she was going to strangle her. In the meantime, she had to stay on her guard. Keep a civil tongue. Live in the present, not the past.

Could they be only friends? Was she kidding herself?

His kiss could still reduce her to a puddle of hormones. Attraction simmered between them just as strongly as it ever had, an attraction she had to fight. She couldn't get involved with Rafe again. She'd never gotten over him the first time.

Chapter 5

Things had gotten too personal last night. Rafe had hurt her and he hadn't meant to. He'd nearly kissed her, too. Hadn't meant to do that, either. *Wasn't* going to do it.

As he slowed on Lincoln Boulevard, then flipped his signal to turn left into the parking lot of the District Eight Sub-Office of Probation and Parole, he slid a look at Kit. She looked cool and composed, as usual, in slim-fitting turquoise pants and a matching fitted jacket. In the soft morning light, there was no sign of the shock or the hunger he'd seen on her face last night. And he'd seen both those things.

Finding a slot near the door in the crowded lot was impossible. Rafe finally found one in the back row facing Lincoln and whipped the 'Vette into it. First on his list this morning was talking to Tony's parole officer. A couple of phone calls to Kent Porter had yielded the exact location of the parole office.

Rafe's mind only half-occupied with the case, he recalled

the shock that had widened Kit's eyes last night when he'd gotten out of the hot tub. He couldn't help a smile. He had done that not only to see her reaction, but also because he knew she'd stop looking at him as if he were the much-anticipated cream in a sandwich cookie.

Sure enough, she'd turned away. Still, he'd caught a flash of hunger in her eyes, and that had caused his entire body to harden. Even this morning, he felt tight and...restless.

Friends. Her request whispered through his mind. Could they be friends? He didn't see how, but he *could* do this job. That's where he needed to keep his focus. He'd find Liz and somehow keep from strangling her for all she'd put Kit through.

He killed the engine but left the keys in the ignition in case Kit might need them while he was inside. He channeled his mental energy to the skittery Liz and Tony, not the memory of Kit's gaze on his body, not the torture of the invitation in her eyes last night when he'd nearly done the ultimate in stupid and kissed her. Not the fact that he'd been up all night trying to ignore the fact that she was in the next room.

"I should only be a minute."

She opened her door and stepped out. "I'm going with you."

He pinched the bridge of his nose and got out, finding her gaze across the top of the car. "Trust me on this. The guy'll be more likely to talk if there's only one of us."

"You mean, if there's only you."

"Well, yeah."

"Forget it." She shut her door, hooked the thin strap of her cordovan leather purse over her shoulder and headed for the stairs leading to the front doors.

It would take as long to argue with her as it would to go in and ask the guy questions. Rafe let out a slow breath, pulled his keys out of the ignition, locked the door and followed. It took deliberate effort to keep his gaze from the exposed velvet of her neck. Or the graceful line of her back. Or the slight sway of her hips. He caught up with her, and his strides quickly outpaced hers.

Once inside the cool, spacious building floored with gray-veined tile, he paused a moment at the information desk to ask a harried-looking bottle blonde for directions to the office of Dennis Baker. A few minutes later, he and Kit walked down the hall and through twin glass doors lettered District Eight Sub-Office of Probation and Parole.

The massive room, easily filling half of the entire first floor, was crammed with desks and paperwork in every corner. Putty-gray filing cabinets crowded between the large windows staring out at the building across the street, in corners behind paper-strewn desks. Phones rang. Men and women in sedate suits worked at their desks, maneuvered the narrow space between desks or bent over filing cabinets. Constant, frenetic motion.

Toward the back wall, Rafe spotted a wood-grained nameplate identifying the desk of Dennis Baker and made his way through a twisted path of chairs, files and outstretched legs of parolees sitting at other desks. Kit picked her way behind him, sticking close.

Baker, a fortyish, washed-out looking guy, was crumpled from the crooked part in his hair to his rumpled gold-on-brown tie. His desk sat in front of a large window, which looked out over a treed yard.

Rafe introduced himself, then Kit as his associate.

When she stepped forward, the man jumped out of his chair, wrestled a pile of files off a creaky wooden chair and placed it in front of his desk, indicating it was for her.

"Thanks." She smiled and sat down, perching on the edge of the chair.

Rafe dismissed the impatience that bit at him over the

man's solicitous attitude. "I'm looking for Tony Valentine."

Baker frowned. "Tony should be at work. He works at Thoma Computer Systems."

"Not today he doesn't," Rafe said.

The muffled ring of a phone sounded, and Baker pushed aside a mound of paperwork, snatched up the receiver. His gaze was riveted on Kit. "Let me call you back," he barked at the caller. After scribbling a number on the top of his desk blotter, which Rafe couldn't even see until Baker shoved aside more paper, the parole officer hung up.

"Sorry." Baker dragged his brown gaze from Kit, who shifted on the chair, and shot Rafe an uneasy look. "Now, what's this about Valentine not being at work?"

The man's gaze returned greedily to Kit, and Rafe squashed the heat that flared in his chest. He explained that Tony had skipped town.

"I spoke to him just this morning," the other man protested.

"Did he say where he was?"

"No, but it was a local number." He pawed through reams of paper on his desk, then leaned over to flip through a calf-high stack of pressboard folders. "I checked my caller ID."

Rafe slid a look at Kit. "Could Tony rig something on the phones to give out a false number?"

Kit nodded.

Baker blew out a breath and flopped back in his chair. "Of course! He's a genius with computer and phone stuff. Why didn't I think of that?"

"You had no reason to think he'd skipped town," Kit offered.

Baker smiled at her, erasing some of the fatigue and transforming his features from homely to average. He pulled his gaze to Rafe, who was biting off an order for

Baker to keep his eyes in his head. The other man said, "I'll have one of my investigators get on this."

The phone rang again, and Baker grabbed it up. After a short exchange, he hung up. "Sorry. Why are you looking for him?"

"Miss Foley's sister might be with him."

"Are you planning to go after him?"

Rafe shrugged noncommittally. "I'm just trying to help Miss Foley find her sister. We thought you might know something."

"No." Baker's mud-brown gaze measured Rafe for a moment. "I have to report it."

"Of course," Rafe agreed blandly. Baker could do whatever he wanted; so could Rafe. His gaze panned over the stacks of paper, the wobbling mountains of files. "If *we* find him, it would save you some paperwork."

"True." The parole officer glanced at the sea of paperwork on top of and surrounding his desk.

Rafe pulled out a card and handed it to him. "I'd appreciate a call if you hear anything. I'm willing to reciprocate."

The other man slicked a hand over his hangdog features, then took Rafe's card. "Deal. Give it your best shot."

"Thanks." Rafe turned to go, glancing at Kit.

She rose, pausing in front of Baker's desk. "Thank you."

The man nodded, frank male appreciation lighting his eyes. Rafe clenched his jaw and put himself at Kit's back as they left.

He closed the door behind them, wondering at her silence as they walked outside.

"The more people looking, the quicker we'll find them," Rafe offered.

"I know." She pushed a hand through her hair. "I think

that man will help us. He seemed overworked and a little…lonely, but honest.''

Baker had been flat-out panting after her, but leave it to Kit to downplay that. Still, her assessment about the overwork and honesty mirrored Rafe's. Had she always had such good instincts about people? He'd never noticed it. Of course, when they'd been together before, his assertiveness could've overshadowed that quality in her. What else had he missed?

The thought intrigued him, but he refused to go down that road. Instead, he forced his mind to the scant information he'd gotten from Tony's PO as he drove to the highway, then took the north exit off the Broadway Extension en route to Thoma Computer Systems.

He tried to keep his mind on the case, tried to screen memories of Kit standing in front of his hot tub, the breeze molding her thin blouse to her high breasts.

Her scent, her heat whispered around him in the car. She was everywhere—in his mind, in his space. And he resented it. He might have to take her with him, but he didn't have to monitor her every move, he told himself even as he felt her shift beside him, thread her fingers through her dark hair.

His chest closed up, and he pressed the accelerator harder. When he'd nearly kissed her last night, he'd seen invitation in her eyes, and as much as he was tempted to lose himself in the taste of her, feel her body come alive beneath his hands again, he wouldn't let her have another go at his heart.

They reached a four-story brick and glass building identified by a huge metal sign as Thoma Computer Systems, one of the largest employers in the Oklahoma City area. This time, they were directed to offices on the second floor. After a few minutes, Rafe and Kit were shown in to see Tony's boss, Vernon Taliaferro.

Their visit was short, as Taliaferro was able to provide only the information Tony had given on his job application.

When Kit leaned forward and asked if they might speak to Mike Green, a man Tony had befriended, Rafe gave her a thumbs-up. No doubt she'd spent her entire life hunting down Liz to get her out of one scrape or another.

Mr. Taliaferro's tall, red-haired secretary led them down a long, waxed corridor and around a corner. Conversation, which had been muted as they passed office doors and a conference room, was nonexistent at this far end of the building. The woman stopped in front of a steel door marked Personnel Only and knocked. When there was no answer, she opened the door, poking her head in.

"Mike! There are some people here who need to talk to you about Tony Valentine."

Still no answer, but the woman stepped away from the door, smiling. "You'll have to go in. He won't hear a thing until you're right on top of him."

Rafe arched an eyebrow.

"He's a little distracted when involved in a project, but I'm sure he'll answer your questions."

"Thanks." Rafe smiled as the woman left them.

He opened the door wider, indicating that Kit precede him. He ducked to get through the door, then found he could stand to his full height once inside.

The muted fluorescent lighting revealed they were in a long, very narrow closet. Machines hummed. Frigid air blasted from vents overhead. As he and Kit moved slowly forward, the walls pressed in on him.

They neared a long mainframe computer, which stretched along the wall to his right, and he turned to negotiate the narrowing space. His shoulder bumped Kit's.

She stiffened.

"Sorry," he muttered. Hell, he hadn't done it on purpose. "Mr. Green?" Rafe called, his voice sounding thick and low in the confined space.

On the wall in the back of the closet, a small lamp glared on the blond head of a man and the earpiece of a pair of black frame glasses.

"Mr. Green?" Kit stopped a few feet from him.

A young man—Rafe put him in his twenties—peered around the corner of a rectangular casing, which stood as high as Kit's waist and fit against the mainframe like the top bar of a T. He blinked. "Yes?"

"I'm Kit Foley and this is Rafe Blackstock."

"I'm a private investigator, Mr. Green. We're here about Tony Valentine."

"Is he all right?" The man, thin with bony arms and fingers, straightened. "He didn't show up this morning. We were supposed to work on this mainframe together."

"We think he's fine." Rafe tried to squeeze between Kit and the bulky computer so he could get a good look at Green. As he edged forward, his shoulder nudged Kit into the wall. "Sorry."

"It's okay," she said tightly. She flattened herself against the wall, and when she did, her breasts pressed against his arm.

She looked quickly away and brought up an arm protectively over her chest. Or tried to. Instead, she jabbed Rafe in the side.

Refusing to acknowledge the tightness in his throat, he snapped his attention to the guy in front of them. "It seems Tony has disappeared, Mr. Green."

"What?" The guy blinked like an owl behind his thick glasses.

Kit put her arm down, looking pained. Rafe faced her, scooting past so he stood slightly in front of her. This way, he could face Mike and so could she.

She moved behind him, inching closer to peer around his

shoulder. When she did, her hips pressed against his, and the touch jolted him like fire.

He sucked in a breath. Holy crap. He'd managed to go all day without giving in to his imagination. Now his arm burned and a low insistent throbbing started in his blood. "Um, do you know him well?"

"Not really. He's only been here, uh, let's see…a couple of weeks." He pushed his glasses up his nose. "Maybe a month?"

Rafe knew it had been less than three weeks. "Mr. Taliaferro says your cubicle is closest to Tony's."

"Right. And we've had lunch together a couple of times."

"But you wouldn't say you knew him well?"

"I was getting to know him, I guess." Thumbing his glasses up his nose again, he glanced from Rafe to Kit. "What's going on? Is he in some kind of trouble?"

"We think he might be. Is there anything you can tell us? Have you spoken to him in the last couple of days?"

"No, not since last Friday, here at work." He slid a small screwdriver into his white shirt pocket, already sagging with the weight of other tools and a rubber-banded notebook. He quickly glanced at Kit. "Oh, you're the one who left me a message about Tony."

"Right." She smiled tightly.

Rafe could feel tension humming through her body and knew it had nothing to do with her sister and everything to do with the tight press of his body against hers.

Mike smiled sheepishly. "Sorry I didn't call you back. I got here early this morning to work on one of the mainframes and I forgot."

She nodded, her breath washing hotly against Rafe's shoulder, which only increased the burn in his veins.

He cleared his throat. "Did Tony say if he had any plans to go out of town over the weekend?"

"No," Green said. "He told me he was going to the movies, some science fiction picture, I think. I'm not big on movies."

"And he wasn't acting strangely?"

"Not that I could tell, but I really haven't known him all that long."

Rafe studied him for a moment, and the guy met his gaze without blinking, again nudging up his glasses. "Did he ever mention a man named Alexander?"

The man's smooth forehead furrowed. "No."

Rafe believed the guy; Tony probably wanted to keep Alexander as far as possible from his new life.

"If you hear from Tony, would you give me a call?" Rafe managed to get his arm up and slide two fingers into his shirt pocket to retrieve a business card. He handed it to Green.

"Sure." Green glanced at it, then at Kit. "I hope everything's okay. Are you his sister or something?"

"Something," Rafe answered for her, shifting to show Kit he was ready to go. "Thanks for your time."

She pressed against the wall, but wouldn't meet his gaze. In the mix of bright and dim light, her cheeks looked flushed. "Do you know Tony's wife, Mr. Green?"

"Liz?" As if startled by the question, the man blinked a couple of times. "Oh, sure. Tony's crazy about her."

"Have you met her, then?"

"We've had lunch together a couple of times." He looked from Kit to Rafe. "Is this about Liz, too?"

Rafe watched Kit, admiration growing. She'd done that exactly as he would've.

"She's my sister," Kit admitted.

The man peered over the top of his glasses. "I don't really see the resemblance."

"Most people don't," she said with a smile, but Rafe wondered at the tightness in her voice.

"Hope you find them."

"Thanks."

"If you find out anything, it would really help us if you'd call," Rafe reminded.

"Yeah, if I hear from them, I'll let you know."

"We'd appreciate it."

Rafe reached the door first, curious to know if Kit's cheeks were really as flushed as they appeared in the closet.

He stepped out, sucking in a deep breath. It was too dang tight in there.

Kit was right behind him, and she seemed as glad for the space as he did. He tried to put out of his mind the feel of her body against his, the way her scent still crowded his lungs.

Color flagged her high cheekbones. Her nostrils flared delicately. She was either turned on or mad. Or both.

"What's going on?" he asked as they got into the elevator to take them to the first level.

"If Mike Green knows Liz, then that means she's been seeing Tony while telling me she wasn't. I mean, Tony's only worked here three weeks!"

Mad. Rafe didn't know why Kit was so surprised. Dizzy Lizzy had always done exactly as she pleased, regardless of what it might mean to or for Kit.

"She swore she'd changed. She swore she was getting her life back together, that she agreed when I told her she should wait and see if Tony was really going straight." Kit shook her head, looking disgusted. "If she's not in danger now, she's going to be when I find her."

Rafe bit back a grin, struggling not to replay the memory of all that passion exploding beneath him at one time. Had Kit always been so verbal? If so, he didn't remember. Another trait he'd squashed with his personality?

As they walked outside and across the parking lot, he

found he had to match her quick steps. Her heels clicked angrily against the asphalt.

"You think Green was telling the truth? About not knowing anything?" For some reason, Rafe really wanted her opinion.

Her nose scrunched up in that cute little way she had when she thought about something. "I do. I thought he was forthcoming. He didn't have to say anything about my message, for one thing."

"True."

"I think his concern about Tony is genuine, also his surprise that Tony isn't at work."

"I agree." Rafe was impressed. Not just by the fact that she was showing anger toward her sister for the first time since he'd known her, but also by the fact that they had actually worked together, and worked well.

As Kit slid into the 'Vette beside him and buckled her seat belt, he reminded himself that they would go their separate ways once this was over. He had to forget about wanting to know more about the woman she was now. He'd been close to her before, let his guard down and had his heart torn to pieces. That engagement ring had burned a hole in his pocket, and his heart, for a year as he'd waited and hoped she'd change her mind about them. She hadn't. Neither would he.

Ten minutes later, Kit's gaze shifted from the green blur of passing trees to Rafe as he hung up his cell phone. He'd put in another call about Alexander to Kent Porter, his buddy at the OCPD, and gotten no information. "I think I've wasted your time."

"How so?" Rafe turned right into the parking lot of a flat-roofed, muddy brown apartment complex in northwest Oklahoma City. They had agreed the next stop should be

Tony's ex-cell mate, Eddie Sanchez, who was also out on parole.

"You heard Mike Green. Liz has been seeing Tony. You were right." Kit shoved a hand through her hair, trying to corral the anger that bubbled through her. As she had a hundred times this morning, she checked the battery on her cell phone. Fully charged. "She probably took off with him to Cancun or somewhere for a wild time. That would be so Liz."

"I don't think so, Kit."

"Why not? You know how she is."

"I found a listening device and a camera in your house, a tracker on your car and mine. I think someone's after them, through you."

"Why haven't I heard from her?" Frustration wound her nerves tight.

"I'm not saying they didn't run off to Cancun, but it's looking more and more as if they had a reason."

Kit stared at him in amazement, then huffed out a breath. "This is a switch, huh? *You* defending Liz."

He grinned. "I'm saying your instincts were right. There's a difference."

She laughed, but felt the same slow roll of her belly that she'd felt while sandwiched with him in that closet. Was it because she couldn't stop looking at him, thinking about him? About *them?* Or was it because of the distance between them? A distance Kit knew needed to be there, regardless of the ache in her chest.

She told herself that ache was more about nostalgia than regret, but she didn't believe it.

She felt more pleasure than she should about the fact that Rafe had agreed with her assessment of the parole officer.

Kit tried to concentrate on Tony's ex-cell mate. Sanchez wasn't home, and they learned from his elderly neighbor, Mrs. Hawkins, that Eddie was working the wheat harvest in Texas but was expected back the next day. Rafe slid a business card under Eddie's door, then pulled out another and asked the woman to call if she heard from him. She promised she would.

As Rafe and Kit pulled out of the parking lot and headed to his office, she found herself staring at his strong jaw, the sculpted profile of his lips. He'd treated her like an equal today, and she liked it. But she couldn't let herself wonder what might've happened between them ten years earlier if she'd felt they were equals then. Their breakup had been her fault for not asserting herself more, and Rafe's for asserting himself too much.

As they walked into his office, Kit again checked her cell phone. In perfect working order and no word from Liz. The tension that had knotted her shoulders upon first learning of Liz's disappearance wound tighter.

The same attractive, middle-aged brunette whom Kit had seen on her first visit rose from the dark pecan desk that dominated the reception area. A striking oil abstract of a serene lake on a canyon floor hung on the wall behind her. Burgundy leather chairs winged the corners of the desk, inviting people to wait comfortably. A credenza, matching the polished wood of the desk, held neatly slotted file folders and manila jackets bearing typed labels with case names.

"Kit, you've met Nita Howard, my office manager." Rafe shut the door behind them and grinned at the other woman.

Nita's short ash-brown hair was perfectly styled, her makeup meticulous and understated. Her deep purple suit gave her blue eyes a hint of mischief. "Hello, Kit. How nice to see you again." She shook Kit's hand warmly, her gaze measuring Rafe.

Kit wondered what Rafe might've said about her to his secretary.

Rafe handed her the photos of Liz and Tony that Kit had given him.

Nita pushed a small sheaf of messages at him. "Kit, have you had any word from your sister?"

"Not yet." She tried to keep the tightness out of her voice. It wasn't Nita's fault that Liz was as irresponsible as they came.

The older woman moved gracefully around the neatly organized desk, glancing at Rafe. "I'll post these photos on the Internet and also e-mail them to your uncle at the local FBI office."

"Thanks."

Nita sank down in her chair, smiling reassuringly at Kit. "If anyone can find your sister, it's Rafe."

"Any more messages, Nita?" he asked gruffly.

"He hates to be talked about," she explained to Kit.

"Especially when I'm standing right here."

Nita waved a dismissive hand at him, and Kit grinned.

"There are a few messages, nothing urgent, but you did have a suspicious visitor earlier. A man. I'd say early forties."

Rafe's gaze sharpened. "What did he look like?"

"About five foot eight, I'd guess. Balding. He had a thick neck, like a bulldog on steroids."

Kit's eyebrows arched.

"What time was this?" Rafe asked with a grin.

"Just after eight-thirty. He wouldn't give his name. He wanted to know if he could speak to you about a cheating wife, but he wouldn't give any details. Kept asking when you would return or if I knew where to find you. He wouldn't leave his name, a number, anything. I found it odd."

"So do I." Rafe's gaze moved to Kit.

At the cool speculation in his dark eyes, her heart gave

a sudden thump. ''You think it's the guy looking for Tony?''

''Or you.''

She stilled, a chill skipping over her skin. ''What do we do?''

''Watch our backs.'' He moved around the corner of Nita's desk and opened the door just beyond, which led into his office. ''Thanks, Nita. We'll be in here for a bit. Could you put a call in to Craig, tell him I've got a computer I need him to check out?''

''Sure.'' Nita turned a warm smile on Kit. ''It was very nice to see you again. I know you'll find your sister.''

''Thank you.'' Kit followed Rafe into his office, taken again with how a sense of him—protective, masculine, strong—filled the room. It was easier to focus on that than dwell on the frustration and uncertainty about when she might hear from Liz.

Tony's computer, plugged in and humming, sat on a round conference table to the right of Rafe's desk. He slid into one of the leather chairs that circled the table.

Still spooked by the possibility that Alexander or one of his goons might have been here looking for her, Kit rubbed her arms and walked over to Rafe. Being close to him made her feel steadier. Even though she knew she shouldn't lean on him emotionally, Kit found it difficult to rein in the urge. Especially since she'd had no word from Liz. *Why* hadn't she heard from her sister?

As he typed commands into the computer, Kit tried to keep her gaze on the screen, not on his strong, elegantly tapered fingers. Or the way his face stilled in noble concentration. Nita's voice crackled over the telephone intercom, and she informed Rafe that his computer expert couldn't pick up Tony's computer until after lunch.

Kit rubbed her neck, moved a few feet away. ''I thought you didn't know much about computers.''

"Just enough to poke around the hard drive."

She nodded, wishing she weren't so aware of his clean-woods scent. The latent power coiled in his broad shoulders just begged for a woman to lean her head there. The confidence that had been tempered from arrogance to a quiet, solid part of him touched a place deep inside her, a place she thought she'd walled up over the years.

That she was still attracted to him was something she no longer tried to deny. Her gaze followed his hands as he massaged the back of his neck. Would she ever *not* be attracted to him?

His gaze leveled on her. "Hello?"

She blinked. "What?"

"I asked if you knew how to handle a gun."

"Handle? You mean, shoot?"

"Yes." His lips curved.

"No. I don't have a lot of need to shoot people on my flights. I mean, they either want peanuts or they don't."

He chuckled as he glanced at his watch. "I think you should at least know how to load and aim. We have time before Craig's due. Let's go to the range."

"Let's not," she suggested brightly. She didn't want to know anything more about a gun than how to spell it. And something about being in close quarters with him caused a flutter of unease to move through her.

"Kit, I carry."

"Good. I don't."

"It'll also be a good frustration reliever."

"I'm not frustrated." At his look, she shrugged. "Okay, I am."

"If things get dicey while we're looking for Liz, I'd like to know you can defend yourself. Without shooting *me*."

"Oh. I guess that wouldn't be good," she murmured.

"Well, thanks," he said dryly. "Seriously, I don't like

what Nita just told us about our anonymous visitor. I'll feel better knowing you're at least familiar with my...weapon.''

Perhaps it was because of her thoughts, but she could've sworn he hesitated over that last word, turned it on a suggestive edge.

His eyes glittered with sultry playfulness, a look she remembered too well.

Her heartbeat kicked up. She stepped quickly away from the table, bumping into the corner of his desk. ''I'm ready.''

His lips quirked, but he said nothing. She followed him out the door, smiling at Nita when the older woman winked at her. Just because Rafe could still turn her stupid with *that* look didn't mean she was going to act on it.

Thirty minutes later, they were in a shooting range on the south side of Oklahoma City. It was cold and loud; Kit had never heard so many guns going off at once. The stringent burn of gunpowder hung in the air.

Rafe set her up with a pair of ear protectors and guided her into one of the many partitioned-off stalls stretching the width of the concrete-floored building. Hanging the protectors around her neck, he leaned down and spoke loudly in her ear to be heard over the frequent crack of gunshots.

''I want you to handle my gun, okay? Just get a feel for it.''

She nodded, her eyes widening as he laid a big handgun on the waist-high shelf in front of her. ''That's huge.''

''I hear that a lot.'' His eyes glinted, and she rolled her eyes, biting back a chuckle. ''Now, pick it up.''

She did, surprised at the heaviness of the weapon.

''This is a .357 Magnum. Automatic. The clip holds fifteen rounds; that should show somebody you mean business.''

''I'll say.'' She had no idea how she would be able to use this thing.

He popped out the clip and showed her how to load the bullets, then slide the clip in. After she repeated his movements four times, he nodded in approval and directed her attention to the paper silhouette of a man's upper body.

The target was clipped to an overhead rod and hung about fifteen feet in front of her.

He leaned close, his breath a warm wash against her cheek. "Lift the gun and aim at the torso. You're going for the biggest area."

She shifted against the feel of his solid chest at her back, cursing the way his body heat seeped into her and prickled in her breasts. How was she supposed to concentrate?

She drew her bottom lip in with her teeth and focused on the target. The gun wobbled, and he put a hand over hers.

"Don't be afraid of it."

It wasn't the gun she was afraid of, but she wasn't about to tell him that. She gripped the handle, let her finger rest lightly on the trigger. Sensation hummed through her, dimming even the boom of a voice over the intercom system. She tried to ignore the way Rafe's body silhouetted hers, all heat and power and teasing maleness. Tried to channel her frustration with Liz toward the paper man in front of her.

"Relax your shoulders." His hands settled there and kneaded for a second or two.

The feel of his hands, big and warm and safe, chipped away at her resolve to keep a distance from him. She stared blankly at the target.

"Center up through the back sight." He reached over and tapped the small metal V at the barrel's end closest to her.

Her gaze moved down the hard muscle of his arm, locked on the way his finger lay atop hers.

His hands curved around her hips, and she nearly jumped out of her skin.

"Steady. Just relax."

How could she do that when her pulse had tripled? "I think I should use a different gun."

"No, mine. This is the one we'll have with us."

His voice stroked over her, fanning the heat that lined her belly. Her shoulders knotted even more.

"Loosen up." His hands flexed on her hips; he pressed against her back, burning like a furnace. Her heartbeat skittered.

Images surfaced, of other times he'd held her hips like this, guiding her down on him, gliding in and out. The gun wobbled in her grip.

He reached up, laid a steadying hand on top of hers.

"I don't think I can do this, Rafe. I'm going to get someone killed, probably me."

"No, you're not. You're doing great." His other arm came around her, reached up to support her wrists from underneath.

She felt him, long and hard and lean against her back. She managed to raise the gun enough to sight the target. "What if I miss?"

"There's no one you can hit."

She snorted skeptically, struggling to keep her attention on the target.

"Sight, then shoot."

She forced herself to think past the solid feel of him, the way his hands felt on her.

Trying to remember all the things he'd told her, she emptied the clip, not quickly but steadily. When she finished, Rafe chuckled. He reached over her and pushed a button on the wall, which brought the paper target zooming toward them on the overhead rod.

"Look at that." Genuine pleasure deepened his voice,

and he pulled the paper from its clip, holding it up for her inspection.

There were several shots scattered down each arm and one in the neck, but there were four shots in the torso.

"I killed him!" she exclaimed.

Rafe laughed. "Good job."

"I've never shot anything before!"

He rolled the paper into a cylinder and handed it to her. "We can practice again if you want."

"All right." She laid the paper to the side and turned back to load the clip as he'd shown her. She couldn't believe the sense of accomplishment she felt. Maybe it was due to the light of admiration in Rafe's eyes.

He'd been right. This small break had drained some of the tension from her shoulders. As she slid the clip into the gun, her cell phone shrilled.

Her breath caught; Rafe's gaze sliced to hers.

Liz! Finally. Kit fumbled in her purse for her phone as Rafe eased the Magnum out of her hand.

"Liz!"

"Becky?"

The feminine voice on the other end was crackly with age and unfamiliar. Kit's heart sank, and a lump of emotion knotted her throat. "No. I'm sorry."

The woman apologized and hung up. Anger changed to disappointment then to concern so quickly that Kit could barely register the emotions. Tears burning her eyes, she punched the End button.

"Kit?"

She knelt to shove the phone into her purse. Her voice wobbled. "Wrong number."

"I'm sorry."

She straightened, worry colliding with frustration. Liz was all right, Kit told herself. She had to be. Kit covered her eyes with one hand.

"Kit?"

He touched her shoulder, and the small bit of control she'd owned shattered. She turned, buried her face in his shoulder.

For one heartbeat, he stiffened. She swallowed a sob, started to pull away.

"Sorry," she mumbled.

His arms went around her. She clutched desperately at him, willing herself not to cry. Leaning on Rafe was the last thing she should've done. And the only thing she could do.

Chapter 6

The need to be held by Rafe had Kit trembling. As a sob rose in her throat, he rocked her close.

"It's all right, Kit. She'll call."

"When?" she demanded, tuning out the sharp retort of intermittent gunshots. She let the strength of him soak through her palms, seep into the core of her. "What if something's happened? What if she *can't* call?"

"Hey." He pulled back slightly, his dark gaze penetrating. "She'll call. In the meantime, we've got people looking for her and Tony, right?"

"Right."

"You're doing all you can."

"It doesn't feel like much." The sharp odor of gunpowder stung the air around them. They were closeted together in the partially obscured space, and she didn't want to let go of him. Holding him, being held by him, leveled her nerves. The acute disappointment over not hearing from Liz had caught Kit completely by surprise. The waiting gnawed at her and eroded the hope she harbored that Liz was in no danger.

Just the feel of Rafe's strength wrapping around her washed away some of the bitter disappointment she'd felt over hearing a woman's unfamiliar voice. She shouldn't be leaning on him, breathing him in like oxygen, but how many times had she done this when they were lovers? She couldn't even count them.

All the times Liz had pulled a stunt and Kit had needed someone to lean on, Rafe was there. It had been so nice to be able to trust someone like that. She'd always had to be strong for her dad and Liz. Rafe had been the first and only man she'd ever allowed herself to need.

Gunshots popped around them, recharging the acrid scent of gunpowder. Exclamations of victory and disappointment echoed in the cavernous room. Her arms tightened around him.

"You okay?" he asked quietly.

"I'm not going to cry." She smiled at him. The dark heat of his eyes caught her, heightened the feel of his taut, muscular body against hers. "I know you're right. If something had happened to her, I think I'd feel it."

"You would." Rapid-fire shots stuttered nearby, and he leaned closer to be heard. "You've always had a good sense of these things, and more patience than Liz deserves—sorry. I'll keep that to myself."

"It's all right," she said quietly, her body molding reflexively to his. Thigh to thigh, breast to chest. His crisp khaki slacks whispered against the light fabric of her pants. Was he as aware of that as she was?

His hands stroked her back. "You're strong, Kit. You always were. Taking care of Liz and yourself, your dad, too."

She stared at him. "You used to say that a lot."

He smiled, and her heart jumped straight to her throat.

He brought up a hand, threaded it through her hair, then buried his fingers there. "Yeah."

Her nerves shimmered and she shifted, fitting her body against his even more tightly. His blue dress shirt, open at the neck, revealed the tap-tap of his pulse in the hollow of his throat. She couldn't tear her gaze away from the confirmation that she was in the here and now with him.

A voice boomed over the loudspeaker, the words mangled.

He dipped his head, his newly shaven cheek brushing hers. "You always had about five things more on your plate than anyone should have to handle. Sometimes including me."

He was apologizing? Surprise warmed her, and she murmured shyly, "I didn't mind handling you."

Heat flared in his eyes, and her breath caught. His gaze fell to her lips. The surrounding voices, the gunshots, the electric whir of the rods transporting paper targets all faded to a dull vibration. She could feel his heartbeat thundering against hers. His woodsy scent invaded her lungs, making her skin tingle. Her hands slid up his back; his fingers tightened on her skull.

Their breath mingled, starting a hum in Kit's blood. He was going to kiss her; she wanted him to.

"Trust me, we're going to find her."

Countless times when they were lovers, he'd held her like this, comforted her, listened to her worries about Liz. Why hadn't she realized that at the time? Back then, she'd focused on his assumption that she would marry and move away with him. Now, surrounded by his strength, familiarity washing over her, she was stunned how she'd forgotten this comfort.

His head lowered, his lips a fraction from hers. She wanted that kiss but couldn't quiet a sudden voice in her mind. The scenario was exactly the same as in the past. Liz in trouble; Kit going to Rafe. The realization jolted through her.

She looked down; he immediately dropped his arms from around her. Her whole body ached with frustration over the aborted kiss, but she knew it would've been a mistake. Rafe knew it, too. She saw it in the clench of his jaw, the fire of irritation in his eyes.

She had walked away from him because she couldn't leave her family. The same reason had brought her back to him.

He stepped away, jammed his gun into the small of his back. "I know you're worried, but you're doing all the right things. The things you can control."

She nodded, her chest aching. How could pulling away from him hurt as much now as it had ten years ago? "What if there's somewhere else I should've looked? Someone I should've called?"

"Don't question yourself like that, Kit. It's not productive."

She rubbed her arms against the urge to step into his arms.

After a quick, impersonal glance, he turned in one lithe movement and started for the exit. As she followed, she felt the warmth of his body drain out of her.

Already she felt an emptiness inside, one that she'd felt for a lot of years after leaving Rafe. The only reason she was with him now was Liz, and for the first time, she felt anger over her sense of family responsibility.

Could she have done things differently ten years ago? She didn't think so. Sliding a look at him, noting the tight jaw, the smoldering anger in his eyes, she wondered how she'd ever been able to walk away from him.

Rafe flipped over in bed, punched his pillow for the fourth time and closed his eyes. The faint rise and fall of her voice down the hall told him she was talking in her sleep again, which served to trigger a flash of images through his mind—Kit's sweet face turned to him this afternoon, her lips parting to meet his before they'd both realized what was going on and stepped back.

He'd wanted to kiss her. With the same mind-burning intensity he'd always associated with wanting to fly. And she'd pulled away. Damn it.

Even now, hours later, her soft floral scent taunted him. Rafe could still feel her lush breasts pressing against him and the itch in his palms to touch them, peel those clothes off and do more than kiss her.

He hadn't been the one to call it quits ten years ago. She had always been the one to pull away, and she still was.

What reason did Kit have to pull away from *him?* He was the one who should've put at least the width of a shooting stall between them.

Feeling the tension in her shoulders, knowing she was more than distracted by waiting for Liz, he hadn't been able to stop wanting to reassure her, wanting to reach for her. So he had.

Stupid. Stupid.

He slid out of bed, went to stand in front of the window. Moonlight showered down on the patio. A fickle breeze played with the shrubbery and potted plants ringing the pool.

When she'd turned to him after that false-alarm phone call, sheer surprise had held him immobile for a half second. She seemed so damn self-sufficient, always had. But the feel of her in his arms had caused something inside his chest to shift. She was where she belonged, and it had been natural to draw her close.

She was concerned about Liz.

He wanted to wring her sister's neck.

He didn't see how things had changed much. He still wanted Kit, wanted her in his bed, but after that, then what?

They could become lovers again. After today, he knew she wouldn't take much persuading, but she'd cut his knees out from under him the first time. He couldn't survive that again.

He wasn't going to, period. His body had throbbed for her at the shooting range. It had been all he could do to hold her while he battled the urge to press her against that flimsy wall and strip her clothes off, push into her with all the fury and lust pounding through his body.

But there had been more than lust. A hollowness he felt deep inside, a hollowness only Kit could fill. And he knew that because he'd tried over the years to fill it with other women.

He'd wanted her, yes, but he also needed her. He'd only ever needed *Kit*. Rafe slapped a palm against the wall and pushed away, disgusted.

Need? What he needed was to keep a clear head and get a grip on his raging hormones. Employ some of the discipline he'd learned in the Air Force, for crying out loud. For once, he found himself wishing Dizzy Lizzy *would* interrupt them. Pathetic.

One phone call from Liz would start a trail. Once they found her, Kit could get the hell out of his life. *That* was what he needed.

It hadn't been only the last few days of uncertainty over Liz that had kept Kit up all night. It had been the undeniable presence of the man down the hall, the masculine musk she'd smelled moments ago in the bathroom while she'd showered.

As she walked into the living room the next morning, she caught a flash of Rafe's bare brown shoulder through the doorway leading to the kitchen. He moved out of her line of vision to the refrigerator.

The aroma of fresh coffee and spicy sausage wafted out to her. She paused in the doorway of the airy, clean-lined kitchen, watching him for a moment. He was always so alert, so intense; it was nice to observe him in a relaxed state.

"Yeah, the name's Alexander. First or last name," Rafe said into the phone snagged between his ear and his collarbone. Standing over a skillet, he forked several patties of sizzling sausage to their other side. "I'm looking for someone who's been here for at least the last two years or had ties here, someone who could've visited my missing person in prison."

He was talking to his uncle, she guessed. Barefoot, wearing only worn, snug jeans slung low on narrow hips, Rafe was enough to make a long breath ease out of her. He was gorgeous. All over. Always had been. Her gaze skated up long runner's legs to the tight butt and over the fluid flex of muscle in his back and shoulders.

She missed his longer hair, but the shorter cut emphasized the strength in his neck, the noble planes of his jaw. Her mouth went dry, and she shifted, drawing his gaze over his shoulder.

He held up a finger, indicating he'd be finished in a minute, and she nodded, moving into the living room.

"Okay, let me know what you find. You've got my cell phone number, right?"

Rafe's voice faded as she skirted the navy leather sofa, edged around the walnut end table, which held a cordless phone and a lamp with a black wrought-iron base. Her feet sank into plush gray carpet, complementing the pale gray walls and clean white woodwork.

She trailed a hand along the sofa's supple back as she slid her cell phone from her pocket and punched in her father's cell phone number. He'd left the day before Liz's disappearance to attend a pharmaceutical sales conference.

She could still feel Rafe's arms around her, and a little ache of want still coiled deep in her belly. Insistent, relentless. The comfort he'd given her at the shooting range had haunted her all night, spinning wishes for things she'd walked away from, making her *want*. Him. A different life.

As the phone rang on the other end, Kit swallowed against a ragged ache in her throat and walked to the patio doors. Rafe had removed the pool's tarp and begun filling the pool with water. Patterned mosaic tiles, a single border around the top of the pool, sparkled green and blue in the early morning sunlight. Rising water glimmered.

Harv Foley answered the phone.

"Dad?"

"Kit! Have you found Liz?"

"No, not yet."

"Any word?"

"No." She hated dashing the hope in his voice.

"She'll call you, honey. I'm sure she's fine."

Kit wanted him to believe that because she was no longer sure she did. She didn't want to worry her father by telling him about the bug Rafe had found in her house or the tracking device planted on his car or the unidentified man who'd shown up at his office yesterday.

"I'm coming down there. I can leave my conference."

"No," Kit said firmly. "There's no need."

"I think we should hire someone."

"I did." Her gaze skipped to the hot tub, her mind flashing an image of Rafe rising out of the water like a nude, ancient warrior. "Daddy, it's Rafe."

Silence. "Rafe Blackstock?"

She hesitated. "Yes."

"I thought he went off to fly jets."

She explained he'd left the Air Force and moved back to Oklahoma to be near his parents.

"And he's now a private investigator?"

"Yes."

"Hmm." Pleasure warmed her father's voice. Though he'd supported her, he'd never agreed with her decision to end her engagement. "Are you doing all right? Are things going okay with him, the two of you?"

"Yes." She smiled. At least as fine as she could be, anyway.

"Shouldn't he know something about Liz by now?"

"It's going to take a little while, Dad. Especially since I have no idea where Liz and Tony might've gone." She filled him in on all the steps Rafe had taken, from putting Liz's photo on the Internet to calling the FBI for any information or leads on Alexander.

"Sounds like Rafe knows what he's doing," her father said.

"He does. And there's really no need for you to come."

"You think I'd be in the way?"

"No, but there's no telling how long this will take. I'm able to take some personal leave. You're not. Besides, by the time you get here, we may have heard from her."

"I've sent you some money. You can put it toward his fee."

"No, Dad—"

"Too late, hon. It's already in the mail. I want to help. Liz is my family, too."

"I know, but I think I've got it under control."

"I never had any doubt."

She smiled.

"All right, I'll stay, but you call me the second you hear anything about your sister."

"Yes, I will."

"And Kit?"

"Yes."

"This is not your fault."

"I know, but—"

"No buts."

"Okay." She smiled, wishing she'd already found Liz in some tropical bar somewhere, not running from a guy who could be connected to the mob. She hated for her dad to worry. "Maybe I'll hear from her today."

"Please call me, Kit. For any reason."

"I will. Love you."

"I love you, too."

She disconnected, staring blankly out the glass door. A dull throbbing built in her head. It wasn't enough that she was fighting these swirling, unwanted emotions about Rafe, but this worry over Liz chewed at her insides like acid.

Kit rubbed at the sudden sting in her eyes. Where was her sister, anyway? If she could know Liz was all right. If she had an inkling that she and Rafe might find her soon. Or hear from her.

Kit wasn't sure how long she could stay with Rafe without doing something stupid, something…physical. Smart had been nowhere around ever since she'd hooked up with him again, especially yesterday.

"Breakfast is ready." His voice was tight.

She turned and found him watching her from the kitchen doorway. His jaw was rigid, his eyes sharp as lasers.

"Come eat."

With a frown at his commanding tone, she passed the sofa and laid her cell phone on the end table.

Balancing two cups of coffee and a small glass of orange juice in his hands, he walked to the table while she sat down. She forced her gaze from the ripple of muscles across his bare belly to the plate in front of her, heaped with eggs and sausage. Two slices of wheat toast sat on a saucer next to her plate, complete with a small jar of black-berry preserves. Her favorite.

The ache inside her drilled a little deeper at the fact that he'd remembered, at the sudden way he'd closed himself off from her. "This looks great. I'm starved."

He slid into his chair and stabbed a bite of eggs. "You should've let him come."

She looked up in surprise. This was about her father? "I didn't want to worry him. I've got everything under control."

He muttered something under his breath. "That won't stop him from worrying. Liz is *his* daughter."

She frowned at the sharpness in his voice. "Why are you getting all worked up?"

"Because maybe he needed to do something, to feel as if he were helping."

"But there's no need. I—"

"You wouldn't let him help, just like you never let me help."

She dropped her fork. "What are you talking about? You're helping me right now."

"That's not what I mean. Why do you have to solve every crisis, Kit? Take responsibility for everything in the family?"

"Because I'm…supposed to."

"No, you're not," he said pointedly. "Liz, and only Liz, is responsible for her actions. Your dad sees that. Why can't you?"

"Just because you're helping me find her doesn't mean my family is any of your business."

"The hell it doesn't! Isn't this why you *really* walked away from me? Because you *can't* let go? Because you can't let anyone help you?"

Anger and hurt exploded inside her. "No, I walked away because of your 'I'm in charge' attitude, because you made decisions without even consulting me. Just like our engagement. You assumed I'd marry you, pick up and leave my family. You never even asked me.''

''At the time, I thought you loved me. I thought you wanted to be with me, no matter where.''

''I *wanted* to be asked.''

He dragged a hand down his face. ''I know. That was stupid and wrong of me. I thought if I could just get you to go with me, sweep you off your feet....'' He shook his head. ''It doesn't matter now.''

''It does matter. You thought if I left with you that I'd stop caring for my family.''

''Of course not,'' he snapped. ''But I did think that maybe Liz would start running her own life.''

''She needed me.''

''So did I.''

''You did not!''

His gaze shot to hers. She saw pain and a vulnerability in the dark depths before they went opaque.

She sobered, picked up her fork, put it down. ''I never felt that you needed me.''

''I did. But I couldn't give you what *you* needed.''

''That's not true.''

''Why were you always pushing me away?''

''I...wasn't.'' Had she done that?

''Then why didn't we work out?'' His gaze met hers. There was no rancor in his voice, just an earnestness that made her chest hurt.

''Because you wanted to make all the decisions without me.''

''I wanted to *help* you. Yes, I made a mistake by trying to control things so that you had no responsibilities, but that's because you already had too many.''

Flustered by the idea of something she'd never considered, she stammered, "I was perfectly capable of making my own decisions."

"I wasn't trying to make your decisions. I was just trying to make things easier on you."

"You thought I'd just go away with you, leave my family."

"But not because I wanted you to abandon them."

She saw a loneliness, a reserve in his eyes she'd never seen, and the truth of what he'd said hit her with enough force to stall the breath in her lungs. She *had* always pushed him away. She hadn't ever recognized that he might need her because it wasn't the consuming kind of need her sister had for her.

The regret in his eyes tore at her. She speared a piece of sausage, chewed. "Why didn't you explain this to me then?"

"It wouldn't have mattered," he said tiredly. "You saw things the way you had to see them. I think you just couldn't stand to give up some of that responsibility."

"What do you mean?"

"Because if you did, you'd have to give up the guilt you feel over your mom's death."

She bit down hard on a piece of toast. "You don't know what you're talking about."

"And if you did give it up, who'd take care of Liz? Who'd be there to mother her? Your mom's death wasn't your fault, Kit."

Hurt stabbed deep. "I'm not going to talk about this with you."

"You're right. Things didn't work out between us. Let's just leave it at that."

"So here we are."

"Right. Here we are."

Their eyes met.

The uncertainty she felt was mirrored in his dark gaze.

The moment stretched between them, then he turned his attention to his plate; she did the same.

With a tightness in her chest, Kit realized how much she'd hurt Rafe ten years ago. She'd leaned on him so many times for comfort, then felt strong enough to handle things on her own. He'd seen that as rejection. She'd never meant it that way, but it didn't change the fact that he felt it. She'd seen the bleak truth in his eyes.

And he couldn't know that her dad had been pushing her for years to make Liz stand on her own. He'd finally quit, Kit realized, two years ago when they'd both thought Liz was really going to straighten up. What would life be like if Kit had to take care of only herself?

She had wondered about it before, gotten a little taste of freedom for the last two years, and she liked it, but at the first sign that Liz was in trouble, she'd jumped right back in with both feet. The possibility of living only for herself opened up a window for Kit she hadn't let herself look into until now. A window with Rafe.

He finished his breakfast and rose, then took his dishes to the sink and rinsed them off. When she moved beside him, he opened the dishwasher, sliding the dishes inside while she wiped the table. The tautness in his shoulders, the wariness she picked up from him pricked at her.

We just didn't work out. Had he really closed the door to their past? Hadn't he ever wondered, just once since she'd asked for his help, if things were really over between them?

He closed the dishwasher. "Let's go out to my folks'."

Kit's eyes widened. "I'm sure I'm the last person they want to see."

"They probably aren't even there. They've been camping at Grand Lake."

And what if Dale and Willa Blackstock were home? Unease curled through her. She hadn't seen or talked to Rafe's parents since her and Rafe's broken engagement. "What about Liz?"

"We've both got cell phones. Uncle Wayne knows to call mine if he finds anything in the FBI database about Alexander. I also gave that number to Tony's parole officer and everyone else we've talked to."

"True," she murmured. Of course, being cooped up inside this house with Rafe, trying to ignore the want humming through her body, would be more agonizing than risking a meeting with his parents. Fresh air and open space might help restore her equilibrium.

"We'll ride horses or walk or fish, whatever you want. Let's just get out of here. This waiting is getting to both of us. If it weren't for that visit from Mr. Mysterious yesterday, I'd even let you have a little time to yourself."

"All right."

"Good. Once we get back from there, we can swing by and check on Tony's former cell mate. He's due in from the harvest today."

"Okay." The admission he'd made a few minutes ago about trying to shield her from more responsibility had ignited a realization that slowly grew inside her. He was quickly becoming the same steady presence in her life he'd been when they were lovers.

Her pulse skipped at the thought of all the times she'd made love with Rafe. They'd never had trouble with the physical part. It would be easy to give in to the attraction still very much alive between them. Just the thought of being with him again quickened her pulse.

He understood her; he always had, except she hadn't seen it. What about now? Was there any hope they might have another chance?

Chapter 7

Almost an hour later, Rafe stood in the barn on his parents' property. Frustration sawed through him, as it had since his conversation with Kit at breakfast. He should've kept his mouth shut. Pointing out Kit's responsibility to her family was not only none of his business, it was futile.

Only Kit could change the way things were in her family, and she wasn't inclined.

She stood at the stall door behind him, watching quietly with those big eyes. The blue-gray depths were clear, interested, but he remembered how they'd gone dark with desire yesterday.

He shoved away the mental image and tightened the cinch on Sugar, the palomino mare he'd chosen for Kit to ride. Sasha, the younger mare, was full of herself today; Rafe would ride her.

Kit moved behind him, stroking Sugar's nose and talking softly to the mare. He glanced back, noting the way Kit's jeans gloved her tight little rear. Rafe determinedly pulled his gaze away. There was no way he could've stayed with her in the house.

All he'd thought about since yesterday at the shooting range was how close she was to his bed, how she'd feel beneath him.

He'd hoped that, out here busying himself with the animals, he wouldn't be so aware of her. He didn't want to feel this frustration, didn't want to feel *anything*. She'd proved once again that when there were problems, she would still push him away, still wouldn't let him help her. She hadn't changed, and he wasn't interested.

He figured if he told himself that a hundred times, he might believe it.

She murmured to the mare, and her voice slid over Rafe like silk on skin. Reminding him of her hands on him yesterday, the feel of her breath whispering against his lips. Her soft floral scent flirted in and out of the more potent smells of horse and hay and saddle leather.

He shouldn't have told her how he'd tried to shield her from more responsibility, shouldn't have tried to justify his take-charge attitude. It didn't matter. None of it did. All that mattered was finding Dizzy Lizzy and staying away from Kit until they did. He wanted her, and no matter how much that fact ate him up, it was still a fact.

Even as irritated as he was, he couldn't dismiss the changes in her he'd noticed, though her overdeveloped sense of responsibility to her family wasn't one of them. She seemed more dissatisfied with Liz, more willing to speak her mind to him, more vulnerable than he'd ever seen her. Those differences intrigued him, planted maverick thoughts in his mind to see just what else might have changed.

In college, he'd always been the one to lend an ear, to try to soothe away any troubles, but he'd never let her do that for him. At the time, he thought he would appear weak to her. Instead she told him at breakfast that she believed he'd never needed her.

Well, it was better for her to continue believing that. He wasn't going to let her hurt him again, and opening up to Kit had hurt written all over it.

"This mare looks just like the one I used to ride."

"You rode Beauty. This is her foal, Sugar." Down the stable a horse snorted, and Rafe grinned. "There she is, saying hello."

Kit turned, then moved down two stalls to where the mare stood.

He pulled another saddle blanket from the weathered wooden wall behind him and shouldered his way past Sugar, who had her head buried in an oat bucket. Sasha, a black-and-white paint, sidestepped, then butted his chest with her nose.

"Yes." He scratched a spot behind her ear, then placed the yellow-and-red striped blanket on her back. "You can run today."

Just outside the stall, he heard Kit speaking softly to Beauty, and the sound torched something deep inside him, something cold and sharp that he refused to define. He needed a lead in this case so he could track down Dizzy Lizzy and Kit could be on her way. That's where he needed to keep his mind.

He tugged the saddle from the same wall that had held the blanket and settled it onto Sasha's back.

Kit stepped inside the stall, bringing that nibble-me scent with her again.

Sugar blew out a breath and moved toward Kit, nudging her jeans-clad hip for a treat.

"Nothing for you yet, baby," Kit cooed as she ran a hand down the mare's neck.

Rafe clenched his jaw, tried not to remember how she'd

grabbed onto him yesterday as if he were the only shelter in a twister.

Sasha bumped him with her rump in protest, and he realized he'd yanked a little too hard on the cinch around her middle. "Sorry."

He patted the mare, then turned to Kit. "Go ahead and mount up. I'll need to adjust the stirrups for you."

As she swung one trim leg over the saddle, the seat of her jeans pulled taut across her rounded bottom. His body tightened.

Disgusted, he yanked his gaze away and moved beside the mare to find Kit smiling at him.

"What?" He reached for the stirrup strap, unbuckled it and threaded it up two notches.

She laughed, a soft, lively sound that pinged across his nerves. "Remember the first time you brought me out here?"

He remembered a hot and desperate session in his car, which was probably not what she meant. "Yeah."

She patted Sugar's neck. "I did all right on the ride until we were on the way back here and Beauty realized we were headed for the barn."

Rafe grunted, hoping she would stop with the memories before she worked her way to the one where he'd started. He stepped around to her other side, reached for the strap.

"She took off like a shot, scared me out of my wits."

"You were howling like a wet cat."

She swatted at him. "I was not. I was…startled."

He grinned. Without thinking, he reached up and wrapped his hand around her calf to place her foot into the stirrup. Firm muscle flexed beneath his palm.

He froze. So did she.

He wanted to slide his hand up, cup the heat between her legs just like that saddle was.

"You didn't catch up to me until she'd stopped in the barn."

Kit's voice was strained, as if she were forcing the words. Hell, he knew he would be.

He clenched his jaw against the memory, but still it flooded in. He'd run his hands over her, making sure she was all right, and she'd fallen full into him, laughing, kissing him hard and deep. Her hands and mouth had been eager, inviting.

"The horse wasn't as rough on me as you were," she said in a shy, tentative voice. "You grabbed me so tight, I could barely breathe."

So, she'd finally remembered. He glanced up and saw that color flagged her cheeks. She leaned over to fiddle unnecessarily with the stirrup he'd already adjusted.

"Hey, I was trying." He managed to speak without snapping. Slowly, he moved his hand away from her. "Beauty couldn't be caught when she had the barn in her sights."

"You were scared," Kit said. "I'd never seen you like that."

"You'd never been on a horse before. I didn't want you to get hurt." He gave one last tug on the cinch to make sure it was secure.

"I was fine."

"Yeah, you were." He saw in her eyes the memory of how they'd kissed with reckless abandon, how he'd dragged her to his car only to stop two miles down the road to finish what they'd started.

"Rafe?"

"That was a long time ago," he said gruffly, fighting the urge to haul her out of that saddle and kiss her until he forgot that she'd walked away from him. "Shouldn't have any problems with that today. Sugar doesn't take off like her mother."

He ignored the hurt in Kit's eyes, just like he ignored

the want drumming through his veins. The way he'd been ignoring it all morning. Hell, ever since she'd popped back into his life. "You're good to go."

She nodded, urged the horse to move into the middle of the barn, onto the packed dirt floor littered with feed dust and hay. He swung into the saddle and followed.

He'd thought coming out here would block the images that had plagued him at the house. Images that involved Kit in his bed wearing nothing but him. Her little trip down memory lane hadn't been good for either of them.

As he guided his mare past hers, she followed, heading for the barn doors. She rode slightly behind him, drawn into herself again. Good, he decided, ruthlessly dismissing the urge to smooth things over. It wasn't his job any more to comfort or protect.

Just as they reached the barn's wide double doors, two people appeared outside. Recognizing their silhouettes against the strong glare of the sun, Rafe groaned inwardly.

"Rafe, we saw your car."

"Hi, honey."

Dale and Willa Blackstock stepped inside the barn.

Rafe glanced back. Kit reined her horse to an abrupt stop behind his mare and shot a look at him. He saw panic then uncertainty in the blue-gray depths.

"Hi, Mom, Dad." His hold tightened on the reins.

"You've got company?" his mother asked pleasantly. Squinting as her eyes adjusted to the dimmer light of the barn, she started around his mare's head, trying to get a look at who sat the horse next to him.

His father snagged her elbow. "Willa."

Rafe saw Kit wince, then she urged her horse forward so that a wedge of sunlight fell full on her face. "Hello, Mr. and Mrs. Blackstock."

"Kit?" Willa's tone was incredulous, and even Rafe

picked up on the indignity beneath the surprise. "Kit Foley?"

"I'm helping Kit with a case," he said quickly, wishing that for once his parents would adhere to some sort of schedule. "We're taking a break while we wait for a phone call." He wasn't opening up the whole can of worms about Liz.

Kit started to dismount. "It's been a long time."

"No, no, it's all right. Stay up there." Willa's gaze went to Rafe, then to Kit. His dad just stood there, Choctaw features unreadable, but Rafe saw the questions in his black eyes. The warning.

"I...hope you're doing well," Willa said stiffly.

"I know this is very awkward." Kit's fingers knotted and unknotted the reins. "I'm sorry."

Rafe's heart clenched. Whatever else they thought of her, surely his parents would admit she had guts.

"Nonsense," Willa said briskly.

His dad nodded.

"I hope everything's okay," his mom said. "Rafe mentioned a case?"

"Mom."

"My sister's missing."

Though he'd given her the opportunity to keep quiet, Rafe admired Kit for not dancing around the truth. She had to expect the disapproval that came into his mother's brown eyes at the mention of Liz.

"I hope she's all right, that everything works out."

"I have every confidence that Rafe will find her."

His parents' features both tightened. Dale pulled on Willa's arm. "Let's leave them alone to get on with their ride, hon. We need to unpack anyway."

Rafe threw his dad a grateful look and kneed Sasha into motion.

Kit followed him out of the barn, then reined up in front

of his parents. "I'm really sorry. I'm sure you didn't expect to see me here today."

"No, but it's all right," Willa said firmly. "Good luck with your sister. I hope you find her quickly."

"Thank you." Kit smiled weakly, said goodbye to Dale and followed Rafe out of the paddock to the open field behind the barn.

They rode in silence for several yards. Kit looked pale, even more so in the glare of sunlight. Her mouth was drawn tight.

"I bet that was the surprise of their lives. Nothing like coming home to find your son's ex-fiancée."

"It's okay, Kit." Rafe fought the urge to move closer to her, to take her hand.

"I never apologized to them for breaking our engagement."

"There's no need," he said tightly. His shirt collar suddenly seemed to choke him. He ran a finger beneath the neck of his cotton polo shirt.

She nodded, but he could see she didn't agree. His mom had handled it better than he might've expected, Rafe admitted, though he knew he'd get the third degree once she could talk to him alone. At least he could reassure her that he and Kit weren't picking up where they'd left off, that this was strictly business. He'd had all the heartbreak he needed for one lifetime.

Kit rode beside him quietly. So quietly that he could hear the tall grass swish against the horses' bellies. Crows squawked and squirrels chattered in the grove of trees to their left. The fecund smells of horseflesh and leather gave way to the fresher scents of clean air and loamy earth. June sunshine buffed Sugar's coat to spun gold.

Rafe shifted in his saddle to peer into Kit's face. "Hey, are you okay?"

"I feel badly. I never spoke to them at all after.... After."

"That was between you and me."

"Your mom probably doesn't see it that way."

"Probably not," he admitted, "but you weren't engaged to her."

Her lips twisted. "True."

"Let it go, Kit. You've got enough to worry about."

The smile she gave him was so forced that it knotted up his gut. "All right."

He'd always wanted what his parents had, that sharing partnership, friends and lovers, trust both ways. He thought he'd found it with Kit, but she'd never been able to fully commit, at least not to him.

In the barn, drawn by the past and the urge to kiss her senseless, he'd managed to keep his hands to himself. That's what he had to do until they found her crazy sister.

He thumbed a bead of sweat from his upper lip. Right. No problem.

The horse was warm and solid beneath her. The fresh air and sunshine should've cleared away the haze of desire, but Kit's body vibrated from Rafe's touch. She could still feel the imprint of his hand on her leg, wanted to feel his touch all over. The thought of him touching her, kissing her because he wanted to, not because someone was watching, was enough to cause a fine sweat to break across her skin.

How could she go from her anger of less than two hours ago to this craving for him? His words at breakfast echoed in her mind.

I think you just couldn't stand to give up some of that responsibility. Because if you did, you'd have to give up the guilt you feel over your mom's death. And if you did

*give it up, who'd take care of Liz? Who'd be there to
mother her? Your mom's death wasn't your fault, Kit.*

She rolled her shoulders. It was unease and not anger
that skimmed through her. It was true Kit had stepped in
as a mother to her sister when their mom had died; she'd
realized that years ago, but who else was going to do it?
Kit was responsible for their mom being gone. She was the
oldest child; it was her duty.

She guided her mare around a fallen branch. Her gaze
locked on Rafe's strong back as he led the way to the creek.
The red knit fabric of his polo shirt molded the long muscles in his back, dipped into the ridges between his shoulder
blades.

He glanced and caught her staring at him. His mouth
tightened. Looking away, he spoke softly to his mare, and
she quickened her step. Kit automatically followed his lead,
her gaze shifting to the strong, copper slope of his neck.

She knew the red shirt covered shoulders that were
bronze and broad, shoulders that had sheltered her more
than once. By touch alone, she knew her way across those
fluid muscles, down the hard arms that had drawn her into
their protection countless times.

She wanted to lay her head against that wide, tempered
chest, skim her hands over his iron-hard belly to his narrow
waist. His tough, sinewy thighs flexed as he guided his
horse up a small incline. One broad hand rested on the
faded denim of his thigh; the other hand held the reins
loosely.

As her horse trotted up the hill behind his, Kit forced her
gaze from him. His stirrups disappeared in a patch of tall
sunflowers. Taking the same path, she spied a sprinkling of
wild pink buttercups and a handful of small purple flowers
that miraculously missed being trampled by the horses.

Liz was the reason Kit was with Rafe, and he'd made

clear he resented that. In the past, that had been more than enough reason for Kit to keep a wall between them.

His words played again in her mind.

Can't let go. Why do you have to take responsibility for everything in your family?

He looked back, his narrow-eyed gaze colliding with hers, peeling away every defense with a painless finesse that made her want to surrender her pride, her common sense.

"Let's race to the creek."

"Is that fair?" She cleared her throat, annoyed at the huskiness in her voice. "You know the way and I don't."

"Over these two hills, then swerve right. Sugar will get you there."

"You're on." Without waiting for a cue, she gave her horse a swift kick in the flank, and the mare lunged, muscles bunching. She reached Rafe's mare, gathered speed from a canter to a flat-out run. Kit laughed.

For the first time in three days, she focused only on what was happening at this moment. Leaning low over the horse, loving the feel of the wind streaming past her face, Kit urged the mare on. She let the motion carry away all thoughts of Liz, of decisions to be made about her life.

Beside her, she felt Rafe closing in. The ground beneath her shook with the force of his horse's hooves. From the corner of her eye, she saw that he leaned low over his horse's neck, gaining speed. Her horse jumped a shallow gully, and she laughed again.

Rafe's laughter rang out, too. He pulled even with her, flashed a wicked grin and passed her.

"No way!" she yelled, tapping her heels against the mare's flanks. Sugar picked up a little speed, her nose coming even with Rafe's thigh.

Both mares swung to the right. A hundred feet ahead, through a clump of pecan trees, the creek shimmered like liquid diamonds. Exhilaration swept through Kit. Rafe urged his horse to jump an overturned tree trunk.

She squeezed her knees tight against the saddle and leaned forward slightly as her mare followed.

Rafe reined up at the edge of the creek a second before she did. He was laughing, his eyes glittering at her in a way that made her senses swim.

"Show-off." Kit's mare skidded to a stop.

His mare reared, spun in a fancy pivot. He held his seat easily, his triumphant gaze finding hers. "I even gave you a head start."

"Don't get cocky, Blackstock. There's still the race back."

He slid to the ground and left the reins hanging loosely over his horse's neck, then led the mare to the water's edge.

When Kit tried to swing one leg over, Sugar snorted and bumped against a tree, trapping Kit's leg.

Leaving his horse, Rafe walked over and laid a hand on the mare's nose. Sugar immediately quieted, and Kit noted that he'd had the same calming effect on her yesterday at the shooting range.

She dropped to the ground, then led Sugar to the creek. As the horses drank their fill of the clear water, Kit tried to dodge the thought that had teased her all morning.

Near the water, the bank was firm and rocky. Trees lined each side of the sparkling creek, which snaked as far as Kit could see in both directions, growing wider upstream. The water disappeared around a curve, lost beneath drooping branches and shade, then appeared again glistening in the sunlight.

"The horses will graze here. Let's walk."

Kit immediately fell in with Rafe's suggestion and dropped her reins. She followed him up the rise and caught up with him in the shade of an old pecan tree. Sunlight dappled the ground, beaming its way between leaves to make delicate patterns on the knee-high prairie grass.

He looked into the distance, across acres of rippling grass, greening winter wheat, the occasional stand of blackjack and cottonwood trees. "It's peaceful out here."

It was peaceful, but tension hummed inside her. Kit knew those shimmering nerves had to do with the man beside her. The man she'd never forgotten. "This was a great idea, Rafe. Thanks."

"You're welcome. I thought it would do us both good. The horses needed it, too. I've only been out twice to ride since my folks have been gone."

He took off, long legs easily parting the grass.

Her steps fell in with his, and she observed quietly, "Everything looks great, almost exactly the same. The barn's a different color, I think."

"Yeah, they decided to repaint with gray instead of red." A cool note slid into his voice. "So tell me what you've been doing with yourself, Kit."

"You already know." She gave her hair a quick finger-combing. "I'm a flight attendant."

"Ten years is a lot of flying. Don't you do other things?"

"Oh. Sure." She thought for a minute. What did she do?

"I finally finished college," she offered tentatively, stopping beneath a sprawling oak.

He stopped, too, looking at her in surprise. Something dark burned in his eyes. "That's great. I knew you would."

Because of Liz and her stunts, Kit had missed final exams twice. She hadn't been able to complete her credits and graduate with Rafe. She'd done so in the months following their breakup, but she hadn't walked across the stage with her class, with him. Until now, she hadn't realized how much she resented missing that.

Tamping the irritation spiraling inside her, she said, "I

was able to help Liz get a job with the day-care center. She's done very well there. She seems to have a real affinity for children.'' She laughed. ''I know, you're going to say it's because she's one herself.''

He reached up, stripped a spring-green oak leaf from its branch. ''No, I'm not.''

The wariness she'd noticed this morning still shadowed his eyes, still showed in the way he carried himself. He was careful not to stand too close to her, careful not to look at her too often.

She knew she'd hurt him years ago. Knew, too, that his parents were justified in being aloof and even angry with her. She didn't want to hurt him again, but she wanted another chance with Rafe. She'd dated enough since their breakup to know that guys like him were one in a million. And she'd thrown him away.

He took off again, moving with fluid grace. She followed, trying to keep at least an arm's length between them. That seemed to be what he wanted. Beneath the shade of a pecan tree, where the grass was short and cropped, he stopped. His shirt sleeves skimmed over biceps that looked as hard as the oak trees around them.

Water gurgled down the hill. Mockingbirds and whippoorwills scolded and squawked overhead. The scent of freshly trodden grass, the newness of spring drifted in the air.

She ached to be close to him, but she didn't move. ''My dad's still in Norman. He said to tell you hi.''

Rafe nodded, a muscle in his jaw flexing. ''What else? Don't you have any hobbies?''

She sensed he was simply making conversation. Something to keep both their minds from the past. Or perhaps Liz. ''I'm involved in the city's reading program. I read to an elderly person at the library once a week.''

''Really?''

"That was one of Liz's community service projects several years ago. She was on probation at college and she had to pick a project. I became interested in it and still enjoy doing it."

"Do you still water-ski? You were hell on a slalom."

She smiled. "I haven't done it in years."

She'd given it up. With her job taking her out of town so much and her spare time spent chasing after Liz, there didn't seem to be time for going to the lake.

He leaned against the ancient oak tree and propped one booted foot on the trunk behind him. "Sounds like you've got a lot going on."

"Not really. I just run around a lot." She laughed, but it hit her then just how little she did for herself, how much of her time revolved around her sister.

He'd been right about Liz, Kit realized. About how she couldn't let go of the responsibility she felt for her sister, that she felt for her entire family.

Dissatisfaction over that had simmered inside her for a long time. For the last year, it had become more insistent, but it was Rafe who'd finally forced her to address it.

Before she could talk herself out of it, she said, "You were right before."

He turned his head, a slight frown between his brows.

"About Liz. About how she should be standing on her own two feet. About how my dad has been pushing for that. He has, for quite a few years."

Rafe slowly brought his leg down, straightened. "I shouldn't have said those things. They're none of my business and I do know there's a reason, Kit."

The gentle sympathy in his voice tugged at her, urged her to move toward him. She could still feel his reserve, see it in the sudden flare in his eyes, but she needed to be close to him.

"You really helped me yesterday, Rafe."

"Hey, I know it's tough, waiting to hear from her, wondering when you will." He stared over her head, a muscle in his jaw working. "But you will."

"I know. I meant, you were really there for me. Just like you always were."

He pushed away from the tree, stepped around her. "Let's don't make more of that than there was, Kit. I was just doing what any...friend would do."

"But I don't want just anyone to do it." She couldn't believe she'd said the words, and the brittle silence behind her told her he couldn't, either.

She was afraid to turn around, but she did, her gaze going straight to his. Wariness and heat smoldered there. He was so solid, so strong. He'd always been those things. And she'd missed them. Missed *him.*

With each moment they spent together, it became clear how much. Keeping her gaze locked with his, she took a step toward him.

"We should probably get back."

She reached out, threaded her fingers with his. He tensed but didn't pull away. She knew what she had to do about Liz. If she could be close to Rafe for just a minute, she knew she'd have the strength to do it.

His fingers were warm and still in hers; his pulse beat a strong tattoo against the column of his throat. Want unfurled inside her, scrambling her pulse, plucking at her nerve endings. She saw desire, felt him fighting it. Fighting her.

She moved closer, lifted one hand to the rugged line of his jaw. "I don't think I'd be able to get through any of this if it weren't for you. I think that's why I had to find you."

He started to shake his head, and she laid a finger against his lips. His chest was deep and strong. His eyes bored into hers, guarded, piercing.

"Don't you ever wonder?" she whispered, unable to keep from dragging her index finger across his bottom lip.

His free hand came up, clamped around her wrist and pulled her away. "No."

She looked into his eyes, saw the lie. The black fire in his gaze turned her bones to water.

"Don't you ever think about how good it was between us? What might've happened?"

"No." But the word was choked, and his gaze fell to her lips.

She could see the same questions in his eyes that had tortured her since last night. She could read the craving to find out, feel it in the way his body tightened against hers. She might regret it later, but for now she had to know.

Keeping her gaze locked with his, afraid he would step away, she raised up on tiptoe. His grip tightened on her wrist, but he didn't move.

One kiss. Given freely. Completely unrelated to hidden cameras or listening devices.

She had to taste him, had to know if they could possibly have another chance. It wasn't over. The smoldering darkness of his eyes, the taut quiver of his body told her he wanted her.

She touched her lips to his, and it was as if a barrier broke. The need and hunger that had slowly swirled between them exploded.

On a growl, he hauled her to him. She wrapped her arms around his neck. He ravaged her mouth, his hands skimming her back, cupping her bottom and anchoring her to him. She felt something sharp and rough at her back, realized he'd backed her up against the tree. She didn't care. All she wanted was him, to have this insane whirlpool of need take her down as it was doing now.

He lifted her, wrapped her legs around his waist. "Damn, Kit. Damn."

Dragging his lips from hers, he nipped his way down her neck, and she clutched at him, kissing his ear, his temple, his cheek. He was hot and hard between her legs, making silver heat lick at her belly.

After tugging her T-shirt out of the waistband of her jeans, he slid his hand beneath. His palm, slightly callused, sent a shiver through her as he dragged it over her rib cage. When his hand closed over her silk-covered breast, she moaned, the pleasure a sharp ache inside her.

He captured her mouth again, and her tongue skimmed his lips, stroked his tongue.

With a strangled curse, he slid her down his body and put her on her feet. Her legs wobbled, and she braced herself against the tree, her hands spearing into his hair as he shoved her shirt up, took her in both his hands.

His thumbs skimmed her nipples, hard and straining against the thin material of her bra. He flicked open the front catch, and her breasts spilled into his hands. She made a sound deep in her throat, her breath stalling at the sight of his hands, bronze against the pearl of her flesh.

He dipped his head, circled one nipple with his tongue. ''I love your breasts. I've always loved your breasts.''

A flush heated her body. The shyness she thought she'd outgrown whistled back, but only for a second. His mouth moved over her, gently, hungrily. Heat shot straight to her core. Trembling, she arched into him, holding on tightly, loving the sensation of being swept into a tide of feeling.

His kiss claimed and demanded. He lifted his head, his gaze scorching as he caressed her breasts again.

''Why didn't we fight harder for this?'' she breathed, clutching at his shoulders to keep him close. ''How did I ever walk away from you?''

It took her a moment to realize he'd stopped. His mouth branded her neck; his hands cradled her breasts.

She opened her eyes, her mind fuzzy with desire. The

disbelief in his eyes, the resentment hit her senses like a slap.

"Rafe?"

With unsteady hands, he pulled her shirt down and stepped away. Barely six inches, but it felt like miles.

"Rafe?" A sob backed up in her throat. Hunger clawed through her, twisting a knot of need.

His breathing was ragged, his pulse jumping wildly in his neck. "We're not going to do this, Kit."

"But—"

"No." He held up both hands as if to ward her off. "I'm not going down that road again."

"But things are different now." Still shaky, she fastened her bra, straightened her shirt and tucked it in. She tried to think around the feel of his hands on her body.

"I was always there for you. You were never there for me. And I'm not talking about sex. I commit, you don't," he said harshly, turning away from her. "Things are *not* different."

"They could be." She snagged his elbow, drawing a savage look. She released him. "What you said about Liz is true. It's time to make her grow up. I'm ready to do that."

"Just like that?" he said doubtfully, the heat in his eyes cooling.

"Yes. I realized that before now, but I couldn't admit it. You made me face it. I've got to stop bailing her out, let her start making her own mistakes."

"Darlin', this is me you're talking to."

"I'm not saying it will be easy, but I'm ready." She sounded desperate and didn't care.

"I know how responsible you feel over your mom, Kit." He reached out, almost reluctantly she thought, and stroked a finger down her cheek. "I don't think you can walk away. Not from Liz, not from any of the responsibility you feel."

"I know Mom's death wasn't my fault." She gripped his arms, granite-hard beneath her palms. "Logically I know it, but if I hadn't thrown a fit for those shoes, she wouldn't have taken me to the mall. And Liz wouldn't have been deprived of a mother."

"You were fourteen, Kit. You were not driving the car. Not her car, not the car that hit her. You tried to help her, and there was nothing anyone could do."

"I know all that." The emotions of the last few minutes, the seesaw between worry and gut-twisting desire dissolved the few defenses she had left. Tears burned, and she swiped the back of her hand across her eyes. "I know you're right."

"Hell." Rafe shifted uneasily, then lifted the tail of his polo shirt. "Here."

"I'm not going to cry," she sniffed, waving away his offer.

"I know." He reached out, thumbed a tear from her cheek. For a second, just an instant, his palm cupped her cheek, then he pulled away.

"Once we find Liz and I know she's all right, I'm going to tell her."

He shook his head. "Kit—"

"I mean it. I'm going to do it."

"Can you, Kit?" He went completely still, his gaze probing hers. "Can you really?"

"You don't expect me to walk away now?" She wiped another tear off her cheek. "She's in danger."

"This certainly doesn't seem to be one of her typical stunts. And no, I don't expect or want you to turn your back on her. But I don't believe you'll be able to let go once she gets back, even if she's safe and sound. Besides, I'm not what you really want anyway. You're confused by the uncertainty of this situation. When we find your sister—"

''No, I'm not confused. I do want you. I want *us*. I know it now. I know what I need to do, what it's time to do.''

''Do you know?'' He advanced on her, backing her against the same tree where he'd kissed the breath out of her. A raw hunger, primal and disturbing, blazed in his black eyes and reached out to her. ''Because I'd want all of you, Kit.''

He was lethal and glorious and undeniably male. The low, harsh edge in his voice sent a shiver rippling through her. A delicious heat started between her legs.

''All of you. No sharing this time. I won't settle for less ever again. And you can't do it, Kit. You can't commit, at least not to me.''

''I want to try.'' She'd never been so excited or frightened in her life. Her heart pounded in her throat; her body trembled. ''I really want to try.''

His gaze locked with hers, searching, measuring. In one split second, she saw it—the decision, the rejection.

''That's good,'' he said, gently removing her hand. ''I hope you can someday.''

She felt more lonely than she had in years. Since the day she'd told him no. Emotion welled in her throat, and she struggled to get the words out. ''That's not enough for another chance?''

He stared at her for a long moment, uncertainty then regret chasing across his carved features. Tension lashed his shoulders.

''No,'' he said simply.

Chapter 8

Just after six that evening, his mood as hot and unrelenting as the sun burning its way down the sky, Rafe drove north on May Avenue toward Eddie Sanchez's apartment complex. Why the hell had Kit decided she wanted to change *now?* Why did she think she *could* change?

She sat beside him, arms folded protectively across her middle, staring silently out the window. She hadn't said a total of ten words since they'd returned from his parents' place. Not even after Nita's phone call a few minutes ago with a message she'd picked up from Mrs. Hawkins on the company voice mail. The elderly neighbor of Tony's ex-cell mate had called to say that she'd spoken to Sanchez in the apartment complex's parking lot.

Kit's scent slid seductively around him. The velvety feel of her soft, delicious flesh still branded his hands, his mouth. And the harder he tried to forget, the more clearly he recalled the creamy taste of her. Sheer sexual frustration had every nerve in his body wired tight enough to relay electricity.

Kit wanted him.

Rafe locked his jaw. While that knowledge could still make his pulse spike, it also made his resolve harden. He hated the distance between them, but it was for the best. She'd said she wanted another chance, but what she really wanted was for things to be the way they used to be.

He rubbed at the knot of tension that had settled in his neck. She could still prime him from zero to ready in under five seconds. He didn't like it, didn't want it, but he had to deal with it. For the present, he wasn't getting the space he needed from her. If he could just get a break in this case, work would go a long way toward keeping his mind from replaying the shadowy pictures of what had happened between him and Kit today.

He'd spent the afternoon outside on the phone, in the garage on the phone, anywhere she wasn't. Kit had stayed in the living room. Lunch and dinner had been bleak, sober affairs. Kit had called Tony's parents again, only to learn they'd had no word from their son. Rafe had lost count of the number of times she'd checked her home answering machine for a message from Liz, without luck.

The calls he'd made—to Nita, Craig, Kent Porter, Uncle Wayne—hadn't yielded much better results. Only Rafe's conversation with Craig had potential. The computer expert was piecing together some deleted files from Tony's computer and might have something later. Rafe had also called a guy who did regular work for him and ordered a background check on Eddie Sanchez.

All afternoon, Rafe had managed to stay busy, but thoughts of Kit tickled the back of his mind. His body, still aching and hard, cursed him for pushing her away, but he knew he'd done the right thing.

She'd made her choice ten years ago, and he'd learned to live with it. He might want her physically, but he wasn't laying his heart on the chopping block again. They could work together, but they couldn't be together.

As he swung the 'Vette into the parking lot of Sanchez's apartment complex, dusk settled in shades of silver over the city, gray sifting over the thin line of red at the horizon. Finding a space in front of Eddie's mud-brown building, Rafe killed the engine and got out. Kit did the same. Dark shadows ringed her eyes; fatigue pinched at her delicate features.

He rubbed a hand across the back of his neck. This enforced closeness made his nerves as raw as those mind-melting kisses at the creek had.

They needed a break in this case and fast. Surely Liz would call soon for money, as she'd told Kit.

Each two-story building had four apartments on the top and bottom floors, two on each side of a set of concrete steps that led to the second floor. Sanchez's apartment was on the lower floor, the back one on the right. As soon as Rafe stepped past the staircase, he froze. Yellow crime scene tape stretched across Sanchez's door.

Automatically, he slammed out a protective arm.

"Hey!" Kit said as he bumped her chest. Then she saw the door, too. "Oh, no."

The chirp of crickets punctuated the stillness. Rafe looked in both directions of the walk-through breezeway. Golden light thrown by a setting sun shone through the opposite open end of the building. He saw the same telltale yellow crime scene tape on the end of a bush. Dread formed a cold knot in his gut.

"Young man!" A paper-thin voice whispered from the next apartment.

Rafe ducked to look under the staircase. One half of Mrs. Hawkins's wrinkled face peered at him. "Are you all right, Mrs. Hawkins?"

"Yes, yes." She motioned them over and cracked the

door barely enough to let them in. Once they stepped inside, she quickly shut the door, locked the dead bolt and slid in the chain lock. "My sister's coming to get me. The police don't think I should stay here. I certainly don't, either."

"What happened?"

The older lady dabbed at red-rimmed eyes. "It was awful, just horrible. I found him, right back there behind the apartment building."

"Maybe you should sit down," Rafe suggested, worried at how frail the old woman looked.

"Thank you." She let him lead her into the small living room and help her onto a nubby, olive-green couch. "I went outside to get my mail. I always return by the back way because I check the bushes. Sometimes the maintenance man here doesn't water them. And there he was. Hidden underneath. Blood everywhere. It was horrible. I called the police right off."

"That was good."

Kit rubbed her arms as if she were cold.

Apprehension snaked across Rafe's neck. "Was it Eddie Sanchez, Mrs. Hawkins?"

"They marked everything off. No one can go in that apartment until they're finished looking around."

He nodded, familiar with the procedure. "Ma'am?"

"The police said he was murdered," she whispered, pressing the handkerchief to her eyes again. Her thin, wrinkled skin was mottled. "That's why I'm going to my sister's."

Rafe struggled to keep his voice level. "I need to know, Mrs. Hawkins. Was it Eddie?"

"Yes. Yes." She dabbed at her eyes again.

Rafe's gaze sliced to Kit. Horror widened her eyes and she covered her mouth with her hand.

The news dropped on Rafe like a hammer. Eddie Sanchez had been their best hope for new information. The one person Tony may have confided in, Sanchez was dead. Had crucial information died with him? This was not the break Rafe had hoped for.

A few hours later, Rafe hung up the phone in his study and leaned back in his soft leather chair. Damn. Kent Porter at the OCPD had just confirmed Rafe's fear, and he did *not* want to tell Kit. Porter's information had forced Rafe to admit that Liz was in definite danger, more than he and Kit had probably suspected.

His desk lamp burned bright over the notes he'd scribbled concerning Liz's case. As they'd left Sanchez's, Rafe had worried at the chalkiness of Kit's face, but she'd insisted she was fine. Once home, she had disappeared into the bathroom for a few minutes, then moved into the living room, cool and calm. He knew she wasn't.

The television hummed at the same low volume he'd worked to all evening. Since he and Kit had returned from Eddie Sanchez's apartment complex, Rafe had sequestered himself in here to work. Kit had watched television. Or rather, she'd had the thing turned on.

His study door was open, and every minute or so, like clockwork, he would see movement from the corner of his eye. Kit pacing.

She didn't cry, didn't ask questions, didn't say a thing. She was wearing a hole in his nerves not to mention his carpet. He knew she was worried about Liz, and he knew, too, she wouldn't say anything to him about it. She'd gone deep into herself after that incident at the creek. Finding out about Sanchez had caused her to withdraw even further.

Rafe knew he'd hurt her. The urge to reach out, try to reassure her about Liz was strong and insistent, but he couldn't risk getting close to her again. If he let her in, it would kill him when she walked away. And she *would* walk away.

It registered then that, aside from the low murmur of the television, no sound came from the living room. Too long had passed since he'd heard the soft give of sofa leather or the crackle of magazine pages. He pushed back his chair, rose and walked out of the study, then crossed the ceramic tile of the entryway. The television droned on, but Kit wasn't on the sofa. Or in the matching oversize chair. Or anywhere in the room.

Panic squeezed his chest. The kitchen was dark. He glanced toward the patio doors. And saw a flash of moonlight and shadow in the pool. Movement.

Striding to the glass doors, he watched for a moment. Kit sliced through the water with the sleek precision of a machine. Long, purposeful strokes. Swift. Single-minded. The water shimmered around her.

Pale light hit the soft curve of her cheek and jaw as she came up for air. Skimming through the water, reaching one end of the pool, flipping a turn, swimming to the other end. She did it again. And again. A relentless, punishing pace.

Rafe's heart clenched.

She just swam. He didn't know how long she'd been out there, how long he stood there. Her strokes became shorter, choppy. Desperate.

Finally, she reached the shallow end and weakly pulled herself up to sit on the edge of the pool. Even from here, he could see how she labored for breath after breath. Except for the frantic rise and fall of her chest, she didn't move. Just sat there, legs half in the pool, limply huddled into herself as she stared at the moon's reflection on the water.

Should he leave her alone?

The trees in his yard swayed with a breeze. Silvery light skipped across the pool. He went and snatched a towel from his bathroom, then took it outside.

The air was cool for June. She had to be freezing. He stopped behind her, his fingers closing tightly over the terry cloth as he saw the points of her shoulder blades thrown into sharp relief with each breath.

"Kit?"

She gave no sign of having heard him. She just sat there, a lonely silhouette with the night curling around her like smoke.

"I brought you a towel." His voice sounded loud and alien against the quietness of the night.

"Thanks." Her voice was as flat as cardboard.

Concern surged through him, and he knelt beside her. "You should probably come on in."

Her chin trembled, as did the rest of her body.

"Here." He held the towel out to her, and when she didn't take it, he unfolded it, laid it across her shoulders.

At his touch, she scrambled up, splashing water onto the patio, onto his boots. Her fingers grabbed at the edges of the towel as she stepped onto the solid concrete surrounding the pool.

Her reaction spurred as much regret as resentment in him. He shoved his hands in his jeans pockets. They were both on edge, and he knew she had to be frightened over what had happened to Eddie Sanchez.

She slid the towel from her shoulders, patted her face and neck. He recognized her one-piece blue tank suit as one from the closet next to the hot tub. The too-large top gaped slightly at the neck, exposing the shadow between her breasts.

She ran the towel down her legs. "Have you talked to your friend at the police department?"

Rafe nodded. There was no need to tell her everything.

Arranging the towel sarong-style around her slender curves, she tucked in one end to secure it. "You might as well tell me. I have a right to know."

"I don't have any news on Liz." He brought one hand up, rubbed the back of his neck.

"But you found out something about Sanchez, didn't you?"

"Yes."

"Tell me then."

"There's no point—"

"Stop trying to protect me." Her chin angled stubbornly at him.

"It has nothing to do with Liz."

"That man was linked to Liz. He knew Tony, didn't he?"

"It has nothing *directly* to do with her." Rafe shoved a hand through his hair, hating how cool and prickly she sounded.

"You tell me, Rafe Blackstock." She stepped closer, moonlight revealing the wanness of her face. Her eyes glittered between wet, spiky lashes. Despite the command in her voice, she looked fragile.

He could still see remaining hurt in her eyes from what had happened between them earlier. Thank goodness she wouldn't know the significance of what he was about to tell her. "The guy was shot execution-style. Two bullets to the head."

She wobbled, and he reflexively reached out to steady her. Before he could, she straightened, visibly gathered herself. "That means something, doesn't it? What does that mean?"

"Kit—"

"Tell me." She bit the words out. "You can at least give me *that,* can't you?"

Her bitter reference to his earlier rejection knifed through him.

"I'm paying you, and that means for anything that might concern my sister."

His jaw tightened at her blatant reminder that he was technically her employee. "It means the job was done by professionals."

Her head came up. "More than one person was involved?"

Hell. He shoved his hand through his hair. "Mrs. Hawkins told the detectives that two men knocked on Sanchez's door earlier this afternoon. She told the men Eddie had stepped out for a few minutes. The next time she saw him, he was facedown in the shrubbery."

Kit went as pale as chalk and walked around him, clutching the towel to her as if it were a shield of armor. She stopped a few feet away, next to his round, white-trimmed patio table. Moonlight skated across the glass top, slanted over the green-and-white striped chair cushions. "So, Mrs. Hawkins saw these men? She described them to the police?"

"Yes."

"What did they look like?"

He chewed on the inside of his cheek.

"I know you got their descriptions, Rafe. You're too thorough." Her voice was taut, as if she'd already guessed.

He shifted so he faced her and met her gaze, which was dark and stormy with worry. "She described one of the men as very slender, six feet tall. And the other as short and balding. With a thick neck."

She stilled. "Like a bulldog on steroids?"

He didn't think she even heard him confirm it. She sank into the curved patio chair behind her. Undiluted fear widened her eyes. "Oh, no."

She put one slender hand to her temple. After a long moment, she looked up. "It's the guy who came to your office."

"I think so."

"He has something to do with Liz. We know that for sure now."

"Yes." And Eddie's execution-style murder was a mob trademark, which was another piece of information that jived with Tony's story.

Kit jumped up, looking around frantically as if unsure where to go. "We've got to find her, right now."

"We're doing all we can."

"Stop standing there! What if that happens to my sister? What if she's shot?" She turned away, the towel falling to the patio. "We can't let that happen. We've got to find her. I hired you to find her."

He knew emotion, not reason, was talking, but that didn't stop the slash of pain he felt at her words. He'd never failed her; he wasn't about to start now. "Until we get a lead, it's stupid to go off on a wild-goose chase."

"There's got to be somewhere we haven't looked, someone we haven't talked to. Have you done everything you know to do?"

"Do you have any ideas? I'm open."

"Maybe I should hire someone else."

"That's your choice," he said coldly, his voice lashing at her. "But you've got to calm down. I'm doing everything that's possible at this point. I'm waiting on a call from Craig, who may have found something on Tony's computer, but even if he hasn't, we're not going off half-cocked. We'll hear from Liz or Tony or someone who's seen them. It's only been twenty-four hours since I put the information on the Internet."

"What if no one contacts us? Then what do we do?"

He refused to even consider the possibility. "You've got to be patient."

"*You* be patient!" She stalked to him, eyes glittering, mouth drawn tight. "That's not your sister out there. It wasn't your sister who was run off the road and could've been killed just like Eddie Sanchez."

Her eyes were angry, but clear. And alive. Relief washed through him. He hadn't seen any emotion since this morning by the creek. "We'll find her, Kit. I know the waiting is hard, but we're covering our bases right now."

Her shoulders sagged. "It doesn't feel like it."

"I know. This is the most frustrating part of any case, trying to wring a lead out of somewhere, waiting until one turns up. I've also ordered a background check on Eddie Sanchez. That might tell us something. But Craig's our best bet right now, until Liz calls."

"So we just need to hope Craig finds something on Tony's computer."

"Right."

She stilled, her eyes narrowing. "Computer! Maybe she's e-mailed me! Why didn't I think of that before?"

"She said she'd call, but that's a good idea. Let's check it out."

Kit suddenly became a blur of motion. She snatched the towel from where it had fallen on the patio, whirled and started for the house. "It'll just take me a minute to change."

"Okay. I'll call Craig again."

"Thanks." She turned at the door. "Sorry for losing it a while ago."

"You're entitled." His gaze met hers. With the towel draped over one pale shoulder, her hair wet and slicked back, she looked small. Vulnerable.

Which made him feel like a class-A idiot for rejecting her at the creek, yet how could he have done anything else? They wouldn't work. They never had.

"I know you're doing everything you can," she said carefully, awkwardly. "I wouldn't have come to you if I didn't trust you."

"I know." His throat went tight. "I'll wait in the study for you. We can check your e-mail from my computer."

"All right." She slid open the patio door and hurried across the living room, then disappeared around the corner and down the hall.

Hating the distance between them, he pinched the bridge of his nose. He didn't want her to get her hopes up, but maybe Liz had e-mailed instead of calling. He doubted it, but checking would make Kit feel she was doing something. And she desperately needed to feel useful, he realized. In control.

That sense of being needed, being responsible was a core part of her, something she probably couldn't change even if she wanted to. Just like he couldn't stop the anger that occasionally still swamped him over the night blindness that had forced him out of his pilot's seat.

He stepped into the house, locked the patio door and picked up the living room extension to call Craig. Why hadn't he ever seen how important being needed was to Kit? By wanting her to force Liz to grow up, was he asking her to turn away from a vital piece of herself?

He *wasn't* asking her, he reminded himself. And Kit wasn't going to suddenly let go of the responsibility she felt. Her cool independence, the remoteness in her eyes when she looked at him was a blaring announcement that she'd gotten his message at the creek. The distance between them pierced something deep inside him. Rafe didn't like it, but he also wasn't going to change it.

There had been no message from Liz on Kit's answering machine, no e-mail on her computer. Disappointment a stabbing pain in her chest, Kit had ached to turn into Rafe's broad chest, cry out her frustration and her growing fear, but she hadn't.

The memory of how she'd cried at the creek kept her

from it. Just another humiliation in a day Kit wished she could forget.

Lying in his guest bed hours later, her thoughts spun from Rafe's rejection to Eddie Sanchez's murder to Liz's whereabouts. Kit's swim in the pool had exhausted her, but she couldn't sleep. All that had happened today had her emotions ricocheting.

There was a link between Eddie Sanchez's murderer and Tony. What if Alexander and his men had already found Tony and Liz? Icy fear slithered through her.

She had to believe Liz was still safe or she'd go crazy. Dealing with Rafe was enough to make her go *there*. She forced her eyes shut, but images of him teased. His woodsy scent was as strong on her now as it had been when his mouth had blazed a trail of fire over her flesh, his phantom touch as provocative as when his hands had curved over her breasts.

Her belly tightened in response, and she forced herself to recall how he'd pushed her away. The memory was enough to send a fresh surge of humiliation through her. What had she been thinking to kiss him like that? Why had she ever thought there could be a second chance for them?

He'd made clear what he wanted from her—exactly nothing. As painful as it was to recall the memory of his unequivocal rejection, Kit did it. She couldn't lean on him any more. For ten years, she'd done fine without him. She'd do fine now.

Mixed with the sting of his rejection was the growing fear that Liz was probably in greater danger than Kit first imagined. Why hadn't her sister called? She glanced at the pillow beside her, saw that the phone was on and charged.

Rafe had called his office manager, Nita, and told her that their mysterious visitor had also likely been seen at Eddie Sanchez's apartment before Eddie's murder. Rafe's suggestion that Nita carry her gun to the office for the next few days, as well as his arrangement for an off-duty police officer to stay in the office during Nita's work hours, only heightened the fear swelling inside Kit.

The fact that he recognized a definite threat to her sister, and possibly others, scared her silly. And kept the horror of Liz's car being run off the road in the forefront of Kit's mind. She willed the phone to ring.

Nerves stretched thin, she threw back the blue-and-white windowpane comforter, then reached across the polished mahogany bedside table to switch on the frosted glass lamp. She picked up the mystery novel she'd started at least four times in the last week. Had Eddie Sanchez known something that might've led Rafe and Kit to her sister and Tony? And if so, had Eddie's murderer managed to get that information? Was one of Alexander's men even now following a lead completely unknown to Kit and Rafe?

The questions twisted viciously in her mind. She forced her attention to the book, only to find her thoughts wandering after a few sentences. The doubt she'd managed to dodge all day seeped in. Rafe had hit, with unerring aim, on a question she could no longer ignore. Could she commit fully to him? She didn't know.

She closed her book, got out of bed and walked to the window, opening the wooden blinds. Moonlight rippled across the pool's water. A cloudless pewter sky sparkled with bright diamonds of light. Her satin nightgown drifted down her body, rousing again the feel of Rafe's hands on her.

Tortured by her thoughts, Kit closed her eyes and struggled to clear her mind.

A phone rang. Her eyes flew open. Her cell phone!

"Rafe!" she called, diving onto the bed to grab the phone. "Rafe!"

She punched the button. "Yes, hello! Hello! Liz?"

"Sis!"

"Oh, thank goodness." Kit choked back a sob and a dozen questions. "How are you?"

"Fine, so far. I can't talk long."

"Tell me where you are. I'll come get you."

"No! Kit, there could be men following—"

"I know!"

The door to Kit's bedroom banged open and Rafe rushed in, wearing only a pair of low-slung gray cotton shorts.

"Is it Liz?" he asked.

She nodded, sitting back on her folded legs and motioning for him to sit beside her on the bed. He eased down, his bare shoulder brushing hers.

"Who's that?" Liz asked. "A private investigator?"

"Yes." Kit wasn't getting into the story of Rafe right now.

"Tell me where you are."

"Tony says I can't say anything directly."

She nearly screamed. "I can't get to you if I don't know where you are."

"I need money, sis. Just wire it. Please. You can't meet me."

Rafe pressed closer, his slightly stubbled jaw tickling her. She positioned the phone so he could hear better.

"We went to see Eddie Sanchez today, Liz."

"He doesn't know anything," her sister said quickly. Too quickly.

"Not anymore, he doesn't," Kit agreed.

"Tell her," Rafe whispered.

"He's dead, Liz. He's been murdered."

"Oh, my gosh!" her sister shrieked. "Tony!"

Liz explained to Tony; Kit heard his deeper voice urging her to do something. Rafe's hand was hot on the sheet behind her; his hair-roughened thigh nudged hers where her gown had ridden up.

"Was it Alexander?" Liz asked soberly.

"We're not sure. We think so."

"It was. Tony, what are we going to do?" her sister wailed.

"Liz, tell me where you are." Kit hoped the startling news about Eddie would scare some sense into her sister.

"Has Alexander or one of his men been following you?"

"They were at first. I haven't seen them for a couple of days. What did Eddie know, Liz? Why would someone kill him?"

"Tony says I have to hang up. Send the money, Kit."

"Get her to tell you where she is," Rafe whispered. "Get a phone number."

Kit nodded. "Where are you? Are you calling from a pay phone? Give me a number."

"Kit, you can't meet me. If those guys are following you, you'll just lead them straight to us! Is that what you want?"

She glanced at Rafe, shook her head. "How much do you need?"

"A thousand dollars, fifteen hundred, if you can. That'll hold us until Tony gets what he needs from Alexander's computer. I'll pay it back. I swear. Tony says he will, too."

"Okay, I'll wire it from my bank first thing in the morning."

"Thank you, sis. Do you think you can do that by eight o'clock?"

"Yes, but you have to tell me where."

Rafe gave her a thumbs-up, his hand resting against her thigh.

"Remember when I was a sophomore in high school?"

"What?" Kit blinked. Where had this come from?

Rafe made a sound deep in his throat.

"Liz, this isn't the time."

"Remember the first time I went to the senior prom?"

"Tell me where you are!"

"I am, Kit. Listen to me."

She noted the uncharacteristic calm in Liz's voice, and the steadiness took Kit off guard. She went still. "I'm here. I'm listening."

"Remember who I went with to that prom?"

Kit frowned. Liz had dated so many guys. Jocks, musicians, race car drivers.

"He drove a red Camaro, jacked up in the back. *Not* the guy who drove a pickup. The red Camaro. That's where we are. Wire the money to this check-cashing place." Liz rattled off a company name. Kit leaned to reach her purse.

Rafe snatched it and gave her a pen so she could jot down the name.

"I've got to go. Tony's about to have a heart attack because I've been on here so long."

"Liz—"

"Oh, one more thing. I thought about moving here once! Love ya!" The phone went dead.

"Liz?" Kit yelled. "Liz?"

Nothing.

She clicked off her phone and bowed her head, trying to focus on the relief she felt rather than the frustration boiling inside her.

After a long minute, Rafe nudged her with his shoulder. "Hey, she's okay. They both are. That's good."

"Yes, and I want to strangle her." She gestured wildly. "We wait and wait on her, then she calls with this?"

"So, who was it? Who'd she go to the prom with?"

"How am I supposed to remember that?" Kit looked at him. "One year, she went with one guy and came home with another."

"Think, Kit. She's giving us a clue." Rafe's gaze flickered to her breasts, then returned to her eyes. Cool, unreadable, all business. Still, she became suddenly, uncomfortably aware that her breast pressed into his arm.

Rafe went on, completely undeterred from his train of thought. "Tony won't let her stay on the phone long and he won't let her say anything directly. He's cautious. That's good. If she's calling and she says she's fine, then she is."

"Okay, okay." Gritting her teeth, she cleared her mind of everything except her sister's wacky clues. "She also said she'd once thought about moving to this place."

"Right. Where?"

"Hollywood with Ryan. Dallas with Mitchell." She unfolded her legs and slid off the bed. The feel of all that hot, hard muscle made her nerves raw. "Santa Fe with Dusty. Kansas City with Lee. See a pattern?"

"Great." Rafe rolled his eyes. "Let's try to figure out the guy's name first. Who was her prom date her sophomore year?"

"Ritchie Sheldon." Kit paced to the opposite side of the bed, tapping one finger on the brass footboard. "No, she went with him to the prom her junior year."

Rafe rose, followed a few steps behind.

"Um, Tony Gibson. No—Ben Doyle." She snapped her fingers. "Ben Doyle."

She turned, nearly ran into Rafe's sleek, bare chest.

He nodded. "Okay. Ben Doyle."

"No. Not him." She sidestepped him, wishing he would put on a shirt. Or a blanket. Something. "He drove a pickup."

"What does that have to do with anything?" Rafe growled.

"She said the guy she went with drove a red Camaro, not a pickup." Her head started to throb. Why couldn't Liz have just told her? "Oh, wait! Benji. Benji." She paced to the head of the bed, then to its foot, trying to picture Liz in her first prom dress. She'd worn a low-cut black dress that year. What was that guy's name?

"Benji who?" Rafe's every step stalked hers.

She turned, looked at him through slitted eyes. "There's a reason I'm not spitting it out here, Blackstock. Benji..." She closed her eyes, his face floating into focus. He'd been gorgeous, dark hair, dark eyes, olive skin. "Wexler! Benji Wexler!"

"Okay, Benji Wexler. Is it Benji or Wexler she's trying to tell us?"

"Wexler. She made sure to say it was a specific Ben. Go by the last name."

"Okay, let's check it out on the Internet. See where we can find Wexler, America."

Instead of going into his study, Rafe strode down the hall to his bedroom, and she followed. The neon green screen of a notebook computer blinked from a small rolltop desk in front of one of his wide windows. He straddled his chair, used his mouse to click up a box and dial onto the Internet.

She walked in and stopped as his scent curled around her. Her gaze went immediately to the king-size bed in the center of the room, which was attractive and unmistakably masculine. Deep greens, stormy blues, a wicked thread of scarlet were jeweled slashes of color against the pale gray walls and carpet.

The straight-edged bedframe, mirrored dresser and highboy spoke of hand craftsmanship and painstaking, honest labor. The walls boasted more black-and-white drawings like those in his office, but these depicted biplanes and early model jets. Next to his window hung a framed oil of Rafe's three horses, chasing each other through a meadow Kit recognized as being close to the creek.

She felt like an outsider and couldn't deny the fierce longing that suddenly clutched at her. To belong to this room, to *him*. She shook it off and walked over to stand at his elbow, leaning close to see the screen.

Once online, Rafe found a search engine, then typed in

the words *Wexler United States.* Kit paced behind his chair, her satin nightdress skimming her knees as she walked.

She stopped, peered over his shoulder again. "They can't be far. Or can they? A car can cover a lot of ground in three days, right?"

"It's hard to know what they've been doing, Kit. They could've been driving this whole time or they could've been hiding out in some hotel somewhere. Even here in the city."

"She should've called me before now," Kit muttered. Skirting his elbow, she looked over his shoulder again. A Web page was loading. She sighed, made another trip around his chair.

She turned, caught his gaze skimming her legs. A cool politeness slid into his eyes. Hating the heat that inched across her skin, she arched a brow. "Anything yet?"

He glanced casually at the screen. "No. It's coming."

She paced to his bed, wrapped a hand around the short, squared newel post of the dark rustic footboard. His plaid comforter, in tones of blue, teal and burgundy, was cornered neatly on the plump mattress. The closet door was closed, hiding rows of clothing she suspected hung as ruler-straight as the navy and green towels she saw through the half-open bathroom door.

Turning, she thought she caught him looking at her again.

She ignored the sudden clench of her heart. "Well?"

"It's coming. Okay, Wexler. Florida."

"That's too far."

"So is...Georgia."

"She said she'd once thought about moving to this place. Look for California, New Mexico, Texas, Kansas. Of course, those are just the ones she told me about. There could be others she didn't, just like she didn't tell me she was seeing Tony again."

"It'll be something you know," Rafe soothed.

Kit was doing her darnedest to keep her gaze off his broad, copper shoulders, the way his sleek muscles flexed and shifted as he bent over the keyboard. He'd acted all day as if she hadn't crawled up his chest at the creek. As if he hadn't had his hands and mouth all over her.

"Aha, Wexler, Kansas."

"Yes!" She rushed over, leaning close to read the screen. Rafe's scent, fresh male underlined with soap from a recent shower, reached out and twisted something inside her. Something hot and primal, something lonely. "That's got to be it."

"Kansas." He typed something; another screen appeared. "Looks like it's about a three-and-a-half or four-hour drive from here. It's in the southeastern corner of the state."

"I'll call my bank in the morning and have the money wired."

"Don't wire it."

She straightened. "What? But I told her I would."

He tilted his head to stare thoughtfully at her. "Let's *take* the money. Drive up there. You want to find her, don't you?"

Kit smiled slowly. "You're brilliant."

He shrugged. "Just doing my *job*."

She didn't miss the way he emphasized the word *job*. So, she hadn't imagined the flare of pain in his eyes when she'd thrown out that threat earlier. She'd regretted the words the second they left her mouth. Regardless of what had happened between them, Kit didn't trust anyone else to find her sister. She just had to remember that's all she could trust him to do.

"I brought fresh clothes from my house earlier," she said. "I can be ready first thing in the morning."

"Me, too."

She started out of the room, encouraged that she might see her sister in less than twelve hours.

"Good job on deciphering that puzzle from your sister. She's nuts."

She glanced back. "Thanks."

"Shouldn't take us too long after finding them to wrap this up. We'll get them somewhere safe until Tony can get what he needs, get him some backup from the FBI."

She nodded. By this time tomorrow, she'd be with Liz. And her time with Rafe would be nearly over. The realization that they could be this close to parting slid a hot needle of regret through her.

Didn't he feel any of that same regret? She could read nothing in the guarded, black depths of his eyes. Nothing about what had happened between them at the creek. He appeared unaffected, as if it hadn't happened, but it had. She wouldn't forget it; she didn't want him to, either.

Impulsively, she said, "I meant what I said at the creek today."

He looked startled; after a moment, he said, "So did I." She saw in his eyes that he really had. He wasn't going to give them another chance. He'd moved on; she had to do the same.

Trying to breathe past the aching tightness in her chest, Kit left the room.

Chapter 9

Even as Rafe drove Kit to her bank the next morning, the blood still pounded hot in his veins. The image of her in that drop-dead-red nightgown made his pulse hitch even now.

She sat in the soft leather seat next to his, close enough that he could feel her warmth. All morning, she'd been polite and reserved. But he noted the way she drummed her fingers nervously on her knee, fidgeted in her seat.

He was tense, too, but maybe not for the same reason. It wasn't that her fluttery slip of a nightgown had bared too much, but that he knew exactly what she looked like under that gown. He clenched and unclenched a fist, downshifted to turn into the parking lot. The memory of those long, sleek legs disappearing beneath berry satin, high breasts peaking with just a look from him chipped steadily away at his common sense. Had they only been together three days? It felt like a lot longer.

I meant what I said at the creek.

He'd told her he had, too. Told her he wasn't going to give them, *her,* another chance. Right now, he didn't feel one bit sure.

Hope, something he thought he had squashed years ago, had flared at the earnest promise in her smoky blue eyes. She made him almost believe that she could really commit completely to him.

Morning sunlight glittered off the large tinted windows of the bank. He swung the 'Vette into a empty space near the front door.

Kit opened the car door, glanced at him. "Any advice?"

"Small bills. You don't want anything that might call attention to Liz and Tony."

"Right." She smiled, the motion easing some of the fatigue in her features. "Be back in a minute."

Rafe nodded, his gaze riveted on her as she moved onto the concrete walk, then disappeared inside. Those khaki slacks curved over her bottom just the way his hands had yesterday. He gripped the steering wheel until his knuckles showed white.

He shook his head and told himself to do something productive. Surreptitiously, he checked the side and rearview mirrors. No sign of the silver sedan he'd shaken a couple of days ago. None of the other cars in the parking lot had followed him here. The cars passing on the busy street behind him didn't repeat. So far, so good.

Rolling his shoulders, he focused on leveling out his pulse, tried to erase the pictures of Kit that still teased his mind. Considering the fact that he felt like his brain had shut down due to pure lust, he thought he'd done a damn fine job of keeping his thoughts, and his hands, to himself last night.

She walked out of the bank and toward the car, her pink cotton sweater molding her breasts and tucking snugly into the thin waistband of her slacks.

As she moved toward him with athletic fluidity, something hot balled in his chest. Something fierce and possessive that he refused to examine. He glanced away, rubbing a hand over his face.

She slid into the car, reaching to put her purse on the floorboard behind him. "I withdrew sixteen hundred dollars. Do you think that's enough?"

"Yeah." Her too-careful tone indicated that she was trying to include him even while maintaining a distance. Which was exactly what he was doing.

He reversed out of the parking space as she fastened her seat belt.

Keeping an eye out for a tail, he headed east on 122nd Street toward the Turner Turnpike. They'd cruise through Tulsa, stay on I-44 East until they neared Wexler.

Beside him, she shifted in the seat, first angling away, then toward him. She reached over and changed the radio station. A rollicking country tune by Vince Gill filled the car. She drummed her fingertips on her thigh.

Rafe kept his gaze trained on the road, but his thoughts seethed. Last night, he'd wanted to tumble her onto his bed, make love to her with no thought about how that would skew things. And it definitely would. Getting naked with Kit would only cloud the issues between them, and he was through letting her confuse him.

Just thinking about those hot, desperate kisses they'd shared at the creek yesterday edged his hormones up an unnecessary notch. Feeling crowded, restless, he settled into his seat, leaning one shoulder into the door.

She reached up and changed the radio station again. As Rafe identified the bluesy soul of Eric Clapton, Kit's soft wildflower scent drifted to him, had him tightening his grip on the steering wheel. This case was nearly over. He hadn't done anything stupid yet. He could last until they met up with Liz.

Somehow he *would* last. Rafe wanted Kit more fiercely than he'd ever wanted anything, including to fly jets. He'd never connected with any woman the way he still did with Kit. And he shouldn't want to connect with her. He knew what she could do to his world, his heart.

But what he hadn't known was how well they would really work together. Last night, for the first time, they'd been a full-fledged team. She'd let him know immediately that Liz was on the phone. She'd asked his advice, followed his suggestions.

Even without his prompting, she'd tried to get the right information out of her sister. The old Kit would've bristled if Rafe had told her what questions to ask, listened in on their phone conversation. This Kit, the one who was even now making his palms damp, had let him in. Just like she'd said she intended to at the creek.

He liked it. Knew he could easily come to crave that give-and-take like an alcoholic craved his first drink of the day. She'd actually depended on him. He recognized that it was satisfaction filling him, rather than the frustration he usually felt when dealing with Kit and one of her family situations.

Quickly, he tamped down the emotion. He couldn't let himself trust that. Right now, he was all she had. That was why she leaned on him.

Liz's prolonged silence had eroded the strength Kit wore like armor. But once she had her sister safely rescued from this latest fiasco, things would probably go back to the way they'd always been. Kit taking responsibility for everyone and everything, giving all of herself to her family with nothing left for anyone else.

She punched the radio buttons again, then again. By now, he'd heard everything from Gershwin to Boy George.

He slid a sideways look at her. "You nervous?"

"Anxious, I guess." She answered carefully, raked a hand through her short, mink-dark hair.

"It'll be over soon."

"Yes. I can't wait." The smile she aimed at him was a combination of relief and uncertainty. Then her eyes widened in horror. "Oh, I didn't mean…not because of you."

"I know." He smiled.

She flashed a shy smile that jolted him to the soles of his feet.

His gut hollowed with want. No matter how he ached to pull her under him, make her go all liquid and limp the way he knew he could, he couldn't afford to let down his guard, couldn't trust her not to hurt him again. Rafe rubbed his neck and eased out a long breath between his teeth.

He needed a clear head, and to get that he needed some space from Kit. After they met up with Liz, he'd no doubt have all the space he wanted, and then some.

He looked at her, the fan of her velvet lashes dark against pale cheeks, the straight, classically boned nose, the stubborn curve of her jaw. Thought about the promise he'd seen in her eyes last night, how they'd worked together like two people who trusted each other implicitly. It wasn't lost on him that they were both making an effort to stay on opposite sides of the invisible line he'd drawn last night.

A dull ache settled at the base of his skull. The only thing he could let himself think about was getting to Liz. He couldn't deal with the confusing tangle Kit was making of his thoughts, his mental balance.

Rafe had really moved on. Kit had spent last night and all this morning forcing herself to remember the unyielding decision in his eyes, his unwillingness to give them another chance. He didn't think she could give him all of herself. And he had every reason to doubt. She doubted, too.

She had to accept his decision, accept that they were

really over, but the four-hour drive to Wexler, Kansas, hadn't brought her any closer to letting go. At the thought, pain squeezed her chest. She slid a look at him, and he glanced over before returning his attention to the road.

In his eyes, she saw the same wariness she'd seen the day she'd walked into his office asking for help. With a pang of bittersweet pleasure, she let her gaze wander over him, admiring the profile of carved cheekbones and jaw, the bronze column of his throat, the smooth V exposed by the opened top of his button-down denim shirt.

She remembered his kisses yesterday, hungry and desperate for *her.* She was trying to stay out of his way, follow his lead, but what she really wanted was to get smack in his way. They'd never be lovers again, but they were partners.

She told herself that was good. Tearing her gaze from him, she studied the scenery. They passed acres of farmland, trees heavy with freshly greening leaves, and finally a sign welcomed them to Wexler, population just under forty thousand.

Being alone with him was what made her wish for things to be different, made her regret walking away from him. Once they found Liz, Kit wouldn't be alone with Rafe anymore. That would help her find the common sense that seemed to have deserted her yesterday at the creek, help squash the urge to beg him to reconsider. Or, if she'd had any hope that it would do any good, to seduce him. But she'd seen that no-trespass look in his eyes before. She didn't have the guts to try it.

Deep down, she knew it was because, no matter how much she wanted him, she couldn't promise that things would be different. Couldn't promise that she could really give up all the responsibility she'd grown used to carrying for everyone else.

She laced her fingers together, trying to calm her jangled

nerves. Just a few more hours and they'd find Liz. Then Kit would get some much-needed space from Rafe. She could do this.

They topped a hill, and he slowed according to the speed limit signs. A charming town spread out before them at the base of the hill, green and lush and built around a square marked by four white stone pillars as well as rectangular planters bursting with red geraniums.

Following directions Kit had gotten by calling the check-cashing business where Liz had instructed her to send the money, he turned right off the exit ramp.

They pulled onto the city's main street, called Center. A half mile brought them to a stoplight. Gas stations took two corners and a newspaper office another. The fourth corner belonged to a locksmith. Past the stoplight was the original section of town, restored to historic glory and steady with foot traffic.

Downtown Wexler boasted businesses on both sides of Center Street. Parking spaces fronted stores that looked as if they could've been there since the turn of the century. A computer business and an Internet company gave evidence to the fact that even this small town had moved into the new millennium. Stoplights marked each block and, as Rafe drove, Kit kept an eye out for their destination.

They passed two jewelry stores, several antique stores and restaurants, a real estate office and a bank. Just past the third light, at what looked to be the end of town, Kit saw the sign for Check It Out, the business name Liz had given her. "There it is."

Rafe swung into the first available space several doors down and they both got out.

Check It Out was snugged between a pharmacy and a jeweler, its front matching the tall plate glass of all the other businesses. Red-and-white striped awnings stretched over the wide, brick walkway, providing shade from the increasingly hot June sun. Butted against each intersection light pole, square concrete planters held flowering dwarf fruit trees and gave a quaint charm to the prairie town.

Kit snagged her purse from the back of the car and stepped up the curb to join Rafe on the bricked walk. Her soft-soled shoes made no sound as she and Rafe walked two doors down.

Feeling his gaze on her, she turned her head.

He looked at her, considered for a moment. "If they're hiding out, she may not be in there."

"I know."

"I just don't want you to be upset if we don't see her right off."

She smiled at him, remembering how he'd tried to re-assure her after they'd learned of Eddie Sanchez's murder and the increased danger to Liz and Tony. "Thanks."

He nodded and opened the door for her.

Kit stepped inside the small open space. Several copy machines crowded the wall to her left, whirring with activity. Across from her, a small counter was protected by a tall sheet of glass. There were only a few customers moving around the worn carpet, none of them Liz. Kit didn't panic. She had the money Liz needed; her sister was here somewhere.

A thin-faced man peered out from behind the glass. "May I help you?"

Rafe touched her elbow, then let go as if he hadn't meant to touch her. She swallowed a sting of hurt and walked with him toward the counter.

She smiled at the clerk. "I wondered if you'd had anyone waiting for a money wire this morning?"

Rafe slid Liz's photo across the counter and through the space underneath the glass. "This woman."

"Yeah." The man, whose name tag read Ronnie, looked to be around thirty. His long brown hair was pulled back

Still the One

in a ponytail. His hazel eyes were curious as he studied the picture. "A woman named Liz. She had blond hair, though, not dark. She took off quite a while ago. Said she couldn't wait any longer."

"How long ago did she leave?" Rafe asked.

The guy pursed his lips as he returned the picture. "More than an hour, probably two."

Kit stuck the photo in the side pocket of her purse. "Did she ask you to forward the money wire anywhere if it came in?"

"We can't do that. She just muttered something under her breath and flew out of here."

"Did you happen to notice her car?" Rafe asked.

"No, I sure didn't." The man's gaze slid to Rafe, and he leaned forward. "She acted like she needed that money pretty bad."

Evidently Rafe didn't feel the need to elaborate. He simply asked, "And she didn't give a phone number in case the wire came in?"

"Nope."

"Do you remember what she was wearing?" Kit asked.

"Oh, yeah." A grin split the man's pinched features. "A lime green zebra shirt. Tight."

Kit rolled her eyes, but Rafe gave the guy a half smile. "Thanks. Do you have a phone book we could look at for a minute?"

"Sure." The man pointed at a small worktable, which held a phone book, phone, stapler and a box of paper clips.

Kit walked with Rafe to the table. "What are you doing?"

"Looking up hotels." He flipped to the business listings. "I don't think there's any sense in waiting around here. We can check out the hotels in town, then swing back. If she comes in, Check Boy there will tell her we were here. She'll wait."

''Yes. There's no way she'd leave without this money.''

Several minutes later, after making a copy of the single page that listed the hotels in Wexler, they thanked the man and told him Liz might show up again. If so, would he ask her to wait? The man agreed.

Rafe held the door for Kit, and she walked past him, more aware than she liked of the strong hand holding the door, the corded forearm bared by rolled sleeves. Once outside, he slid his sunglasses on, hiding his eyes. His features closed, his jaw set, he looked intimidating. And unfamiliar.

''She'll call.'' She suddenly felt the urge to fill the silence that had followed them all the way from Oklahoma City. ''She won't be happy that I didn't wire the money.''

''Maybe we'll hear from her soon.'' He unlocked the 'Vette's door and opened it for her.

Once in the car, he circled the block, then turned the opposite direction down Center Street. The town stretched about four miles along the busy main street. The first hotel was a little over a mile through town, on the other side of the highway overpass. They drove past fast-food restaurants, a tire store, a statuary, several florists.

The Wexler Inn resembled an old English cottage. Made of light stucco and dark timbers, it boasted the same old-world charm as the downtown area. Inside, they spoke to a reservations clerk. The young woman didn't recognize the photos of either Liz or Tony, but she offered to fax the pictures to the night manager, who was at home. The night manager didn't recognize them, either.

Kit thanked the woman and walked out with Rafe, fighting irritation. Where was Liz? Had she led them on a wild-goose chase? ''She never could stay anywhere longer than a minute.''

Hands braced on his hips, Rafe surveyed the long avenue of businesses, the steady stream of noon-hour traffic. ''If she's here, we'll find her.''

"She's here," Kit said quickly, running a hand through her hair. "She's probably just getting me back for not sending that money right away. Too bad. I've been waiting on her, worried out of my mind."

Rafe turned his head and looked at her, his dark eyebrows arching.

"What?"

A small smile tugged at his lips. "Tough looks good on you."

She waved him off, walked to the car, but she couldn't squelch her smile. Nor could she dismiss the warmth his words sent through her. For the first time since last night, he'd said something personal, and it had been a compliment. She thought she'd long ago outgrown the need for male approval, but evidently approval from Rafe was different.

There were five more hotels in town, and they checked them all. Finally, at the last one, the desk clerk who'd just come on his shift recognized both Tony and Liz. "Sure, they stayed here. Checked out early this morning."

Kit, who'd been turning away in anticipation of failure, pivoted. "How long were they here?"

"Just the one night."

"Did they register as Mr. and Mrs. Tony Valentine?" Rafe slid off his glasses, shifted to make room for Kit as she stepped up to the counter.

"No." The older man typed something into his computer, then looked up. "Mr. and Mrs. Washington."

Kit shared a look with Rafe, who nodded to show he recognized her mother's maiden name.

"Thanks." Rafe took her elbow and guided her outside. This time, he didn't seem to notice he was touching her.

"So now what?" Kit's arm burned with the imprint of his fingers.

"We definitely know they've been here. We know Liz was at Check It Out a couple of hours ago."

"We know she wouldn't leave town without that money," Kit offered.

"Probably. Unless something happened."

"Like Alexander?"

"Maybe. I haven't spotted anyone following us since we left Oklahoma City, but that doesn't mean Alexander didn't get a line on Liz and Tony."

He let go of her to slide the sunglasses on. She could feel his gaze, intense and penetrating, from behind the reflective lenses, and she fought the urge to squirm.

He walked toward the 'Vette. "I think we should check in with the police."

"There's no way Liz or Tony would go there." Sunlight bounced off the car's hood, shimmered in the lenses of Rafe's glasses.

"If we're going to find them before Alexander's goons do, we need to spread the word about them."

Kit nodded, determinedly shoving away her admiration of the way his broad shoulders filled out the soft denim of his shirt, the way his jeans molded sleekly to his long legs. She settled into the car.

He drove the way they'd come, into downtown Wexler, past Check It Out and pulled up in front of a white-painted brick building that took up about half a city block. Black stenciling on its front identified it as the Wexler Police Department.

A pair of glass doors led them into a small tiled entry with an elevator. Cool air swirling around them, they walked through another set of glass doors to their left and past a row of chairs lined up against the wall.

A petite, gray-haired woman smiled at them from behind a tall sheet of bulletproof glass that stretched from wall to wall. In a small alcove to Kit's right was a door marked Personnel Only.

Rafe fished his wallet out of the back pocket of his jeans and nudged it through the bowl-shaped opening beneath the glass. "Hi, I'm a private investigator from Oklahoma, and I wondered if I could talk to your duty sergeant?"

The woman flipped open his wallet, studied his license then picked up the phone close to her right hand. After she hung up, she said, "Sergeant Smith will be right out."

A few minutes later, the door marked Personnel Only opened. A tall, lanky man with shrewd eyes and the freckled face of a farm boy identified himself as Sergeant Smith and invited them back. Rafe put the man's age close to his own thirty-two.

Open doors, marked with name plaques, lined both sides of a long corridor. The walls, painted a soft blue, sported framed photos of various officers receiving awards, posing on motorcycles in full dress uniform and lined up for group shots. The sergeant showed them into the break room, the sixth and last door on the right. A big poster of a classic, cherry-red Corvette was mounted on the wall next to an old refrigerator.

Rafe smiled in admiration. "A sixty-seven Stingray. I've got a black one."

"That's mine," Smith said. "Great cars."

"Yes."

The sergeant eased down onto the corner of a long table holding foam cups and an ancient coffeemaker. "Esther said you're a P.I.?"

"That's right," Rafe confirmed.

Kit sank down on a scratched metal chair, content to let Rafe do the talking but paying close attention to every word.

"I'm working a missing persons case." He showed the officer pictures of Liz and Tony while filling him in on what had happened. "We got a call from Liz last night that they were in this area, but we haven't been able to locate them yet."

Smith looked at the pictures, then shook his head. "Sorry, haven't seen them."

"Her hair's blond now," Kit offered, scooting forward in her chair.

"Sorry." He gave her a sympathetic smile before shifting his gaze to Rafe. "You say there's a mob connection?"

"Yeah. And I've got descriptions of two guys suspected of murder who are probably following them. One's very slender, six feet tall, and the other is about five foot eight, balding with a thick neck."

Smith had taken out a small, well-worn notebook while Rafe talked and now scribbled a note. "I'll put the word out. Give you a call if I come across anything."

"Thanks, I'd appreciate that."

"Yes, thank you," Kit added.

Rafe circled his cell phone number on his business card and passed it to Sergeant Smith.

The officer rose. "Let's get copies of your pictures, then check with the guys who aren't out on calls right now."

"Great."

As Smith led them around the corner and down another hall, he looked at the photos again. Holding up Liz's picture, his gaze sliced to Kit. "I see a resemblance in the eyes. Related?"

"She's my sister," Kit said.

He nodded, stopping inside the doorway of a small room, cramped with half a dozen desks and computers. Two officers, one male, one female, sat in front of computer screens, hunched over keyboards. Two other males leaned back in wooden-legged chairs with their feet propped on their desks.

Sergeant Smith held up the photos of Liz and Tony.

"Hey, guys, anybody seen these two people? The woman's gone blond."

Chairs creaked as the four officers rose to their feet and ambled over. The auburn-haired male officer who'd been working on the computer and was about Rafe's height studied the pictures, then passed them back. "No, haven't seen 'em."

Kit pressed against the doorjamb, peering around Rafe.

The lone female officer, a pretty brunette, bent her head over the pictures. "No, sorry," she murmured, her gaze lingering on Rafe a little longer than Kit liked.

The next officer, a young man with a crew cut and massive biceps that strained the sleeves of his uniform, reached across the brunette. He straightened when he saw Liz's picture. "Hey, Georgie, we've seen this woman."

Kit's heart leaped, and she clutched a handful of Rafe's shirt. She couldn't help it, almost didn't care when he stiffened.

The younger officer, Scott, motioned over a barrel-shaped man with stubby legs and a cigar clamped between his teeth.

"Yeah, we've definitely seen her," Officer Scott said.

Georgie, identified as Pollack by his name tag, leaned close, then removed the cigar stub and grinned. "We were in the diner earlier this morning and she walked in. Ordered two breakfasts to go."

"You're sure it was her? Did you see Tony, too?" Kit stepped around Rafe, encouraged.

"Didn't see him, ma'am, but I ain't likely to forget a woman with a set of—er, a woman like that." His eyes glowed, and Kit could just imagine his thoughts. She'd seen it all before and for the first time was really thankful that Liz's looks drew such notice.

"We knew she wasn't from around here."

"Did you happen to notice as she was leaving," Rafe

asked with a male-bonding grin, "what kind of car she was in?"

"Actually, we did." From the sheepish grin on the younger officer's face, Kit figured they had watched Liz as long as possible. Typical male response, especially if her sister had dyed her long, thick hair blond. "They were in a Ford pickup, white. Probably eight or ten years old. Oklahoma tags."

"Great." Rafe shook hands with both men.

"Her hair's shorter, too. About here." Officer Scott indicated his collarbone.

Kit was shocked Liz had cut her hair. "Thanks."

"You're not the only one looking for 'em."

She stilled, looking at Rafe.

"No, we're not." His gaze narrowed slightly. "How'd you know that?"

"About fifteen, twenty minutes later, a bald guy walks in, shows the waitress a picture and I heard her tell him that a woman matching that same description had just left."

Bald guy. With a thick neck, Kit thought, concern worming into her excitement over getting a lead.

Rafe asked, "Did you happen to see which direction the woman in the truck went?"

"Looked like they were heading north, for US-69, but I couldn't tell you for sure."

"That's great. We really appreciate your help."

"Any time," Sergeant Smith said, shaking Rafe's hand. "We don't want any trouble, especially with the mob. We'll keep an eye out."

Once outside, Rafe paused next to Kit's door after opening it.

"Sounds like they've already left," she said.

"Probably, but now we know what they're driving. At least for now. Let's sweep through the parking lots in town."

"All right." Captured between the car and Rafe's broad chest, Kit told herself to get in the car before she did something she'd regret, like touch him. As she settled in her seat, he shut the door, then walked around and got in.

"I'm surprised Liz hasn't called yet." Kit fastened her seat belt as Rafe started the car.

"Until she does, we should probably stay put. Do you have a problem with that?"

"No. Of course not." But she did. She needed desperately to get some kind of space from him. She'd been counting on her sister to provide that. Maybe Liz was still here.

An hour later, they'd made a sweep of every parking lot in town, including the hotels they'd already checked. No sign of an old-model white Ford pickup with Oklahoma tags.

"Looks like we missed them," Kit said.

He turned into the parking lot of the Wexler Inn. "How about if we hole up here and wait until we hear from Liz?"

The prospect of spending another night alone with Rafe snapped her nerves taut. "You don't think we can catch them?"

"Which direction, Kit?"

"Good point." She noted the tight lines of his body, the white lines that fanned out from his generous mouth. "Look, I'm sorry about this—"

"Hey, none of this is your fault. We'll find them. I just don't think it's a good idea to take off without having some idea where to go."

"I agree." She watched the cars whiz by on the busy street in front of them.

"So, we'll check in here. We can get separate rooms. Since it seems that Alexander's goons are ahead of us rather than behind, there's no reason we have to crowd each other."

Crowd each other? She wouldn't have put it that way, but then she hadn't been the one to put their past in a box that would never be opened again, had she? She forced a smile. "Great. Two rooms. Then what?"

"Find something to do while we wait."

Her gaze met his. There wasn't one bit of suggestion in his tone, in his look. Just a cool steadiness. "All right."

What was she wanting to see? Desire? Regret? He'd made it clear where they stood.

A muffled ring sounded, and Kit jumped, then grabbed her purse from the back seat. Another ring and she had it out. "Yes! Hello!"

"What happened?" Liz demanded. "Could you not figure out my hints?"

Kit's lips twisted, and her gaze shot to Rafe. She stabbed a finger toward the phone, indicating that it was Liz. He leaned close, and she held the phone between them so he could hear. "I figured it out, if you meant Wexler, Kansas."

"Yes, so what's the deal?" Her sister's voice rose. "I waited almost three hours for that money."

"Are you guys all right?" Kit asked.

"Yes."

"I brought the money. I'm here. We can meet right now."

"You *brought* it?" Liz's voice turned shrill, and Kit moved the phone a fraction away. "I thought I could depend on you. What are we going to do? We need that money, Kit! I can't believe you would trick me this way."

"Give me a break, Liz. I'm trying to help you."

"Then why don't I have that money?" her sister snapped.

"You're going to meet me and get it," Kit said, warmed by Rafe's thumbs-up. "Rafe can get protection for Tony while he—"

"Rafe!" her sister exploded. "Rafe Blackstock?"

"Yes, and he—"

"Oh, good grief. No wonder you're not thinking straight."

Kit ignored that, though her blood started a slow boil. "Liz, he's a P.I. now. He's been helping me all along."

"It was probably his idea not to wire that money."

"It was a good idea," Kit said tightly.

"Tell her you'll wire it now," Rafe whispered.

Kit frowned.

He nodded, his gaze urging. "Go on."

"I'll wire it now, Liz, if you don't want to meet me."

"We're gone, Kit. We're not coming back there. We think we saw one of Alexander's men."

"That's why you should let us meet you somewhere."

"So they can do to us what they did to Eddie? No, thanks."

The scorn in her sister's voice needled Kit, but she recognized the fear underneath. "Tell me where to send the money."

"Will you really do it this time?"

Rafe nodded, his cheek nudging hers.

"Yes," Kit said, refusing to dwell on the feel of his warm, supple skin, the smooth jaw.

"Promise?" Liz asked.

"Yes." Kit gritted the word out, about ready to pass the phone off to Rafe.

"Okay. Remember the first boy I ever kissed? Second grade."

Frustrated, Kit let her forehead fall forward. Rafe's breath washed against her neck, her earlobe. "No, I don't remember."

"Second grade, Kit. And it's in the same state we're all in now. Wire the money to the First State Bank there."

And she hung up.

With careful deliberation, afraid she might scream, Kit also hung up, then shoved the phone in her purse. "She makes me so mad," she said between gritted teeth.

"I know, but we've got to focus on what she said, figure out where she wants to pick up that money."

"The First State Bank of Nowhere, Kansas," she muttered, her relief at hearing Liz's voice short-lived. "All right, all right, I'm trying."

Rafe chuckled, his shoulder lifting against hers. "You gotta admit no one else could figure out where they are. Not from tapping the phone, anyway."

"Ugh." Kit shoved a hand through her hair, trying for all she was worth to remember the first boy Liz had kissed.

Rafe moved away, casually angling back against the door, but Kit felt the withdrawal like a slap. This was the way things were going to be; she had to accept it.

"Okay, second grade." She drummed her fingers on her knee, too aware of Rafe's spicy scent, the way his broad shoulders blocked the window behind him. "Oh, Will…Grady. Yes, that's it."

"Okay, let's take a look." Rafe reached under his seat and pulled out the atlas he'd brought.

Leaning over, her shoulder against his, she scanned the map of Kansas. "A town in Kansas named Will? William? Williams? Williamstown?"

"Grady City." Rafe stabbed a finger at a small dot on the opposite side of the state. "Straight west of here, clear across Kansas. Looks like four hundred miles or so."

"They must be planning to drive all night."

"If she wants to pick up that money tomorrow, I'd say you're right."

"So, we go, too, right?"

"Right."

She took the atlas from him and dropped it in the back seat. "First stop Check It Out?"

"Yes. We'll wire the money, drive on to Grady City and be there to meet Liz at the bank in the morning."

"I like the way you think."

He flashed her a grin that caused a flutter in her stomach. She flat out gave up on ignoring it; she just couldn't. The man got to her quicker than lightning to a rod, and she was out of resolve to fight it.

Less than half an hour later, they had wired sixteen hundred dollars to the First State Bank of Grady City and were headed north on US-69 to US-54 West. Her nerves were stretched thin from keeping up a casual front. This was going to be a long night.

Chapter 10

He was doing fine, Rafe told himself as they drove. Even if his car had never felt so small. For nearly twelve hours, he'd been sitting mere inches from Kit, breathing the same air, feeling every one of her movements in nerve endings that were too sensitive. About three hundred miles back, he had put himself in a holding pattern, refusing to allow his mind to go anywhere but the case. He hadn't and *wouldn't* think about Kit and the need closing around him like an insidious fog.

He shifted his legs beneath the car's dashboard, his knees banging into the glove compartment. He had the passenger seat as far back as it would go. Once the sun had set, Kit had offered to drive because of his night blindness.

He'd wanted to drive, wanted something to occupy his mind and his hands, but he could see that she needed to feel as if she were helping. Since his night vision in the last year had become noticeably worse, he'd agreed.

They'd talked about music and movies, even waterskiing, and Kit had followed his lead, not once broaching a subject with more personal relevance than that. The whole time, he'd kept an eye out for a silver sedan or any sign of a tail.

She'd been in such perfect sync with his thoughts and suggestions today that they were starting to operate like two old partners. Satisfied with what they'd learned in Wexler, he couldn't stop his admiration over the way she'd handled Liz. Better than he'd ever seen.

He'd always wanted to be the one person with whom Kit could let down her guard, release the lock on that iron-maiden control. Maybe when they'd been together before, he'd asked too much of her, too quickly. Since they'd hooked up to find Liz, she'd let him see frustration, uncertainty, fear. The old Kit never would have shown such vulnerability.

Too late, he reminded himself. The time for regret was past. Yet, he wondered what it would be like if she turned that intense, single-minded focus on him.

He slammed the door on the thought. It wasn't going to happen. And he wasn't letting his mind wander to silky, tantalizing corners like that anymore.

Discipline and self-control were second nature to him, right? He was Air Force, after all. He could do this. He *was* doing it. He refused to be distracted by something he didn't know how to deal with. He cared for her—she'd been his first love, and he supposed he would always have feelings for her—but he wouldn't go back.

They reached Grady City limits just after one in the morning and pulled up under a single red flashing light at an intersection in the middle of the prairie. Flat wheat fields, barren of trees, rippled unendingly into the sooty night. Silver clouds, trimmed in midnight black, scudded across the sky in front of a translucent, milk-white moon.

After consulting the map, they turned right at the intersection and drove into town. Seeing Kit stifle a yawn for the third time, he suggested they stop at the first hotel they saw. Within half an hour, they were settled into clean, moderately priced rooms across the hall from one another.

He told Kit good-night, trying not to notice how sexy she looked with her short hair tousled by repeated finger combings. Or how the smudges under her tired eyes tugged at him.

He stood in the open doorway of his room, waiting until she locked herself in and he heard the dead bolt slide home. Restless and edgy, he moved into his room, closed the door. Walking to the window, he nudged back one edge of the nubby oatmeal-and-turquoise striped curtain. He'd requested rooms on this side of the hotel so he could keep an eye on the parking lot.

The night was dark and still, the parking lot empty of people. Tall fluorescent light poles sent pools of yellow light onto the asphalt, slithering under and around bodies of cars. Everything was quiet. Too quiet.

Eyes gritty from fatigue, he rubbed a hand over his face. He was wound up from being so close to Kit all day, listening to her soft voice strum over his nerves. Images of her chased through his mind. Snatches of the conversation they'd had about her mom's death. The complete surrender on her face when he'd kissed her at the creek. The way she'd faced his parents.

He was tired, his defenses down, he told himself as he put a mental brake on the thoughts. A good night's rest was what he needed to clear his head. Again, he scanned the cars in the parking lot, then froze as his mind registered where his gaze had stopped. A silver sedan.

It looked like the same make and model as the one that had tailed them in Oklahoma City.

He picked up the phone and called to tell Kit that he was

going down to check out the parking lot. No need to alarm her until he got a close look.

She answered, her low, drowsy voice causing the muscles in his belly to pull tight. The conversation lasted less than thirty seconds, but his body still throbbed as he took the stairs from their second-floor rooms to the lobby level.

Once outside, he walked across the parking lot and double-checked the silver sedan. Yes, it was the same car. And it was empty.

Sensation buzzing at the base of his spine, he spun toward the hotel. He was the only soul out here, his the only footsteps scuffing along the pavement. So, where was Alexander's baboon?

Spurred by the reminder that Kit was alone, Rafe jogged inside and to the stairwell door. He took the steps two at a time, not questioning the increasing pace of his strides or the concern that knotted the muscles in his neck.

He opened the door to the second floor, his gaze shooting down the short hallway. A man stood in front of Kit's door, holding the handle.

"Hey!" Adrenaline hit his system like a live current and Rafe took off running.

The guy didn't even look at him, just spun and bolted down the hall, rounded the corner. Wall sconces cast a soft light and provided enough illumination for Rafe to get a good look at the man. Short. Balding. One of Alexander's apes.

Concern shot through him, and he raced past eight rooms before he cornered at the end just as the man had. He didn't see the guy anywhere, knew he could easily be led into chasing the man around the entire floor, which was laid out in a square. Nearby, a heavy door slammed shut. The door leading to the stairs. Rafe heard the muffled sound of footsteps pounding down the steps. The man was gone.

Kit!

Rafe pivoted and raced to her room. That guy hadn't had time to get into her room. Had he?

Rafe pounded on her door. "Kit!"

No answer.

He pressed an ear to the door but heard nothing. Rattling the door's long handle, he pounded harder. "Kit!"

"Hey, keep it down out there, will ya?" A scratchy female voice sounded through a half-open door behind him.

"Sorry." He fought down panic that lodged in his throat like a stone. "Kit!"

Why didn't she answer? Was she asleep? He snatched his card key out of his pocket, raced into his room and grabbed the phone. Dragging the cord and phone box as far as he could, he propped open his door with one foot, his gaze glued to her door. Willing her to pick up the phone.

The corresponding rings sounded in her room, but there was no answer. She was all right. She had to be. If that bald-headed bastard had done anything to her...

Rafe dumped the phone onto the bed and hurried across the hall, pounded on the door again. Nothing.

By this time, several other guest doors had opened. Sleepy-eyed people poked their heads out, grumbling and demanding quiet. "What's going on?"

"Was there a robbery?"

"I chased a man out of here a while ago," Rafe said, fear sliding icy fingers down his spine. "Now I can't get any answer from my...from Kit."

"Let's call the manager," the raspy-voiced woman suggested.

He tried to shoulder the door open. Tried his own card key with no luck. Again, he pounded on the door. Still nothing. Apprehension closed over him, suffocating, pinching his gut.

The elevator bell dinged, and he glanced down the hall, recognized the swarthy features of the night manager.

"Waz de trouble?" the man asked in thickly accented English.

Rafe was glad one of the guests had called the man. He tried to sound calm against the dread welling like a tide inside him.

"I need to get into Ms. Foley's room right now. I've been knocking and there's no answer. I'm afraid something may have happened."

"I can't let you in unless—"

"I know you remember me from checking in earlier." Rafe advanced, hoping the six inches he had on the guy would intimidate him. "I chased a guy off this floor a while ago, a man who was trying to get into this room. He is not one of your guests. Understand?"

The manager's olive skin paled, and he nodded. "I did see a man rush out of the hotel."

"I need in that room," Rafe said, his chest hurting at the possibility that something might have happened to Kit.

"Yes, yes, of course." With a shaking hand, the manager slid in his card key.

The lock clicked, and Rafe grabbed the handle, yanked open the door, sliding his Magnum from the small of his back.

"Should I—"

"Wait here." He stepped inside, his gaze sweeping the room as he thumbed off the safety on his gun.

By the soft, white light of a corner lamp, he quickly registered that the bed, dresser, closet were all undisturbed. But just behind the room door he held open with his arm, the bathroom door was shut. He heard the shower, had visions of Kit lying in there hurt.

Apprehension a slick, greasy knot in his belly, he

snatched open the door just in time to see her sweep back the shower curtain.

His gun was already up, leveled, when he yelled, "Kit!"

She screamed, plastered the shower curtain across her breasts.

He registered naked glistening flesh, surprised eyes.

"What are you doing?" she demanded, raking back her wet hair. "How did you get in here?"

No blood. No sign that anyone had been in here, either. She'd been taking a shower the entire time. His knees nearly buckled in relief. He thumbed the safety on, returned his gun to the small of his back.

"I'm taking a shower here, Blackstock. Are you crazy?"

"Be right back." He leaned around the still-open door and met the wide-eyed stare of the night manager and the three guests who'd joined him.

All hid smiles behind their hands.

Heat crept up his neck as he spoke to the manager. "Looks like she's all right, but I do want to talk to you later about the man you saw."

The man nodded, his curious gaze going past Rafe. "Is she—"

"She's fine." As Rafe shut the door, he heard the swell of excited voices, the night manager trying to calm everyone. Rafe slid the dead bolt, set the chain and twisted the knob lock before turning to find Kit standing in the shower just as he'd left her, her eyes huge.

She clutched the beige plastic curtain to her as if it were a family heirloom.

Stepping into the doorway of the bathroom, he stared into her blue-gray eyes, losing himself for a moment, reassuring himself that she was all right. Relief drummed through him, though it didn't quiet the thunder of his heart or thaw the frigid knot in his belly.

At his look, she went still. A frown puckered between her dark brows. "What happened?"

Concern flickered in her eyes, and he knew she'd recognized the same emotion in his. Her fingers tightened on the shower curtain.

"Everything's okay," he said automatically.

"Rafe," she snapped. "I know you didn't come in for me…uh, because you wanted… *Why* did you come in here?"

She had never looked more beautiful. Her mink-dark hair was wet and slicked back from her oval face, her lashes spiky. The scents of fresh soap and shampoo and woman steamed around him.

He ached to touch her, to feel that she was all right. He told himself it was enough that he could *see* she was. He wasn't aware he'd moved until the shower spray misted his face. Water jetted against the curtain, pinged the sides of the porcelain tub. Diamond droplets of water shimmered in the cleft where her bare shoulder joined her neck.

Unable to take his gaze from her, he curled his hands into fists at his side. "I went downstairs to check out the parking lot."

"Yes, you told me." Her skin was flushed pink from her shower; her eyes glowed like smoky jewels.

The thin beige shower curtain clung to her body like plastic wrap, revealing the vague impression of a nipple, the flare of a hip, the slope of a lean thigh. His mouth went dry.

Apprehension flashed across her features, and she reached up to turn off the shower. In the ensuing quiet, she said, "Tell me."

"When I came up, there was a man standing in front of your door."

Her body went rigid. "A man?"

"A short, bald man." He crossed his arms against the urge to gather her to him when her eyes widened with fear.

"He was in here?"

"I don't think so. I've checked your room and nothing looks disturbed. I think I interrupted him before he could get in."

She gripped the curtain so tight it strained at the shower rings. "I thought that guy was in front of us. You've been watching for his car ever since we left home. Where did he come from?"

"I wish I knew," he said, thinking it probably wouldn't hurt if he just touched her cheek.

She was fine, he told himself. He didn't need to put his hands on her. Hurting with the effort, he turned away.

"Rafe?" Her voice trembled slightly.

That was to be expected. He'd burst in and scared her to death. "I'm an idiot. I'm sorry I scared you. I saw that car and went down to check it out. Which gave Ape Boy a perfect opportunity."

"How could you know he'd come up here?" she asked. He heard the slide and click of shower curtain rings, felt her move behind him.

He forced his suddenly wooden legs to move, to take him out of the bathroom and to the foot of her bed.

"He's never approached us before. If he's the one who put that bug in my house, he did it while I was gone." She sounded close.

He turned, saw she stood only a foot away. She wore that same berry-red gown she'd worn last night at his house. Hunger twisted in his belly. He ached to pull her to him, slide his hands over flesh that was probably still warm and damp from her shower, feel her heart beating next to his.

She must've read something in his face. Moving to the bed, she reached into the small suitcase that lay open on top and pulled out a robe to match the gown, belting it around her slender waist.

The satin clung to her in all the places he was trying to avoid looking.

"Why didn't you use all those locks?" he growled, pacing to the far side of the room. He had to put some distance between them before he touched her.

"I would've locked them all before I went to bed," she said defensively. "Besides, you should be glad I didn't. Otherwise you couldn't have charged in here like the Lone Ranger."

He braced his hands on his hips, staring blankly at a bland pastel watercolor on the wall. His pulse still wheeled; his heart still pounded in his throat. "I thought—I saw him standing in front of your door. I couldn't tell if he'd been in here or not. As soon as he saw me, he took off."

"Did you catch him?"

He turned. "I wanted to check on you first."

Her eyes went liquid, which flashed an immediate danger signal to his brain. But his body was deaf to all except the flirty soap scent of her, the sleek curves silhouetted in red satin.

Frustration and lingering panic had his hands curling into fists. He would *not* do something stupid like haul her to him and kiss her until he drowned in her. "The night manager said he saw someone run out of the hotel about that time. I'll call him in a few minutes."

He moved around her and prowled the room, cataloguing details. Her shoes were placed beside the closet. Her travel bag, full of neatly arranged cosmetics and a hair dryer, lay open next to the small suitcase on the bed. The comforter, done in a southwest motif, showed a small indentation where she'd sat. Nothing had been disturbed.

At the foot of the bed, he stopped and bent his head. What if something had happened to her? He would never have forgiven himself. How, *when* had Alexander's goon found their trail again? "He won't come back, Kit. He won't want us to get another look at him and he knows we'll be waiting."

"Rafe?" Her palm flattened against the small of his back as she stepped beside him. "I'm okay. Really."

"No thanks to me."

"There's no way you could've known that guy would show up." She came around to face him. "We thought he headed out of Wexler after Liz and Tony. Maybe he lost them. Or maybe he planned to follow only us all along. We've been watching. There's been no sign of him or anyone else."

Words welled up, apologies, pleas. He tried to rein in his seething emotions. "I won't let anything happen to you, Kit."

"I know that." Her gaze burned into his like smoky sapphires. "I've always known that."

There was such confidence in her eyes, such trust. Something dark and sharp twisted deep inside him. "You're really okay?"

"Yes." Her gaze drifted over his face; she smiled.

He couldn't help it. He reached out, stroked one finger down her velvety cheek. It surprised him to see that his hand was shaking. She was alive and fine.

She caught his hand, held it in both of hers. But it wasn't enough.

He didn't give a damn if he was an idiot. He had to feel her, all of her. Soft and sleek and warm up against him.

He slid his free arm around her, pulled her to him. And just held her. Breathed in her freshly showered scent, savored the cool wetness of her hair against his cheek, felt her heartbeat thudding against his.

He closed his eyes, emotions he'd corralled so tightly

pushing at his weakening restraint. "I'm staying in here tonight," he said gruffly.

She pulled back to look at him, and he thought he saw a flicker of panic. "You don't have to. I'm fine."

"I'm not letting you out of my sight until this thing is wrapped up."

She still held his hand cradled in both of hers, pressed between her breasts. Her gaze, uncertain and dark, searched his face. For a minute, he thought she might argue.

Then she smiled, a sweet, teasing smile. "Okay, but you're not getting the bed."

He grinned even as his arm tightened around her. After a moment, she laid her head on his chest again, relaxing into him.

She was really all right. And she would continue to be, he told himself. No matter what he had to do.

His reflection stared back at him from a gold-framed wall mirror set over the room's desk. It wasn't just that he wanted her; it was that he still felt something for her. There was no denying the paralyzing panic that had squeezed his chest when he'd thought something had happened to her. And it told him that all the emotions he'd dismissed and stuffed into a tight corner of his heart had now erupted. Not just searing lust, but fear and need and regret.

He didn't think he could let her walk away this time. And he had no idea in hell if he had the guts to give her the one thing that might stop her—his heart.

An hour later, Kit lay on her side in bed, staring into the darkness with her back to Rafe. She could hear him breathing, smell the woodsy hint of him. And while it reassured her to have him stretched out in that overstuffed chair at the foot of the bed, her nerves flickered like tiny, secret flames.

She'd been frightened earlier, that split second when he'd

burst into her room and then again for a moment when he'd told her about Alexander's man outside her room. That man could very well have been the one to run Liz off the road. He *had* been spotted at Eddie Sanchez's before the murder.

Even so, right now she felt perfectly safe. Rafe had said he would never let anything happen to her, and she believed him completely. What had her stomach dancing was what she wanted to happen…*with him.*

After missing Liz this morning in Wexler, Kit had known it was a double-edged sword that her time with Rafe had been prolonged. As difficult as it was to be near him, she was glad for the extra time. And because of that, an urgency pushed at her, tried to wash over her conscience.

He'd told her where he stood, where *they* stood, but she wanted him. It was as simple and as complicated as that.

After seeing the panic in his eyes turn to relief when he'd found she was all right, she knew he still felt something for her. Things weren't really over between them. They couldn't be. Not when just the thought of leaving him again blasted a cold in her that made it nearly impossible to breathe. She would do whatever it took to keep him in her life this time.

She'd been kidding about taking the whole bed, but he'd firmly declined her offer to share. He spent several long minutes on the phone with the night manager and then the local police to report the incident. He'd given them a description of the man and the car and asked them to be on the lookout.

After pulling the wide overstuffed chair to the foot of her bed, he'd slouched down where he would have a full visual of the door in case anyone tried to come in. Beside him, on a round, glass-topped table, lay his gun.

She didn't have to turn over to know that he was finally asleep. She heard his breathing go deep and even, felt the subtle shift in her pulse from steady to standby. His familiar scent clung to her from their earlier embrace and plucked at the tension ticking against her nerves.

Each breath she took pushed her breasts against the satin of her gown and made her long to feel his hands there. An insistent ache built between her legs.

When he'd burst in on her in the shower, she'd seen something more than concern in his face, something she couldn't dismiss. Vulnerability and need, the same need that whispered through her. She couldn't forget it. Certainly couldn't sleep.

Every time she closed her eyes, she saw his go dark with relief upon seeing that she was all right, recalled how the hunger in the black depths had quickly cooled with caution.

Rolling to her other side, she studied his shadowed silhouette. Small slivers of light peeked around the ends of the curtains. His dark head tipped back on the chair; his chest rose and fell steadily. He angled into the chair, which was almost too narrow for his broad shoulders.

An invisible cord seemed to connect the pulse in her throat to the soft throb between her legs. Her skin tingled; a fine heat inched under her skin, urging, promising.

She couldn't forget that hunger in his eyes, couldn't forget the way he'd simply held her as if he would never let her go.

She pushed back the covers, slipped out of bed and walked to him, her toes bumping against his boots. One touch. That was all she wanted. He'd made it clear where they stood, where he wanted things to stop. She wanted to touch him while he slept, just once without seeing that wariness in his eyes, being reminded of the line he'd drawn between them at the creek.

Hazy light filtered over him, defining a slash of brow, the carved cheekbones, the angled plane of his jaw. Lips that could be both generous and cruel.

She'd walked away from him, broken his trust.

She swallowed against the ache in her throat. Imagined having the freedom to touch him as she wanted, her hands curving over his shoulders, sliding across the buckled muscles of his abdomen, kissing him and having him kiss her back with no thought to the past or anything except the white fire that had always been between them.

How she'd wanted to kiss him earlier when he'd taken her in his arms and simply held her. She'd come close to doing just that, nearly pressing a kiss to the underside of his jaw, but she hadn't. Now she wished she had, wished she had risked him pushing her away again.

They were here, they were together. In the silent darkness, Kit wanted to believe they could stay that way. She wanted *him* to believe it. To believe in her again. With a shaking hand, she reached out to stroke his thick, raven hair.

She never saw him move. Strong fingers clamped around her wrist, tugged hard. She cried out and tumbled onto his lap, against his hard, deep chest. She stared into eyes black and sultry enough to tempt a man-hater. Kit didn't stand a chance.

"What are you doin'?"

His breath washed against her lips. Her pulse skipped into a harsh staccato.

Her legs dangled over the edge of the chair. Her hip was wedged into the V of his thighs. Licking suddenly dry lips, she stared into his eyes, mesmerized. "I was just…touching you."

His eyes narrowed slightly. "It's not a good idea to sneak up on me."

His heat surrounded her. Had her body ever tingled like this, from her scalp to her toes? "I thought you were asleep."

"I was." His gaze roamed over her face, paused on her lips.

Her pulse throbbed hard, then skipped when she felt his palm slide across her rib cage. She held her breath and watched as his hand stopped achingly close to her breast. His fingers, dark and strong against the satin of her gown, burned through the thin fabric.

She looked at him then and darn near stopped breathing. His eyes glowed with promise and a fierceness she'd never seen.

His hand tightened on her ribs. "You should go back to bed," he said in a rusty voice.

Beneath her shoulder, his heartbeat was as erratic as hers. Short breaths feathered her lips. She read a flash of quicksilver heat in his eyes.

"I don't want to go back to bed," she whispered. Her gaze dropped to his lips, and she shifted so that her body curved into his. Breast to chest, shoulder to shoulder.

He still held her wrist, and her movement brought his curled fist to rest against the curve of her other breast.

The involuntary flex of his hand gave her the courage to go further, to say, "I don't think you want me to."

His body tensed beneath hers. "We talked about this."

"We could talk about it again."

"Are you shaken up from what happened before? Alexander's goon won't come back."

"I know. I'm not shaken up."

He hooked one arm beneath her legs and got to his feet, asking gruffly, "What do you want, Kit? What are you—"

"I want you to kiss me."

A stillness settled over his face, and he slowly set her on her feet.

She felt every hard inch of him slide against her. Denim against bare legs and satin. The hard ridge of his erection against her belly. She curled her hands over granite-hard biceps.

Her voice shook from the stark excitement racing through her veins. ''Right now, I just want you to kiss me.''

''Is that all you want? And you better be damn sure when you answer.'' He wrapped a hand around her nape, pulled her to him so that their lips nearly touched.

Between thick, sooty lashes, his eyes glittered at her, feral and male and heart-stopping. ''As I'm sure you can tell, I'm hard enough to drill rock right now, Kit. I'm not man enough to say no this time. If you're not sure, go back to bed.''

She'd never seen that savage, sensual gleam in his eyes. It made her swallow hard.

The only thing she *was* sure of was that she wanted this. This moment, this night. She knew she could commit to that.

Chapter 11

She looked straight into his eyes, her pulse beating in her throat. "Kiss me—"

His mouth covered hers.

She lifted trembling hands to his face and surrendered. One strong arm hooked around her waist, anchored her to him. His tongue skimmed her teeth, delved deep into her mouth, demanding, taking.

Knees wobbly, she looped her arms around his neck, went on tiptoe so that there was no space between them. His hard chest pressed to her breasts. His belly nudged hers. One lean thigh insinuated itself between her legs, pressed hard against her center; she went hot and wet. His jeans were rough against the satin curling around her thighs. Sensation poured through her like liquid fire.

His tongue stroked hers, making her weak, torching the flame low in her belly. She clutched at his shirt, managed to release the buttons and spread it open. Her hands curved over his smooth, muscled chest, measured the width of his shoulders. She'd missed him. No one had ever filled her up the way Rafe did.

He shrugged off his shirt, his mouth busy at her neck. His hands curved over her bottom, pressed her tighter into him.

He kissed his way up her neck, across her jaw. She turned her head and slanted her lips across his, drawing his tongue in with hers. He tasted faintly of toothpaste and sin.

Her heart soared. This was what she had wanted, another chance with him. She'd thought it would never happen.

He gathered her gown in his hands, palmed off her panties, pushed them to the floor. The satin of her gown drifted against her bottom, heightening the feel of his slightly rough palms.

She made a greedy sound in the back of her throat, holding his face between her hands, kissing him hard and deep. Her hands smoothed over those magnificent shoulders, down brick-hard arms that banded her like steel, relearning the feel of muscles that were bigger and harder than before.

His hands were everywhere, his kisses consuming and urgent.

Pulling his mouth from hers, he nipped his way down the side of her neck, nibbled at her collarbone before nudging aside one skinny strap of her gown. The bodice sagged low on the swell of her breasts, and his teeth followed, then his tongue.

Her nipples hardened. With one hand, he slid off the other strap, pushed the satin down her body until it bunched at her feet in a crimson pool.

She stood naked before him, trembling with anticipation and the little doubt that suddenly sprang up. What if he rejected her again?

He lifted his head, his gaze intense, penetrating. "You're incredible. Even more than I remember."

When his gaze riveted on her breasts, she felt that old

shyness creep through her but forced her arms to remain at her sides.

With a look of near reverence, he reached out, gently cupped her breasts in hands that were bronze against the magnolia paleness of her skin.

He skimmed a thumb over her nipples, then leaned down and pressed a gentle kiss to one breast.

She nearly melted at his feet, saved herself by hooking one finger into the waistband of his jeans. Taut muscles spasmed across his belly at her touch. Against her stomach, she felt his erection throb. As he drew one nipple into his mouth, pulling tight an invisible cord of tension at her center, she flicked open the button of his jeans. Her thoughts scattered, but her hand kept moving, cupped him through his jeans. She felt him hard and insistent in her palm.

He nipped at her breast in response, and a breath shuddered out of her. Hands trembling, quick and clumsy, she slid open his zipper, worked down his jeans and briefs.

He moved his mouth to her neck, to her ear. "Get closer, Kit. Closer."

She wanted to. Running her palms down his bare, hard flanks, she marveled at the fluid flex of muscle beneath her hands.

She dragged her hands around, skimmed the front of his legs and found him, huge and hot and straining at the V of her thighs. Her hand curled around him, and he stilled, his breath harsh against her neck.

He pulled back to look at her, eyes glinting with dangerous intent, peeling away her breath, her reason. "Don't take me all the way. Not yet."

Her breath mingling with his, she nodded, watching his face as she stroked him. He stared at her through slitted eyes, pleasure sharpening his noble features as she dragged her hand the length of him.

She measured him again, and a breath shuddered out of

him. He moved a hand between her legs, lean fingers sliding into her sleek wetness. His arms shook. His breath was just as ragged and labored as hers, yet she felt restraint in his touch, in the lashed tautness of his shoulders.

How could he be so in control? She felt as if she were about to splinter, operating solely on sensation and instinct. She wanted him to lose control, too.

His fingers stroked her, deep and hard; she sagged against him, feeling the tide swell inside her.

"Not close enough," he growled, anchoring his arms beneath her bottom and lifting her.

She hooked her legs around his hips, bringing his erection against her and triggering a wildness inside her. She moved against him. "Rafe," she moaned.

He turned, set her on a desk that held a phone and a lamp.

She arched against him, kissing him, her head bumping the mirror behind her. She kept her legs locked tight around him. She didn't want to lose one moment, one second of feeling him like this, had thought he would never let her in again.

He moved his hand and with two wicked strokes, he stripped the last of her control. The climax ripped through her, quicksilver and searing, consuming the way only Rafe had ever been able to give her. She moaned his name, wanting more of him, needing him.

He held himself stiff-armed over her, head bowed, breathing hard, his copper skin flushed.

"Rafe?" she panted. She needed to feel him deep inside her body, her heart.

She could tell he was searching for control; she didn't want control. Reaching down, she took him in her hand, and his muscles lashed tight.

"Kit," he rasped.

She couldn't tell if it was a plea or a command. "I want

you. I need you. Rafe, please.'' The words were thick in her throat; a greedy flame ate at her from the inside.

He paused, his gaze searing, peeling away every defense.

''I'm safe,'' she said.

''Me, too.''

''Now, Rafe.'' She tightened her legs around his lean waist, urging him closer.

He slid inside, deep and full, his eyes black and steady on her. Her body fitted to him perfectly, as she'd known it would. She clutched his shoulders, lifting her hips. He thrust deep inside her. Sensation drove her, a hot, whipping wind that reached for her.

Her hips rose, lifted, met each of his measured thrusts. He bowed his head, tendons cording in his neck and arms as his body stroked hers.

His hands curled into her hips, flexed with each long slide of his body. She reached up, framed his face in her hands, moving with him. She pulled him to her, covered his lips with hers.

He kissed her back, keeping rhythm with his movements inside her, driving her steadily higher and out of her mind.

Finally, he began to move faster, and she kept pace, her heart overflowing. She'd nearly given up on this, hadn't even dared hope.

And yet, she reached for something…elusive, something she recognized, but couldn't define.

The tension coiled, then snapped inside her. She gasped into his mouth. The first climax hit her, then another, strong, hard, fast.

He threw his head back, thrust harder, faster and finally stilled, bowing his head against hers. For long moments, they stayed like that as their breathing slowed. His flesh was damp beneath her palms, and she felt complete in a way she hadn't since leaving him.

Slowly, she became aware of the corner of the mirror digging into her hip, and she shifted.

He raised his head. "You okay?"

"Yes." She gave a weak smile. "The mirror's getting a little friendly."

He gathered her to him and staggered to the bed. Boneless, she slid down beside him, trying to catch her breath. She turned her head to look at him. His chest rose and fell; a fine sweat slicked his body as it did hers.

His arm still held her loosely to him.

She curled her hand around his and rolled into him. "Very nice, Blackstock. You certainly have not lost your touch."

"Neither have you," he said in a rusty voice.

His hand curved over her hip, pressing her into him. She nestled her head on his shoulder and closed her eyes.

Sunlight brought her slowly awake. She blinked at the ceiling, then squinted at the strip of light streaming through the center part of the draperies. The small ache between her legs brought the memory of last night flooding back.

She smiled and slid a hand across the sheet, reaching for Rafe. When she encountered only cool sheets, she rose up on one elbow, pushing her hair back.

He sat in the oversize chair, pulling on his boots. His hair was neatly brushed, his face freshly scrubbed.

"Morning," she said, rolling to her stomach to watch him.

"Morning." He stomped his foot into his boot, stood.

How long had he been up? When had he left her? She glanced at the clock, saw it was after seven. "You should've woken me."

"Looked like you could use the sleep."

The words were soft, polite. Stilted.

"Is something wrong? Has something happened?" A

chill skittered across her shoulders. She sat up, pulling the sheet around her.

"No word from Liz so I'm assuming she's fine." He didn't meet her eyes, didn't look at her at all. Instead he checked the ammunition in his clip, then slid it into the gun's chamber. "I've already used the shower, so it's all yours."

Despite the ache in her body proving how close they'd been last night, Kit felt a chasm growing between them. Making love with Rafe hadn't felt wrong, but *something* did.

He regretted making love with her.

Her head came up as the realization slammed into her.

He turned, glanced at her, and she knew she was right. His eyes were flat, remote. That, combined with the rigid set of his body, drove a painful wedge beneath her ribs. Her mind could barely compute what it meant.

He'd made love to her with all the finesse and hunger that she remembered. At the end, he'd finally surrendered to the same reckless pulse thundering through her. Almost, she realized, as if he'd surrendered against his will.

She'd thought making love had symbolized a new start. She'd felt him in her soul, surrendered completely to him for the first time in her life. Just as he'd always done. But not this time. Not with her.

The hope she'd held close to her heart crumbled. Tears tightened her throat. She stood up, sweeping the sheet around her and starting for the bathroom. "I'll be out in a minute," she managed to say.

"Kit?"

Hands knotting the sheet, she paused. Waited for him to apologize or explain. The seconds ticked by, scraping against nerves already raw from the extreme plunge in her emotions. He said nothing. She wasn't sure she could bear it if he did.

She walked into the bathroom and shut the door, her body trembling.

He hadn't once called her darlin'.

Hadn't lost all sense of time and place as she had.

Making love had been a purely physical act for him without investing one bit of his heart. And she knew exactly why.

Her heart clenched; she bit her lip to keep from crying. Would he ever trust her again?

Riding a razor edge of anger and guilt, Rafe watched Kit disappear into the bathroom. Last night, she had made herself completely vulnerable to him for the first time in their lives, but he hadn't been able to do the same. The last time he had opened up, she'd walked away. His world had shattered. He couldn't let that happen again.

When she'd told him she wanted him, she'd seemed so certain. When they'd made love, she had committed totally to him. Hell, she'd about committed him right off his feet. He had thought he was ready, but he wasn't.

Being buried tight inside her had only sharpened his awareness of her and his sense of loss. He hadn't been able to tell her how much he'd missed her, missed the way she said his name just before she came apart in his arms, missed the way she held his face when they were both going over the edge. Blocked by the memory of how she'd hurt him before, the words had stayed locked in his throat.

"What do we do about Liz?" Kit's voice was cool and steady as she walked out of the bathroom. She stuffed her toothbrush into her makeup case, then zipped her travel bag. "About that guy who was here last night?"

"We'll keep an eye out for Ape Boy." He noticed her eyes showed no sign of the hurt that he'd dealt her. They were cool, even remote, but he remembered the bleak sharpness there. "As for Liz, we don't want to lead Alexander's goon to her and Tony, so we can go to a dummy bank and throw him off their trail. Or we can stay here.''

''Let's go to the bank,'' she said quickly, gathering her purse and travel bag, then moving to the door.

She said the same thing he would've. Staying in this room, cornered by guilt and second thoughts, would be impossible for him. Evidently for her, too.

He slid his gun into the waistband of his black jeans and picked up the room's phone book along with his bag as he walked out. They could choose an alternate bank in the car.

They rode down in the elevator, the silence abrasive and thick. Rafe slid a look at her features, composed, guarded.

''I'm really sorry, Kit. About last night.''

''Oh, look, we're here,'' she said brightly, practically clawing the door open and hurrying into the lobby.

He snagged her elbow, turned her to face him. ''We need to talk about this.''

She stared at him, anger and hurt warring in her eyes. She sighed. ''Can we talk later? Take care of this first?''

''Yes.'' He released her even though he didn't want to. ''And we will talk, all right?''

''All right.''

They paid for their room. Rafe paused at the hotel's double glass doors and scanned the parking lot before proceeding outside. ''I don't see the silver sedan or Baldy.''

''That's good, right?'' Subdued, Kit walked beside him, her gaze sweeping the lot carefully.

''Yes, but the guy's not an idiot.'' He unlocked her door, then took her bag and put it in his small trunk along with his luggage. ''He won't get that close again. He may have even switched cars. He knows we'd make that sedan in a heartbeat.''

Once in the 'Vette, Kit directed him to a bank on the other side of town. The moderate population was spread over wheat fields interspersed with strip malls and grocery stores. The silence built around them, echoing with hurt and regret. He kept seeing the devastation on her face this morning when he'd turned away from her.

Just as they pulled into the parking lot of Farmer's Home Bank, her cell phone rang.

She leaned close so he could hear as she answered.

"Kit!" Liz shrieked, sounding hysterical.

"What is it? What's happened?" Kit demanded. "Are you guys okay?"

"The money! Where's the money?"

Kit shot Rafe a panicked look; he swung into a parking space and put the car in Park.

"You didn't get it?" she asked Liz.

"No!"

"I had it wired from Wexler." Kit held the phone close to Rafe's ear. "I'll make a call—"

"It's too late. We've already left Grady City."

He could feel the warmth from Kit's scalp; her soft hair brushed against his cheek. Setting his jaw, he narrowed his focus to the phone call only.

"Why did you leave?" Kit asked sharply. "If you'd stay in one place long enough, you could get the money."

"I'm not the one who messed this up," her sister reminded acidly.

Rafe wanted to take the phone and tell Liz to simmer down, but he didn't.

"I'm still in Grady City." Kit shifted beside him, her shoulder nudging his. Her scent drifted around him. "I can go to the bank right now, make sure the wire gets to you this time."

"We really need the money, sis. The bank said they never received wire instructions at all."

"I'm sorry, Liz. I didn't know. I can send it to you now; just tell me where."

"Okay, Tony says we can stop before we get to where

we're going. Remember that year we went to Yellowstone?''

"Yes." She'd been thirteen, Liz ten. The year before Mom had died.

"And the car broke down in Colorado? That old brown Fairlane?" Liz asked.

"Yes," Kit said with visible relief. "You're going to the town where we had it serviced."

"Right, but only for a couple of hours. You can send the money there." She gave Kit the name of a local bank.

Rafe nodded, giving Kit a thumbs-up. He couldn't stop a flare of admiration at the way she calmed her sister down.

"I'll make sure it goes through this time, Liz. Call me after you get it."

"Tony doesn't think I should. We're heading for a cabin not far from there, and you won't hear from me for a while. He's sweeping the hard drive, and he has almost everything he needs off Alexander's computer."

Rafe shook his head, mouthing, "No. Tell her not to break contact."

"Liz, please call. At least to let me know you're all right."

"I can't promise. Bye." And she hung up.

Kit did the same, sighing loudly. "I guess we need to go to the bank and make sure the money goes through this time."

Rafe nodded, reversing out of the space and turning onto the main avenue. "So, where do you send the money?"

She pulled away from him, stuffed her cell phone in her purse. "A bank in Pueblo."

"But they're not staying. They're heading for a cabin somewhere?"

"Yeah, a cabin in Colorado. Like nobody has one of *those*. How are we going to figure that out?" Kit asked wryly. "She said she might or might not call."

Rafe drummed his fingers on the wheel. "If they're planning to stay there a while, maybe that's where they were headed all along."

She shot him a thoughtful look. "And Liz did say they didn't want to leave a straight trail to where they were going, which would explain all their zigzagging."

"Right."

"So maybe," Kit said slowly, "this is the information Eddie Sanchez had. This is what got him killed?"

"Very likely. And maybe he knew about this cabin because it belonged to him."

"Do you think?"

The possibility put a hint of life in her eyes, more color in her cheeks than she'd had all morning. "Could be. Once we get to Pueblo, we can check it out."

"How?"

"I'll do a property search on the Internet." He stopped at a light, pointed through the intersection. "We'll stop at this bank first and send Liz the money."

"Then drive to Pueblo and make sure she picked it up."

"Exactly. After that, we'll see if we can locate this cabin or some kind of information to help us find it."

"So this might really be over soon?"

He hated how the anticipation in her voice sliced at him, but he didn't blame her for wanting some space from him. "Yeah."

"That's good." She let out a deep breath. "That's really good."

After Kit contacted the check-cashing place in Wexler, she issued instructions for the money to be wired to Pueblo. She and Rafe waited an hour, until they were told the money was received on the other end, then they drove out of Grady City, straight west on US-50 for Pueblo.

The drive took almost seven hours. They arrived midafternoon, and once there, Rafe drove to the bank Liz had designated. Kit went inside to make sure the wire had indeed gone through. While she checked on that, he got directions to the police department.

Some of the strain seemed to vanish from around her mouth once she learned that the wire had come through and Liz had picked up the money.

He drove to the police department and explained the case to the desk sergeant, who took careful note of Liz and Tony's descriptions, as well as Alexander's goon. The sergeant then generously agreed to let Rafe hook up to the Internet via one of their phone lines.

For over an hour, Rafe searched Colorado property records for Eddie Sanchez. He saved the files to his laptop to look over once he and Kit left the police department. After thanking the sergeant for his help, he and Kit climbed into his car.

He was tired, his brain was fuzzy, and guilt sawed at him over the distance he'd put between them.

After Kit agreed quietly that she was hungry, he chose a nice restaurant off I-25 South, and they shared a meal in near silence. The smudges under her eyes were darker; the quiet way she held herself gouged at his conscience. Rafe knew he couldn't let things go on like this. She deserved better, regardless of how determined he was to protect his heart.

Finished with his steak and potato, he laid down his fork and napkin. Crawling over broken glass held more appeal, but he jumped right in. "Are we just going to pretend last night never happened?"

"Isn't that what you want?" She gave him a cool if exhausted look across the table. "Just to forget it?"

"Not really. There were things I should've said. Hell, I should've said anything, but I just…didn't. I was wrong and I owe you an apology."

She stared at her plate, then lifted somber eyes to his.

"You can't help it if you think our making love was a mistake. I just wish you'd said something before...before."

"I didn't say it was a mistake." He leaned forward, urging her with his eyes to look at him, but she looked at her glass, the tablecloth, her half-empty plate. "I didn't say that."

Her gaze searched his. She carefully folded her napkin and leaned over to pick up her purse. "Let's find a hotel for tonight. We can talk about it there."

"Okay, good." He hoped he hadn't screwed things up beyond redemption.

Chapter 12

They checked into a hotel off I-25, not far from where they'd eaten. Even though Rafe hadn't spotted the tail all day, he didn't feel comfortable getting separate rooms.

As he filled out the registration card and pocketed the key, Kit's mouth tightened, but she didn't protest. In fact, she didn't say anything. Well, he thought wryly, he certainly didn't need to worry about a repeat of last night.

While he put her bag on the bed and his in the space between the wall and an armoire holding the television, she walked toward the window and stepped around a red floral chaise lounge to flip on a lamp in the corner. She stayed at the window, staring blankly at the khaki curtains. He wasn't sure if they had another shot. He just knew he was miserable and he'd made her the same way.

The room smelled of pine air freshener and cleaner. He slid his gun out from the small of his back, double-checked the safety and laid the weapon on top of the armoire.

He watched Kit for a moment. She was a small, solitary

figure; lamplight washed across her soft features, traced her curves with silvery light.

"I'm really sorry, Kit. I know I hurt you."

"You did." She took a deep breath, then turned to face him. "But I hurt you, too."

"I didn't do it to punish you."

"I know." In the pale light, her features looked worn from exhaustion. Anxiety darkened her eyes. "I've been thinking about it all day and I finally get it."

"Get what?" It had been his suggestion to talk, but he suddenly felt as if he were maneuvering around quicksand. "There's no excuse for what I did."

"You were there for me last night. Just like you always were."

"I should've said no, should've told you I wasn't ready. I should've *known* I wasn't ready."

She stepped toward him, looking up earnestly. The tantalizing scent of wildflowers and woman drifted through the room. "I was *never* there for you. Last night, I finally realized it. Or rather this morning. Why did you even put up with me as long as you did?"

The question hit him like an ambush. Rafe stared at her. Of all the things he'd expected, this wouldn't have made the list. "Do you think I was such a jerk this morning because I was trying to get back at you? I wasn't. I thought I was ready. I wanted to be ready, but—"

"No, I don't think you pulled away to punish me or get back at me or anything like that. I don't think you meant to hurt me at all."

He exhaled a huge sigh of relief. "I didn't."

"But I do think you pulled away because you don't trust me. You don't trust that I won't hurt you again. And the reason you don't trust me is because all I ever did was hurt you."

"That's not true. It hurt when you walked away, but that's all."

"No, it's not. I was always crying on your shoulder, then taking off to deal with family problems."

"I never looked at it that way, Kit."

"Not once?" she challenged. "Be honest."

"What difference does this make now?" Frustration raking through him, he scrubbed a hand over his face. He didn't like the turn of the conversation. "It was ten years ago."

"I know you resented that. You still do."

"Don't put words in my mouth." Tension strung his body taut.

"Until we talk about it, until you admit it, how are we going to move on?"

The walls pressed in on him, squeezing his lungs. He stepped around her, gained a few feet of distance by walking to the bed. She was right. As much as he wanted to be over the anger he'd felt, he wasn't.

"I know one reason you can't trust me is that you think I'm going to run out on you again. Just tell me, Rafe. Please. I want to get this out in the open. I want to fight for us, Rafe, and I can do it for both of us if I have to. But I have to know the problem. You have to tell me."

He shoved a hand through his hair. "Okay, yes, I think about that."

"And you felt abandoned. Not just when I ended our engagement, but all those times I walked away before. All the times I left when you needed me."

"Maybe." He felt cornered, edgy. "I wanted to talk about what happened last night, Kit. I don't want you to dissect me."

"Why can't you admit you resented me? That you still do?"

There it was, black and ugly and cold. "Because I don't.

I didn't.'' He skirted the end of the bed, found her right in front of him.

She touched his arm lightly, yet it held him in place like a truss. ''What about that time your grandfather died and I left before the funeral to chase after Liz?''

The memory touched a raw place; he shook off her hand, moved past her. ''Things happen.''

''And what about when you made the All-State team in basketball, but I wasn't there for the announcement or to watch any of your games? I was with Liz.''

''We both know all this, Kit.'' The light scent of wild-flowers trailed him, knotting the muscles in his neck even more. ''Talking about it won't change anything.''

''I want to move on, Rafe. I want to move on with *you* and I don't think you can trust me until we deal with this. You've got to tell me how I hurt you. I don't want to do it again.''

Was she right? If they talked about it, could they put it behind them? She had this thing between her teeth and she obviously wasn't letting go. ''But if I tell you, *that* will hurt you. Hasn't there been enough of that?''

''Please, Rafe. I need to know.''

''Damn.'' He paced to the closet on the far side of the bed.

She followed. ''Don't you think this will help? Can't you tell me? You told me I should tell Liz to grow up. You're the one who told me I should let go of the responsibility I feel over my mom's death, and I think I'm doing that.''

He pinched the bridge of his nose. ''I was angry when I said all that.''

''Then I'll tell *you*.'' She sat behind him on the corner of the bed, pushing in that steel-velvet way she had. ''I was never there for you. I made you feel second to my family, especially to my sister. And then I left you because of them." Her voice quavered. "How *could* you ever trust me again?"

He stared into those big, liquid eyes, amazed that she would open herself up for this. Maybe she was right. Maybe talking about the past would allow them to put it behind them.

"I want to trust you, but you're right." He finally gave in, sat next to her on the bed and looked her straight in the eye. "I wonder how long it will last. I wonder if you'll only stay until the next time Liz needs you or the next time she runs off. I wonder if you'll leave when I want something you don't want to give."

A tear rolled down her cheek, and he thumbed it away. "This isn't what I want. I don't want to hurt you."

"No. I need to know. I need to hear it from you." She reached out, took his left hand in both of hers. "I swear, Rafe, I want to try with everything in me, but all I can do is try. I can't promise. This is all new for me, too. But I want *us*, if you do. I can't swear I'll never look back, but I really want to look forward."

The plea, the total vulnerability in her eyes undid him. And it was her honesty that finally allowed him to admit the level of resentment he'd denied feeling. He searched her face. "I can't make promises, either. I'm not sure I can forget what happened the last time I let you in. You owned me heart and soul, Kit. I don't know if I can give that up again."

"That's fair." She squeezed his hand tightly. "I know I have to earn your trust—"

He placed two fingers over her lips. "You don't have to earn anything. I just need to be sure. *We* need to be sure."

She nodded, her eyes glowing. "I don't think our making love was a mistake, but maybe it was too soon."

"It was, for me. It made me lose perspective, Kit, and I need to keep that." Reaching out, he stroked a finger down her velvety cheek, tried to ignore how close she was to him, how easy it would be to make love to her and pretend everything was all right. "My heart wants to trust you, but my head keeps getting in the way."

"I understand."

He slipped one finger beneath her chin and tipped her face towards his. "I want you, Kit, but I need some time with the rest of it."

"Okay." A tremulous smile curved her lips, making his gut pull tight. She leaned forward, brushed a soft kiss against his lips. "I'll be here. I'm not going anywhere this time."

He kissed her gently, deepening the contact only when she pressed him closer, her mouth opening under his. A new tenuous connection fluttered between them, fragile yet cementing the feelings that had never died.

She ended the kiss, pulling away with a sigh and cupping the side of his face. "It will work out. If we both want it to."

He wanted to believe her.

She smiled and stood. "Guess we'd better get busy looking at those property records."

"Right." His body ached for more of her, but he knew now wasn't the time.

He plugged in his laptop, trying to calm the steady thrum of want in his veins.

After an hour of poring over the reports, Rafe groaned and flopped back in the chaise lounge. "I don't know what we're missing."

"Maybe it's just not there." Kit rubbed her neck, sagging back in the chair she'd moved next to him.

"Maybe not," he admitted.

She stifled a yawn. "I'm about ready for bed."

"Me, too."

She disappeared into the bathroom.

When she emerged, wearing her gown and robe, her face was scrubbed clean of makeup. Her short, dark hair was brushed into a sleek wedge. The room's fluorescent light picked up a hint of auburn in the dark brown.

She padded to the window but left the curtains closed. "Do you think the bald guy's out there?"

"I don't know." Rafe ignored the ache that settled in his chest at the sight of her in that curve-hugging robe. Looking at her long, lean legs only reminded him of how she'd wrapped them around him last night.

"Do you think it will be much longer before Nita hears something on Sanchez's background check?"

"I hope not. I'm not having much luck here. There are a lot more guys named Eddie Sanchez than I anticipated." Somehow, he tore his gaze from her. He needed to keep his focus on the case, sort out his feelings about Kit, not confuse them further.

"I know Nita passed on to my investigator that I wanted him to dig deeper, so hopefully she'll learn something useful soon. She'll call as soon as she does."

Kit smiled, her gaze softly devouring him.

Sensation hummed through his body. "You shouldn't look at me like that."

"Close your eyes so you won't know."

He grinned, the want sliding deeper. "Craig called while you were in the bathroom. He said he's pieced together a trail of e-mails between Alexander and Tony. Even one threatening Tony's loved ones if he didn't do as Alexander wanted."

"Good," she said fiercely, her eyes shifting from dreamy to sharp. "I hope they're enough to put that jerk in jail."

"Me, too. I told Craig to get it over to Uncle Wayne, let the FBI start compiling evidence." Rafe sat up, sorted through his files until he came to the beginning of the property records. He might as well go through them again.

She walked to the bed, sank down on its edge. For a long moment, there was only the sound of his mouse clicking as he scrolled down and read a file.

"I don't guess you want to sleep here tonight?"

His gaze shot to hers. Images flashed through his mind, mirrored in her eyes. Their bodies moving together last night, the friction of damp flesh against damp flesh, the way she'd closed tight and perfect around him. He could still taste her, wanted to do more than that. "I don't think so. Probably not a good idea."

"I didn't mean..." A blush stained her cheeks. "I meant I'd sleep on the chaise or on the floor. This bed feels pretty comfortable. I don't mind if you want to use it."

"Oh. No, you take it." His body already throbbed; it would be sheer hell to lie in that bed and think about her being in there with him.

"Let me know if you change your mind."

He nodded, watching her slip out of her robe and slide into bed, reach up to turn out the light just above her head.

He swallowed hard.

Her eyes glowed as they sought his. "Good night."

"Night." A tightness stretched across his chest, and he rubbed at it. For several seconds, he watched her. Her mouth was relaxed, her features vulnerable as she fell asleep. It was with some effort that he pulled his gaze away.

She had hit upon his resentment like a sharpshooter. Surprisingly, he did feel better after talking about it. She amazed him with her willingness to open up, lay her feelings on the line after the way he'd hurt her this morning.

But he had no idea how far he could go from here. He couldn't reject her any longer, but he couldn't commit, either. Would he ever be able to?

The phone shrilled. Kit rolled and reached for it, only to realize the ring belonged to a cell phone. Rafe's cell phone.

"Hello." His deep voice rumbled, rusty with sleep.

Groggy, she sat up, blinking the sleep from her eyes. Dawn-pink light crept into the room.

"Great." He rose from the chaise lounge where he'd spent the night. "Tell me what you've got."

"Is that Nita?" she whispered.

He nodded, moving to sit down on the bed next to her. Only the sheet and thin bedspread separated them. His lean thigh silhouetted hers; his heat reached through the fabric. The sight of his dark, tousled hair and his black T-shirt wrinkled and untucked sent a surge of warmth through her. She had gotten some sleep, and Rafe looked as if he had, too.

"Hang on," he told his office manager. Leaning forward, he jotted a note on the hotel's stationery pad that lay on the bedside table.

When he settled back, Kit breathed in the deep, woodsy scent of him. She curbed her impatience to know the news.

"Thanks, Nita. I'll give you a call and let you know what's going on."

He hung up and ripped the sheet of paper from the pad. "She heard from my investigator. The reason we couldn't find a cabin for Sanchez on the Internet is that it's listed under his mother's maiden name, Harper."

"So, where are we going?" His warmth coaxed her closer. Kit wanted to snuggle up to that broad chest, press a kiss on the side of his neck.

His gaze traveled over her face, lingered on her lips long enough to make them tingle.

Reflexively, she licked them. "Rafe?"

"Yeah." He jerked his gaze to hers, and she saw desire flare in the black depths, saw him bank it. "Uh, let's see. We're going to Fort Towell. The cabin is located just east of there, on the edge of a wildlife preserve."

"Where's Fort Towell?"

"South central Colorado, down by a town called Alamosa in the San Luis Valley."

"How long will it take us to get there?"

"Probably two and a half hours." His gaze dipped to the swell of her breasts, revealed by the scoop neck of her gown.

Her hands tightened on the sheet. She wanted him to kiss her, wanted to know if his feelings were the same as they had been last night before they'd gone to sleep. But he wanted slow, and she'd promised.

He looked away, stood. Walking to the window, he glanced at his watch.

"I'll shower and dress." Kit slid out of bed, her nerves shimmering. How could he notch up her pulse with just a look? "It won't take me long. Do we have time?"

"Yes." He turned, kept his gaze trained carefully on hers. "I'll jump in once you're finished. It's early enough that we should get there by mid-morning."

"And what about Ape Boy?"

He grinned at her use of the nickname he'd given their tail. "We'll keep an eye out. Once we get to Fort Towell, we'll stop for directions to the cabin. I only have an address. We'll also make sure we're still alone. Anyone following us will find it a lot harder to hide in such a small town."

"What if we don't see him? We didn't yesterday."

"If he's still tailing us, we'll spot him."

"And what if he's not?"

"We've either lost him or he's following Liz and Tony."

She swallowed against the possibility, then told herself not to borrow trouble. She turned and walked into the bathroom.

An hour later, they were ready and in the car. While Rafe filled up with gas at a convenience store on the way out of town, Kit bought two large, steaming cups of coffee and two sausage biscuits.

Leaving Pueblo, they drove south on I-25. As Rafe smoothly maneuvered the Corvette through early-morning highway traffic, she savored her coffee and watched him. Broad shoulders made the most of the moss green T-shirt he wore today. Beneath the aroma of roasted coffee, she caught a whiff of the hotel soap he'd used.

Her gaze slid over the flex of sinew on his forearm as he shifted gears, moved down to muscular, denim-clad thighs and scuffed boots. He was one gorgeous man.

He kept one hand on the wheel as he drank his coffee. His gaze switched frequently between the rearview and side mirrors. Kit regularly checked her side mirror, but she saw nothing suspicious.

They drove in the opposite direction of most morning traffic, and the number of cars thinned quickly. If the bald guy was still following them, and if he was still in the silver sedan, he'd be easy to spot on this flat stretch of land.

Wildflowers along the side of the road provided an occasional splash of color against greening farmland. Just to the west and behind Kit's shoulder were the Wet Mountains, a subrange of the Rockies, their gray-purple face and snowy peaks wreathed in clouds. Kit's gaze kept returning to Rafe, as did her thoughts.

She was glad he'd finally opened up to her about his resentment. For the first time in the days since they'd begun working together, he'd let her in.

Why had it taken her so long to see the way she'd put him second to her family? It had finally hit her after they'd made love, after he'd withdrawn from *her*.

At first, she'd been angry and hurt, but that had soon dissolved, leaving her to stare at the cold, hard truth. His distance from her had allowed her to see that she'd always done the same thing to him. When they'd been together before, she had only committed fully to him when they'd made love, holding back at all other times. She thought she needed to be self-sufficient, and she had been. So much so that Rafe had believed she never needed him.

Shifting her gaze out the window, she admitted the real reason she'd left him in the first place. He'd wanted to relieve her of some of the responsibility she carried, and that had frightened her. She'd felt threatened. Because if she had let go, she realized, she would've felt she was giving up a part of her identity, the part that had taken over and become a surrogate mother to Liz.

It wasn't just being with Rafe, but also the past ten years that had taught her that. During those years, she'd battled giving up that responsibility a fraction at a time. Could she live her own life without taking on her sister's? There was a balance somewhere, and Kit wanted to find it.

Her cell phone rang, and she pulled it out of her purse. "Maybe it's Liz," she said to Rafe. "Hello?"

"Kit?"

"Yes." Her head came up and she grabbed Rafe's arm, mouthing, "Tony."

She slid closer to Rafe, leaning over to hold the phone so they could both hear.

"This is Tony. Tony Valentine."

"Of course, I know it's you, Tony." She bit back her impatience and the flare of worry that he, not Liz, was calling her. "Is everything okay?"

"Liz is fine, yes. I wondered if you guys would meet me?"

"Absolutely. Where?"

Rafe's gaze sliced to her. He shook his head as if he couldn't hear.

She angled the phone toward him, her shoulder flush with the hard line of his. Their heads touched.

"I'm in a little town called Fort Towell. I left Liz back at the cabin asleep."

"But she's okay? And you're okay?"

"We're both fine," Tony reassured her. "She needed to sleep, and besides, she doesn't blend too well."

Rafe chuckled.

Kit grinned, her anxiety lessening somewhat. "Tell us where to meet you. We're already on our way there. We found out about Eddie's cabin."

Tony gave them directions to a place called Pet's Diner, right off US-160. "I'm driving an older model Ford pickup. White."

"Okay."

Rafe motioned for her to give him the phone.

"I'm going to pass the phone to Rafe. He wants to talk to you."

She took Rafe's coffee cup then she handed him the phone.

"Tony, Rafe Blackstock. We're less than two hours away. Keep a low profile. You've been doing great at that."

Kit dug a pen out of her purse, then a receipt. On the back of it, she jotted down the name of the diner.

Rafe said, "Good. Put that evidence in a separate place from the computer. Right."

After another pause, he said, "Have you noticed anyone following you? That's good. Okay, we'll see you in a couple of hours."

He hung up and handed the phone to her. "Tony said he hadn't seen a tail, but he left Liz at the cabin in case he did. He's protecting her."

"He darn well better be. He got her into this mess," Kit muttered, stuffing her phone into her purse.

"Are you sure?"

She looked into those steady black eyes. "No. You're

right. She got herself into it. She probably just jumped right in the car with him and took off, no matter what he said.''

"Kinda like her sister," he teased.

"Hmph, you needed me and you know it."

He chuckled, his eyes sparking with humor and a softness that made her stomach dip.

She was supposed to be with this man. Only him. Would she ever be able to tell him?

He'd made no promises last night—neither of them had—but Kit felt encouraged. They'd reached a level beyond what they had shared before.

For the first time, she'd let him in, really let herself depend on him, and though it was intimidating, it was also freeing in a way she'd never expected or experienced. That mix of emotions played through her. She was thrilled Rafe hadn't rejected her, but could she be what he needed this time? Could she really let go of the responsibility she'd carried for so long?

She was going to try with everything in her. She didn't want to lose him again. If anyone walked away, this time it would be him.

And that was a possibility, she told herself. The thought unleashed the same swelling panic in her that it had before, but she fought it down.

Less than an hour later, they took the US-160 West exit off I-25 and drove west through Walsenburg. Seventeen miles took them through La Veta Pass. The flat prairie began to roll and dip, becoming a valley. After several minutes, Rafe pointed out a sign declaring that Fort Towell was less than an hour west. The Sangre de Cristo Mountains, visible only as bluish-gray summits while they'd traveled south, rose to their north, looking close enough to touch. Clouds haloed the peaks; the sun beamed through, splashing gold onto slopes of evergreen trees.

Kit noted that, while she and Rafe had driven in silence

at times, it had been comfortable. She slid a look at him, her heart clenching.

Memories washed through her—his burning kisses, the bone-melting stroke of his hands on her flesh. She'd never stopped loving him and wanted to tell him that, but now wasn't the time. He didn't trust her not to walk away again. Those three words wouldn't mean anything until he did. *If* he ever did.

Knowing these thoughts would drive her crazy, she focused on her sister. "What's the plan once we meet up with Liz and Tony?"

"First, we'll make sure Alexander's goons aren't around, then we'll see just how safe their cabin is. If necessary, I'll move them to a motel somewhere. I'll call Uncle Wayne for backup and also connect him with Tony. By now, Craig's delivered what he found to the FBI. Wayne will tell me how he wants to proceed. I'll either take them back to Oklahoma City or meet my uncle somewhere."

"*You* sure are going to be busy." She arched a brow, unable to resist jabbing him a little. "What about me? You're not planning to ditch me, are you?"

She had only meant to tease, but the words too closely mirrored her secret fear. An awkward silence grew between them.

"No," he said quietly, then shifted his attention to the road. "*We'll* do all that, okay?"

"Okay."

"Uncle Wayne will probably want Tony in protective custody, possibly Liz, too. Will you be all right with that?"

Kit smiled as she realized she really would be. "At least I'll know where she is and that she's safe."

"True."

Since the beginning, she'd been nervous about the outcome—they were talking about Liz, after all—but she'd never doubted Rafe would find Liz. Never doubted he'd keep her, Kit, safe. She had every confidence he would see this through to the end with her, but what about afterward?

He glanced over. "How well do you know Tony?"

"Not well. He's a likable guy and smart. Computer smart, anyway."

"Bad influence?"

She shrugged. "At first, I thought he'd be the one man to make Liz feel settled, but I was wrong. I was disappointed when he went to prison. Sure made Liz the more steadying influence in that relationship."

"There's obviously something still between them."

"Yeah." Kit ran her fingers through her hair.

"Think she'll see him once this is over?"

"I don't know. She obviously wanted to before all this started. It may depend on whether he goes back to prison."

"Are you okay with it if she gets back together with him?"

"Do you think it would matter if I weren't?"

His lips twisted. "I imagine you're anxious to see her."

"I'm anxious to smack her, but that's never done any good."

He chuckled. Kit angled into her seat so she faced him, her gaze following the golden wash of sunlight over his features, his muscled arms. "I'm just glad they're okay."

"She always seems to land on her feet." Rafe passed a car, then moved into his lane again.

"Yes," she murmured. He was exactly right. Liz *would* manage to land on her feet whether Kit were there to catch her or not.

Studying Rafe's sculpted jawline, the noble profile, Kit realized he'd been right about something else, too. For years, she had struggled with letting go of the responsibility she felt over her mom's death. She knew it would break her mother's heart to know Kit blamed herself. Getting her own heart to let go of that blame was a different matter altogether.

Every time she thought she had managed to do it, her sister would pull a stunt, and all the uncertainty would well up again.

Kit saw that maybe she'd used that as an excuse. Maybe she'd been afraid to let Liz go rather than really believing that her sister depended on her completely. That realization drew her up short, but it fit, settled something deep inside her that had felt restless and out of place since her mom's death. Part of her would probably always feel responsible for her mom's death, but she was tired of carrying it, especially by herself.

She looked at Rafe, and a new determination filled her. She was willing to do whatever it took in order to keep him in her life this time. But regardless of what he decided about them, it was time for her to make some changes, starting with how she dealt with Liz.

Before long, she and Rafe could focus on themselves, sort things out. Once Liz and Tony were safe, Kit could tell her sister about her plans for a new life.

Chapter 13

The closer she and Rafe got to Pet's Diner, the more edgy Kit became. Not just because she wanted to see for herself that Liz was all right, but because she wanted this finished. The fact that neither she nor Rafe had spotted the bald guy tailing them also had her nerves jangling.

"What do you think happened to Baldy?" she asked as Rafe flipped on his signal and turned into the gravel parking lot. "We haven't seen him since Grady City."

"I don't know, but we need to keep an eye out. I don't like the way he suddenly disappeared."

Kit nodded, taking in the long white building in front of them. A red-trimmed door and windows, along with a tasteful back addition, nearly disguised the fact that the front section had originally been a mobile home. They drove between the two rows of vehicles parked along its length. She pointed out Tony's white pickup at the far end of the front row.

Rafe nodded. "If Alexander's goons are around, they won't miss it, either."

He eased the 'Vette into the first available spot, between an old Chevy sedan with peeling green paint and a grungy brown four-door Jeep.

He killed the engine, and they both got out. The early summer air was comfortably cool, the sun bright in a pale blue sky. To the north rose four mountain peaks Rafe had learned were Mount Lindsey, Little Bear Peak, Blanca Peak and Ellingwood Point, snow visible on their summits.

Kit scanned the row of cars behind where they'd parked, noticed that Rafe did the same, but she didn't see the silver sedan or any car that looked familiar. She should've been relieved, but like Rafe, she wondered what had happened to the guy who had attached himself like their shadow.

Semis and sports utility vehicles zoomed past on the highway. Tufts of sagebrush dotted the sandy pastureland across the busy roadway.

"There he is."

Kit turned toward Rafe, her gaze going past him to the end of the row. A slender man in a baseball cap, Denver Broncos shirt and jeans stood at the tailgate of a white Ford pickup.

Tony made eye contact, then turned and walked around the truck to the side of the diner.

Kit started toward him, and Rafe fell into step with her. "You doing okay?"

"Yes, just ready to see Liz." She smiled at him, wishing she weren't so jumpy. "I'm glad this is almost over."

"Won't be long now."

She hoped so, hoped they could get Liz and Tony out of here before Alexander's goons showed up. They rounded Tony's pickup and Kit saw him standing in the shadows of the building.

She glanced at Rafe. "I'm glad you're here."

"Not going anywhere." He squeezed her shoulder.

Grateful for the support, she reached up and touched him.

Even in the shadows, Kit could see how strain had hardened her brother-in-law's usually soft mouth. His short brown hair was hidden beneath the ball cap, and he'd grown a full, if spotty, beard to go with his mustache. His wire-framed glasses did little to hide the anxiety in his gray eyes. "Hi, Tony."

"Hi, Kit. Sorry about this."

"Me, too." She gestured to Rafe. "This is Rafe Blackstock. He's my...a private investigator. He's got contacts with the FBI and can get you some protection."

The men shook hands. Even though Tony stood only an inch shorter than Rafe, he seemed smaller due to his narrow shoulders. He backed against the stucco wall, edging farther into the shadows as he glanced nervously behind him. She and Rafe moved closer; Rafe stood on her left side, keeping an eye on the parking lot.

Tony's eyes were red-rimmed and tired-looking. "Thanks for meeting me. I want you to take Liz with you. There could be trouble, and I don't want her involved. I hope you'll have better luck at talking her into leaving than I have."

Kit nodded. "We'll get her out of here. What about you?"

"Thanks." Relief flashed across his sharp features. "I'm going to the FBI. I've got three disks in my truck, taped under the seat. They contain all the evidence I could find against Alexander on his computer. From the first time he approached me about running a scam for him to where he threatened to hurt someone close to me."

"That's good," Rafe said.

"Should I give them to you?"

"No, you hold on to them, turn them over to the FBI yourself."

Tony nodded, his gaze darting to the parking lot. "We

can go to the cabin if you're ready. I wasn't followed. I've tried to be careful about noticing that.''

''Great. We didn't spot a tail, either.''

Kit pressed closer to Rafe, reassured by his easy handling of their covert meeting. She'd hired him because she trusted him, had known he would help her; in the bargain, she'd gotten a confident, more-than-competent professional and maybe a second chance with him. ''Should we follow you to the cabin?''

''Yes,'' Tony said, ''but I wanted to give you directions, too. In case you lose sight of me. We'll turn right onto this highway and go four miles west. Take a dirt road marked by two brick columns. From there, it's about fifteen more minutes, past a mesa and some thick forest. Liz will probably be awake by the time we get there.''

''And mad,'' Kit said with a smile.

''Very mad. But this is for her own good.'' Tony's smile eased the lines of fatigue and worry in his thin face. His gaze searched Kit's. ''I really tried to keep her out of it. She wouldn't listen.''

''I know how she is.'' Kit was past being angry with either of them; she just wanted them to come out of this safely.

''I'm glad you're here,'' he said. ''Maybe you can talk some sense into her, tell her to get on with her life and forget about me. I imagine I'm looking at more time, seeing as how I skipped out on my parole.''

She admitted to a flare of admiration. He really seemed to have Liz's best interests in mind. ''We don't think your parole officer turned you in yet. A few days ago, we talked to him and he indicated that he'd let us have a chance to find you.''

''Really? That's great. He's a pretty nice guy.''

Rafe stepped behind Kit, his body a solid shield at her back. He eyed the parking lot carefully before turning to

Tony. "Once we get Liz and make sure you two are some-where safe, I'll call my uncle at the FBI. They've started building a case against Alexander with some evidence re-covered from your computer."

He explained about Craig and the information he'd turned over to Wayne Blackstock.

"Your guy must be good." Respect lit Tony's eyes.

"It took him a while," Rafe said with a grin, "but he got it."

He put a hand to the small of Kit's back, his touch warm and reassuring as the three of them walked toward Tony's pickup.

"Ready?" Rafe asked.

Tony nodded and slid into his truck while she and Rafe moved to the 'Vette.

"Did you ever see the bald guy?"

"No."

She studied Rafe, trying to determine if he were uneasy or nervous, but his black eyes revealed only caution.

Twenty-five minutes later, after bumping and twisting along a rutted dirt road past cedars and pines and a pair of deer who skittered away at the sight of them, she and Rafe pulled up behind Tony's truck in front of a small, A-frame cabin.

Tony started up the pine steps. Kit followed with Rafe, admiring the beauty of Liz's temporary home and inhaling the scent of pine on the cool air. Leave it to her sister to find a gorgeous spot to hide.

The cabin was nestled in a lush grove of evergreen trees. Framed by a pale blue sky and sun-tipped branches, the picture was as inviting and perfect as a travel brochure. Birds chirped, and a slight breeze whistled through the trees. Since Kit had left Pueblo, the temperature had dropped slightly. Though still pleasant, it was cooler in the valley. She rubbed her arms, wishing she'd brought a light jacket to wear over her short-sleeved cotton shirt.

Rafe waited at the bottom of the steps for her. Five steps, carved from the same golden pine as the cabin, led to a wide deck. Sunlight glittered off two triangular windows situated on either side of the door. She and Rafe started up the steps.

"Whoa."

The alarm in Tony's voice had Kit's head coming up. He stood in the open doorway, his hands in the air.

"Tony!" a woman screamed. "They work for Alexander!"

Liz! The voice jolted Kit. Before she could call out, Rafe grabbed her wrist. She jerked toward him, stunned. *What was going on?*

He silenced her with one quick slash of his index finger.

"Hey, man, don't shoot." Tony stayed frozen in the doorway. "I don't have a gun."

A masculine voice murmured something, then Kit heard another unfamiliar male.

"Run, Tony!" Liz cried.

Rafe ducked under the stair rail, pulling Kit with him. She stumbled onto the ground beside him. Apprehension clogging her throat, she followed, her steps barely making a sound on the pine needles and grass, the tiny bits of gravel.

Her brain tried to catch up to what her eyes had seen. Rafe tugged her to the side of the cabin, put her behind him.

For a moment, his hand flat against the curve of her hip to hold her to him, he listened.

Trying to do the same, Kit pressed close against his back but heard only the roar of her heartbeat in her ears. Sweat slicked her palms. She clutched a handful of Rafe's T-shirt as her stomach dropped with a sickening thud. Alexander's men were here and they had Liz.

His mind racing for a plan, Rafe turned, took Kit's hand. It was cold in his. Her face was pale, her eyes wide with shock.

"Kit," he whispered. "Look at me."

She focused on his eyes, and he squeezed her hand. "Good. Listen. We don't have much time. Tony's trying to get them all out of the cabin, into the open. He told them the disks were in town."

"Why?"

"If he can get them outside, we have a chance to get to Liz."

The shock disappeared from her eyes, and she gripped his hand. "What do we do?"

He released her, pulled his gun from the small of his back. "I've got fifteen shots here. You have to help me."

She nodded, still pale.

"Get behind the cabin. Stay out of the line of fire."

"But I want to help."

"This is the best way. You're not armed. You can't protect yourself unless you stay covered. I'm going to try to get to Liz, send her your way."

"Okay."

He touched her cheek. "Are you all right?"

"Yes, yes." Her eyes were dark with worry, but clear.

He walked her to the back of the cabin. "No matter what, stay covered until this is over."

Her hand tightened on his arm. "Be careful, Rafe. Please."

"I will. We've got plans after this, right?" He smiled at her.

"Right."

He allowed himself one hard kiss, then edged along the

back of the cabin to the opposite corner. After one glance to make sure Kit was safely in place behind the cabin, he eased up the side, thumbing off the safety on his Magnum.

He hoped Kit would do as he'd asked. If there was any chance of her being in the line of fire, he wouldn't be able to think of anything except her.

He looked back once more. She was there, waved at him. Thank goodness, she was playing it smart. She'd stay out of sight.

Putting all other thoughts out of his mind, he slipped silently to the front corner of the cabin. Tony stood at the bottom of the steps, still talking.

He had managed to get Alexander's goons and Liz outside. The two men, Baldy and a tall, skinny guy, matched the descriptions Rafe had gotten after the murder of Eddie Sanchez. Skinny stood on the middle step, his gun trained on Tony. On the top step, the bald guy held Liz in front of him like a shield, one arm hooked around her neck.

The lush body and tight black outfit were classic Liz, but Rafe had to look twice at the blond bob. He'd only ever seen her natural medium brown hair. She whimpered, her body pulled awkwardly into Baldy's.

When the man shifted, Rafe finally saw his gun, drilling into the underside of Liz's jaw.

"I'm telling you, those disks are in town." Tony's features were drawn, his gaze trained on the man who held Liz. "If I don't pick them up by tomorrow, they'll be mailed to the police."

Good thinking, Tony, Rafe commended silently, trying to gauge his chances of taking Baldy from this angle. *Move down another step, you slimeball.*

Skinny stepped to the ground, backed Tony into the hood of his pickup.

The bald guy pushed Liz down another step, then another. Rafe moved silently toward them.

"Leon!" the skinny man called. "There's a car back there. Behind this truck. It's a black Cor—"

Rafe jammed his gun into Leon's back. "Let her go."

The man tried to angle away from Rafe, put Liz squarely in front of him, but she dug in her heels. He yelled, "Junior!"

The skinny guy whirled, aimed at Liz. Tony roared and tackled him from behind. The gun went off. Liz screamed.

"Drop, Liz!" Rafe ordered. "Fold your legs and drop!"

His words were drowned out by more gunfire from Junior. He and Tony grappled on the ground, fighting for the gun.

Rafe yelled at Liz again, and she folded her legs. Caught off balance, Leon stumbled, slamming her into the railing.

"Tony!" she screamed. "Tony!"

Junior's gun fired again. Leon draped himself over Liz like plastic wrap. Rafe couldn't get a clear shot.

Tony yelped, frantically pushing at the man on top of him. Scrambling off the ground, he stumbled and bumped into the grill of his truck. "He's dead. Crap, he's dead."

Before Rafe could tell Tony to get Junior's gun, Leon exploded into motion. He pushed Liz to the side and bolted down the steps.

She tumbled over the rail, on top of Rafe. Under the sudden impact, he stumbled. They both fell to the ground.

A shot rang out. Tony cursed. Another shot cracked the air. By the time Rafe moved Liz and darted under the steps, Tony had taken cover behind the passenger side of his truck and was shooting at Leon, who had ducked behind a tree.

Tony fired twice more, peeked over the hood to squeeze the trigger again. This time, the gun clicked, empty.

Leon popped out from behind his tree, shot twice. Tony dove for the ground.

Liz screamed, getting to her feet.

"Stay down, damn it, Liz!" Rafe motioned her down. "Get behind the cabin. Kit's waiting for you."

Another shot sounded. Liz dropped to the ground, stayed low.

Rafe fired in Leon's direction. Saw the guy's shoulder and fired again.

He had no shots to waste, no chance of getting to his other clip in the car.

Leon fired. One shot whizzed past Rafe's ear; another buried itself in the wood over his head. The other man bolted into the woods.

Rafe squeezed off two shots, aiming for Leon's leg. The man tripped, then fell. Silence descended so abruptly that Rafe's ears still buzzed from the sound of gunfire. The acrid smell of gunpowder burned the air. Rafe blinked. Had he hit the guy? If so, where?

After several moments with no movement from either Leon or Junior, Rafe moved carefully from under the steps. He knelt to check Junior. No pulse.

"Tony, you okay?"

"Yes." The man's voice shook as he rose slowly from behind the truck.

"Check on Kit and Liz." Rafe started toward the edge of the woods where Leon had fallen.

Rafe could see him, sprawled facedown on a bed of pine needles, unmoving. Keeping his gun at the ready in case Leon planned to surprise him, Rafe stood over the man. No twitch of a leg, no moan, nothing.

He knelt, placed two fingers on the guy's neck. He was dead.

He'd never killed anyone before. A wave of shock rolled over him, left his chest clammy. His hands unsteady, he thumbed on his safety.

For a moment, he dragged in deep breaths, trying to ease

the greasy knot in the pit of his stomach. Sweat trickled down the side of his face, and he wiped it away.

He turned and started toward the cabin, looking for Kit's dark head. Just as he slid his gun into the small of his back, he reached the steps and saw her on the ground hugging Liz. Tony was on his knees beside them.

"They're both dead." Rafe strode toward them. Liz was exactly where he'd last seen her.

He had a clear view of them. Kit wasn't hugging Liz; she was *holding* her. Liz's head lolled against Kit's breast, her eyes closed. Tears streaked Tony's dusty face.

Dread fisted in Rafe's gut. "Kit?"

He didn't even realize he'd moved, but he found himself in front of her. Dropping to his knees, he gripped her shoulder. "Are you okay?"

She looked at him with anguished eyes. "Liz. She's been shot."

Fear a cold fist around his heart, Rafe moved quickly. He and Tony carried Liz carefully to Tony's truck while Kit raced ahead to open the door and slide in. They situated Liz so her head rested in Kit's lap, her feet across Tony's.

Outwardly, Rafe was calm, but inside his nerves were a hot, jumbled mess. How close had those wild shots come to Kit?

He followed them to the highway, calling an ambulance on the way. Then, he called Kit to let her know he'd meet her at the hospital. He stayed behind to wait on the police and tell them what had happened. The sight of Liz's blood on Kit's blouse had given him a brutal jolt, made him admit what he'd been trying to deny ever since she'd come back into his life.

He needed to see her, make sure she was okay, but it was three hours before he finally reached the San Luis Valley Regional Medical Center in Alamosa where the paramedics had transported Liz. Due to the nature of her wound, they thought she needed a larger facility.

Rafe had given his statement to the local police and stood by Kit as she and Tony had both given theirs. Rafe had told her the cops were willing to wait until her sister was out of surgery, but she wanted it finished.

Just as the police officers left, a young, blond doctor with kind blue eyes stepped out of the operating room. He introduced himself as Dr. Warren and told them that the bullet had nicked Liz's spleen. He'd performed a splenectomy, which had progressed fine, and they'd removed the bullet, but she had a pneumothorax—a hole in the lining of the lung—in her right chest from an errant central IV line placed by an intern.

He recommended a three- or four-day stay in the ICU to recover from the blood loss and the puncture. Just after Liz was taken to ICU, Harv Foley arrived. Rafe hadn't seen the man in over ten years. He was still built like a linebacker, broad but lean.

His big build was a perfect match for his big heart. Not a speck of gray shone in Harv's dark hair. Kit's hair was the same mink shade as her dad's, and both Harv's daughters had inherited the man's stubborn chin. Rafe was pleased to learn that Kit had called her father, glad she was letting him and Harv help her.

The days passed in a blur of bad coffee, medical updates, an emotional seesaw of alarm and relief. Kit looked worried but never became overtly upset. Just handled everything in her cool way and looked increasingly gaunt.

By the fourth day, Liz was recovering well enough from the surgery and a mild pneumonia that they removed her chest tube and transferred her to a regular floor. Despite Liz's progress and the fact that Harv was there, Rafe was the only one who could convince Kit to leave her sister's room. To eat, walk the grounds, to shower. But he couldn't get her to sleep, not even when he told her he'd sit with her. He marveled at her composure, her stamina.

He loved her. The words he hadn't let himself think for so long burned in his chest. He'd always loved her, figured he always would. Wanted to get her off somewhere alone and tell her, *show* her, but now wasn't the time.

She remained upbeat with him, steady with Liz. Still, Rafe sensed a subtle shift in her. Because of all the medical commotion, dealing with the police and Tony's parole officer and getting updates from his uncle on the case against Alexander, Rafe couldn't put his finger on what it was about Kit that seemed off. It was something he should recognize, but he didn't.

She was incredible, so strong. He'd always recognized her independence, but he'd never given her credit for what those years of self-sufficiency had done for her. She was the core of her family, made all the decisions for Liz's care, made sure her father slept and ate regularly, even when she didn't. She never wavered.

Until the fourth day. Even though it was just past sunrise, Rafe had been outside talking to his uncle on the cell phone. The FBI was waiting on Tony and his evidence. Once they had it, they planned to pick up Steve Alexander, whose name was really Sergio Alejandro. Rafe should get home, but Kit needed him.

He walked in from the parking lot, the tap of his boots echoing on the tiled lobby floor. The doctors had pronounced Liz out of danger early this morning and said she looked as if she would recover fine, but they wanted to keep her at least two more days. He didn't want to leave Kit but didn't see how he could put it off after tomorrow.

Pride filled him that she had, at last, allowed herself to lean on him. Even so, she hadn't cried, had barely expressed anger or shock over what had happened to Liz.

She'd been as steady as the mountains surrounding them. Spending time with Liz, time with him.

Needing to stretch his legs, he took the stairs rather than the elevator to the third floor. As he stepped into the empty corridor, the squeaking clank of a food cart drew his attention. An orderly and the cart he wheeled disappeared around the corner toward the nurses' station.

Rafe saw Kit leaning against the wall ahead of him. She stood with her back to him. Her shoulders looked slight in the coral linen cropped top she wore; the slim capri pants hung loosely on her. Had she lost weight?

She was so still that for a moment he thought she might be asleep, then she reached up to rub her temple.

He walked toward her, glad she was taking a minute for herself. Her legs buckled and she wobbled suddenly. He lunged for her.

"Whoa, darlin'." He caught her arm, steadied her. "You okay?"

"Yes." She smiled brightly, but it looked like a desperate effort to him. Exhaustion lined her pale face. Dark circles ringed her eyes.

"You need to get some rest."

"I'm fine. I took a nap a while ago."

"Liar," he said softly, gathering her to him. He spotted a couple of empty chairs in a small alcove by the stairs and walked her there.

Sitting in one of them, he pulled her onto his lap.

"Rafe," she protested. "I'm fine."

"Just sit here for a minute." He pressed her head to his chest. She looked like she was about to crumble. "Everything's under control. Your dad's with Liz. Just take a minute."

"I want to be with you, talk to you."

"We can be together right here, like this. Why don't you close your eyes for a while?"

"I don't want to sleep. I'm doing all right," she said stiffly.

"Yes, you are." He moved one hand up and down her arm, kneaded the nape of her neck, trying to loosen the tension he felt bowing her back and shoulders.

She stared at him for a moment, the determination in her eyes giving way to resignation. Finally, she rested her head on his shoulder and let out a deep breath.

"You're one amazing woman, Kit Foley, and you've been strong for everyone, but it's okay if you want to cry. Or get mad. There's only you and me here."

"I'm fine, really." She sat up, flashed a smile that didn't quite reach her eyes. "Did I already thank you?"

"About a hundred times." Breathing in the soft shampoo scent of her hair, he narrowed his eyes. There it was again, that fleeting sense that something was wrong.

"She was almost out of danger," Kit murmured. "Almost."

He tipped her chin up with one knuckle. "You know that wasn't your fault. You're not blaming yourself."

"No. I know it wasn't my fault. And I know it wasn't your bullet. I know where it came from. You were firing away from her."

"Good." He was glad she'd reached the same conclusion as the local police. He would die if he thought she believed it had been his shot that wounded her sister.

He resumed his soft massage of her neck.

"Tell me what your uncle said." She began to relax against him. "Tell me what the FBI is doing about Alexander."

With all that had been going on, Rafe hadn't given her the latest developments on the case. She did know that Tony had been remanded into his custody by Oklahoma's parole board, and now that Liz had been pronounced out of danger, Rafe would take Tony home.

"The FBI is ready for Tony. They've been surveilling Alexander and are ready to move as soon as they see what Tony has on him."

"What's his real name?" She stifled a yawn.

"Sergio Alejandro."

"Is he really connected to the mob, like Liz said?"

"Looks that way. He changed his name to Steve Alexander so that his Mafia ties to a Boston crime family wouldn't be so apparent. He moved into the Midwest five years ago and has been taking over territory in Oklahoma and Texas."

She let out a deep breath. "Wow. My sister can pick them, can't she?"

He chuckled, kneading the tight muscles in her shoulders.

"Thanks for the massage." She pressed a kiss to his lips.

He pulled her closer, but didn't deepen the kiss. He wanted more, but not here, not now.

"I'm good to sit with my sister for another hour. Then maybe you and I can eat or something? I can give you an hour, too."

"I wish you'd sleep. I'll sit with you."

"I don't want to spend our time together sleeping. I want to be with you." She kissed him again, then stood.

He rose, watching her thoughtfully as she turned and walked around the corner, her footsteps echoing on the tile.

I can give you an hour, too.

Her words bounced back, triggered that sense of something being off. Mentally flipping through the last few days, he realized how she'd gone between him and her sister with the measured regularity of a metronome. Like a checklist. Time with Liz. Time with Rafe.

It all fell into place then. His own words to her at the creek crashed back.

I want all of you. You can't commit to me. I was always there for you. You were never there for me.

She'd sworn she was ready to walk away from the responsibility of her sister—*for him.* Sworn that she wanted to choose him over that responsibility.

He'd thought by being here with her, he was supporting her. But when she should've been focused solely on Liz, she felt she had to give him equal time. She was choosing between them, and she didn't have to.

He groaned, sank down in the chair. What had he done? Now he could see how she carefully rationed her time between them like the last bit of water in a drought.

If he hadn't come upon her in the hallway, he doubted he would have seen the toll this was taking on her. She certainly wouldn't have knowingly shown him. Between the time she spent with Liz and the time she spent with him, she was driving herself into the ground.

He had told himself he was helping her, told himself that *he* was the only reason she hadn't fallen apart. That *he* was the one who kept her on an even keel. What a lie. His presence presented a distraction for her, a demand on her time she didn't need. This constant juggling act wasn't what he wanted for her, this feeling that she had to choose between him and her family. Was this how it would always be?

A sharp pain pushed up under his ribs. He couldn't watch her tear herself apart like this. He didn't want that for her, for either of them. Even though he might lose her forever, he knew what he had to do.

Chapter 14

"**Y**ou're leaving? But why?" Kit demanded, panic flashing across her delicate features.

A little over an hour later, they once again stood in the small alcove by the stairwell.

Rafe had asked her to walk with him. It had taken him four flights of stairs and a cup of coffee to get the nerve to tell her.

"It's time. I need to take Tony back." He wasn't sure how to say it, but he knew he had to tell her. The timing couldn't be worse, but he couldn't stand by and watch her drive herself into the ground. He knew she would never say anything about it, much less admit it. It was up to him.

"I thought you could stay until tomorrow." She searched his face intently. "I thought Tony's parole officer wasn't expecting you back until tomorrow night."

She paused, indecision flitting through her eyes, then she said, "I can go with you."

"No." He hadn't expected that, hated the dilemma he read on her face. "It's too soon. Liz can't leave—"

"My dad can stay."

"That would kill you, Kit." He took her empty coffee cup, walked to the wall and tossed both his and hers into the trash bin.

"But what about us?" She followed him. Mid-morning sun streamed through the window, picking out the blue in her eyes. "I don't want to give up. I want this to work. I can make it work."

He turned, gently cupped her shoulders. "You're killing yourself trying to make it work," he said quietly. "Right now, you shouldn't be worrying about anyone except Liz."

She stiffened. "Are you saying you've decided you don't want me?"

"No. I haven't decided anything like that."

"Then what—" Her chin lifted. "You don't trust me. Maybe you never will. At least be honest."

"I am, Kit." He shook her gently, looked straight into her eyes. "Listen to me. I want you in my life. If I didn't know that before yesterday, I for damn sure know it now, but not like this. When I told you I wanted total commitment from you, I didn't mean for you to tear yourself apart trying to make everyone happy."

She pulled away, her eyes stormy with denial. "You don't have to leave."

"I think that's the best way I can help." To keep from reaching for her, he rubbed at the lash of muscles in his neck. "You shouldn't have to feel torn between me and Liz. You should be focused on her."

"I am."

"Can't you see what you're doing? An hour with her. An hour with me."

She blinked, then shook her head. "That's compromise."

"No, Kit. I never should've given you an ultimatum that

day at the creek. It wasn't fair.'' And now it had jumped up to bite him.

"This isn't right, either.'' She paced to the stairwell door, then back, worrying her lower lip with her teeth.

"When I said I wanted your total commitment, I didn't mean this.''

"What *did* you mean then?''

"I never thought it would come to this, Kit. You shouldn't have to choose, darlin'.''

"I don't feel that I am,'' she said hotly, planting her hands on her hips.

He gave her a level look until finally she tossed her hands in the air. "Okay, maybe I do feel that way right now, but Liz is healing. What about afterward?''

"I have a lot of things I want to say to you. *Need* to say. But now's not the time. You've got too much on your shoulders right now. When Liz gets better, we'll talk. There's time enough for that then.''

The anger drained out of her face; she looked at him sadly. "Will we be able to work this out?''

"I hope so.''

Pain and uncertainty welled in her eyes. "Can I call you?''

"You'd better.'' He pulled her to him, folded his arms around her. He wanted to be there for her, but instead he was in the way.

Her arms tightened around him. He closed his eyes, savoring the feel of her against him, the silk of her hair tickling his jaw. He didn't want to go, but he couldn't stay. "How much longer do you think they'll keep Liz?''

"Maybe only another two more days. I'll let you know.''

He drew back, searched her face. "I'm counting on it.''

She nodded, the vulnerability in her liquid blue eyes tugging at his heart. He dipped his head, covered her mouth with his. She rose on tiptoe, fitting herself tight against him.

Her hand moved to his nape, pressed him closer. The kiss was long and slow, making it even more difficult to stick to his decision. He ached clear down to his toes.

She made a little sound and pulled away. Tears glimmered in her eyes. "I wish you weren't going."

"Me, too." That was the hell of it.

She framed his face in her hands. "We'll talk?"

"Definitely." Pulling her to him, he took her mouth again, devouring this time, intense and savage, frantic to possess her. She kissed him back with a desperation that clutched at his heart.

"You've got my cell phone number." He breathed against her forehead when they came up for air.

"Yes."

"And my office and home numbers."

"I'll call. Be careful. Will you let me know when you get home?"

"Yes."

He walked her to Liz's room then kissed her goodbye, wondering if it was for the last time. As he and Tony drove away from the hospital, Rafe couldn't help feeling as if he were leaving his future in that third-floor room. But he couldn't make her choose, even if it meant they would never be together.

Rafe had left her. Two hours later, Kit stood at the single window in Liz's hospital room, wanting to hope, but uncertain. Her hands curled over the sill, painted the same misty green as the room. The walls, along with coordinating pastel floral prints above and across from Liz's bed, were chosen to soothe, but they couldn't calm Kit's churning thoughts.

Rafe had said they would talk after this, that he had things to tell her. She hoped he wanted to tell her he loved her, that he wanted another chance with her, just as she did with him. But what if he wanted to tell her just the opposite?

Was this the end? He thought she couldn't balance her time between him and her family. She thought she'd been doing a pretty darn good job of it. The concern, the regret in his eyes as he'd said goodbye told her he really believed leaving was the best thing.

Eyes burning with fatigue, she stared at the sunshine, remembering the pain in his face, the possessive promise in his kiss. Had he been right about her? She could see how she had been meticulous about making sure neither Rafe nor Liz felt slighted or ignored.

"Why don't you go after him?" Liz said from her bed.

Kit turned to look at her sister, still not used to the sight of Liz's short, platinum hair. This was the first time Liz had ever said anything about a man she'd dated. "We have things to work out."

"Who doesn't." She fluttered a well-manicured hand, somehow managing to look demure in her hospital gown.

"She has a point, Kit." Harv Foley walked into the private room and eased down onto Liz's bed as he pulled a small carton of chocolate ice cream out of a brown paper bag.

Liz's eyes, the exact blue of their father's, lit up. She took the spoon from him and waggled it at Kit as she opened the carton. "You shouldn't give up on Rafe."

Kit looked at her in surprise. Liz sounded more mature than she had ever heard.

"Rafe made you happy, Kit. You two are a good fit. He's a doll, plus one gorgeous hunk of man. I don't know exactly what happened when you guys broke up, but if it was because of me—"

"It wasn't. Not exactly anyway."

"That plus your guilt over Mom's death?"

"Have you been going to a psychiatrist?" she joked.

"Ha. I just know how you are, and I know you've always felt responsible for what happened."

"How could I not?" She frowned. "If it weren't for me, you would've had your real mother, Liz."

"You lost your mother, too, sis. I see it as a loss, not something you stole from me. You didn't *take* Mom from me and you weren't responsible for her death. It could easily have been Dad or I in the car with her that day."

"Or no one," Harv put in quietly, his round features somber.

Liz nodded. "And for the record, I've never felt deprived of anything. I had you, didn't I?"

"Oh, Liz." Kit's eyes burned. "Thank you."

"Thank *you*." Her sister reached out and took her hand. "That's a lifetime of thank-yous, by the way."

Amazed and touched, Kit sank down on the corner of Liz's bed. "Why haven't we ever talked like this before?"

Liz popped another spoonful of ice cream into her mouth. "You were too busy telling me what to do all the time."

"Oh, please." She noted how much improved her sister's color looked today; her blue eyes sparkled like they had before that awful confrontation at the cabin. "So, if I told you things were going to be different from now on, that I had to take a more hands-off approach to your life, you'd understand?" She hoped Liz said yes because it was really time. "I'm not abandoning you, sis. I just think we both need to stand on our own two feet."

"I hear that," her sister said without missing a beat.

Kit's eyes widened. "Do you know what I'm saying? No more getting you out of jams, no more intervention in your jobs or with your boyfriends."

"I get it, sis. And I'm glad. I love you, Kit, but I know it's time for you to live your own life." She sobered. "It's time for you to stop trying to save me from mine."

"Oh, Liz, I've never felt that way." Kit reached out and took her sister's hand.

"I know." Liz's gaze was thoughtful. "But it's true all the same. I know what I've cost you. I know what a pain I've been and I'm going to do better."

Had her sister ever been so reflective? So decisive? "Wow."

Harv Foley took both their hands in his big ones. "You girls have been the other's whole world for a long time. Your mom would be the first to tell you to build one of your own."

Kit smiled, noting the pride and encouragement she saw shining in his eyes. He'd been telling her the same thing for years, but since she had said goodbye to Rafe today, the words took on new meaning, opened the door to a freedom she wanted to experience.

"You're right, Dad." Kit wasn't exactly sure how to proceed, but she would figure it out.

Liz gave her a level look. "I appreciate how you're always there for me, Kit, but you're the one who just told me things were going to be different. Get on with it."

"I will. As soon as we get you home and settled—"

"I can do all that, hon," her dad said. "Liz is coming along. Dr. Warren said she'll probably be discharged in a couple of days."

"But won't you need—"

"Dad and I can manage just fine." Liz capped her ice cream and dropped the empty carton into the wastebasket beside her bed.

"Are you sure?" The possibility of leaving before her sister had never entered Kit's mind. Her heart urged her to go after Rafe, but what if he needed more time? What if *she* did?

"We'd like you to stay," Liz said, "but we don't *need* you. Rafe does. And you need him. Go."

A flurry of excitement tickled her belly. Kit folded her arms, stared at her dad, then her sister. "When did you get so smart and mature?"

"When I was being chased by those two jerks from Alexander." Liz's reminder sobered them all for a moment, then she smiled. "Dad can stay. I'm out of danger."

"She is," Harv added.

"But you can't say the same about you and Rafe."

Harv chuckled. "Go, Dr. Liz."

"If it were me," Liz said, "I'd be getting to Tony as fast as I could. In fact, when I get out of here, that's what I'm going to do. Not that you asked, but I think you should do whatever you have to in order to keep Rafe this time."

Really liking this side of her sister, Kit grinned. "Got any ideas?"

"Something to do with naked and whipped cream?"

"Liz!" She burst out laughing. "That's really more your speed."

"I don't know. You might like it."

"I don't know about the whipped cream, but you should definitely go, honey." Harv Foley hugged her. "Definitely."

Rafe had said he wanted to talk. She did, too. And she should go now. Today. Find out if this was the end or a new beginning.

She was afraid to go, but as she recalled the promise she'd made to him, she was more afraid not to.

Rafe should've been sleeping like a rock, but he wasn't. He was restless and edgy after the twelve-hour drive from Colorado, and his eyes wouldn't close. Even four hours after arriving home, he kept seeing the panic, the rejection on Kit's face, kept wondering how badly he'd hurt her. How badly he'd screwed up.

As he'd promised, he'd called the hospital to tell her he

had made it home all right. Liz had answered, saying Kit couldn't come to the phone. She'd said she would give Kit his message and have her call, but she still hadn't.

He got out of bed, went outside, shoved off his briefs and dove into the pool. The June night wrapped around him, warm and silky.

He'd thought he was doing the right thing by leaving, but if so, why did his chest feel ripped open? Why did it feel so wrong?

He stretched into his stroke, recalling the night he'd seen Kit out here, swimming for all she was worth. That same frustration pushed him now. He sliced through the water, going another length of the pool.

Due to the late hour, he had dropped Tony at Uncle Wayne's house rather than the office. The FBI had arranged to put their chief witness against Alexander in protective custody until the trial was over. Even now, they were making their move on the mafioso to put the man behind bars.

Rafe turned, swam to the far end of the pool, his strokes smooth and measured. His uncle had informed him the FBI had found evidence that Alexander had killed a man in Kansas and run another woman off the road, just like he had Liz.

The case was wrapped up except for the trial, in which Tony and Liz would testify. Rafe would be called on to identify pictures of the two men who had tailed him and Kit, tried to kill them at the cabin.

Surfacing at the far end of the pool, he stared at the black velvet sky.

Kit. His heart ached. He wanted to know she was all right, wanted to make love with her and try to erase the memory of the last time they'd been together. That night when he'd taken her body, then withdrawn from her.

He turned and swam toward the opposite end of the pool, his muscles finally unknotting.

Today's long drive had given him more than enough time to think. He loved her, had always loved her. And he decided he'd rather have her any way he could get her than not at all.

He was ready to take a chance on them. No more ultimatums. They'd find a compromise, even if it meant seeing her only when her family wasn't in crisis mode.

Cutting through the water, he pictured her face, her eyes soft and liquid blue, her sweet lips. He'd call her again. *Now.*

He reached the middle of the pool, stood and ran a hand over his wet face. That's when he saw her.

Standing only feet from him, water barely covering her breasts. Her bare breasts, her bare body.

His heart kicked against his ribs. He blinked. Wondering if his mind had transferred her image to the water, he moved forward. "Kit?"

"Hi," she said shyly. Pulling her bottom lip between her teeth, she stared at him uncertainly, then stepped toward him. Moonlight shimmered on the water, washed her in liquid silver.

"You're here." He couldn't believe it. He sounded hoarse and winded and stupid.

"Yes. My dad drove me up to take a flight out of Colorado Springs." She stopped inches away, water rippling around her, reaching out to lap against his chest. Her eyes were deep with longing and need and something he wasn't sure he could name.

"What happened?"

"I told you I wanted to be with you and I meant it."

"You should be with Liz."

"This is why I didn't call and tell you I was coming." She reached him, ran her hand up his chest. "I didn't want you trying to talk me out of it."

He grabbed her wrist, as much to make a point as to

steady himself. "You don't have to give them up for me. I don't want that."

"I'm not. I thought about what you said. You were right. I was making a choice when I didn't have to."

He felt the heat of her under the water, the shadow touch of her body. Sensation hummed through him. He was already hard, his pulse throbbing. "I don't want you to feel torn. We'll work something out. I want you in my life, Kit."

She pressed closer, her breasts nudging his chest and driving his pulse into orbit. "I want that, too. I need you, Rafe."

His hand slid up her arm, trailed over her bare, velvety shoulder. "Was I an idiot? Want me to beg first?"

"You were right." She dropped a kiss on his chest, looked up at him. "And I want you to make *me* beg."

"Damn," he said hoarsely. He pulled her to him, his hands curving over her bottom. She lifted herself and wrapped her legs around him.

Her center pulsed hot against his erection. "I hate what happened last time, darlin'. I want to make that up to you."

"I like the sound of that." She shifted, pressing hard against him.

"You're really here." He moved his hand between them, found her sleek and hot as he slid one finger inside.

She clenched tight around him, her hands moving down to stroke his erection. "I want to feel you. All of you."

Her hand slid the length of him, and he nearly lost it right then. Using all his willpower, he held back, concentrating on watching the pleasure flash across her features. They touched each other, stroked. Harder, longer. Sinuous movements that took him to the edge, had her breath shuddering out.

She whispered his name, her gaze locked with his. "Now, Rafe. I don't want to wait any longer."

Somehow, he made it to the side of the pool, braced his back against the concrete edge so it wouldn't scratch her and held her as she slid down on him, slow and steady.

A perfect fit.

She kissed him, sank down to take him even deeper.

His hands moved to her breasts. He plucked gently at her nipples and curved his hands around her fullness. "I love you, Kit Foley."

Her eyes darkened; love and trust shone in the smoky depths. "I love you, too. I thought you'd never say that to me again."

"I never stopped. I never will."

"Me, either."

For the first time, they made love with absolute trust. No shackles from the past, no concerns other than the rhythm of her body meeting his.

He watched her eyes, and the lock on his heart fell away. He gave to her the way he had before, completely, without inhibition. The way he thought he never would again. And she did the same, for the first time meeting him with full abandon. The stroke of his body into hers felt familiar, but there was a freshness, a deeper comprehension of years lost, regret buried that made their lovemaking seem new.

The same awe that had locked his breath in his lungs the first time he'd taken her still held him. He saw that same wonder in her eyes and a vulnerability shining out at him that he knew he'd never take for granted. They'd paid a ten-year price to get here.

They moved slowly together, making it last. Committing to each other with every stroke, every whispered word. Giving, taking, reaching.

His hands flexed on her hips. He remembered this, the velvet feel of her skin beneath him, the delicate woman taste of her. As she came apart in his arms, he stored away the memory of moonlight gliding down her arched neck.

The sultry steadiness of her eyes on his, the way her hands urged him on, the open surrender in her face. And when he finally let himself go, they climaxed together.

She moaned deep in her throat, and he kissed her, catching his name as she clenched around him. Tight and deep and complete.

Breathing hard, he braced his weak body against the concrete. She sagged against him, her heart thundering in time with his.

She peeked at him through spiky lashes. "Miss me?"

He grinned and kissed her, hungry for the taste of her, making up for lost time.

She looped her arms around his neck. "I want to stay."

"My bed's big enough for two."

"No, I mean I want to stay always." Uncertainty slid into her eyes. "With you."

He stilled, feeling goose bumps rise on her back as the water cooled around them. "Are you sure?"

She touched his face. "Absolutely."

He lifted her so her eyes were level with his. "We'll figure out a way to make it work."

She kissed him, then pulled away breathless and tugged him with her to the steps. She got out of the pool, picked up a towel and wrapped it sarong-style around herself. As he climbed out behind her, she handed him one.

He held her close as they walked into the house. On the cool tile of the foyer, she stopped, lifted serious eyes to his.

"Hey." His hand moved up to caress her bare shoulder.

She licked her lips nervously. There was a mix of doubt and excitement on her face.

"Kit?"

"I'm ready to commit one hundred percent. I want you to know that."

"I know, darlin'."

She took a deep breath; words tumbled out. "On my way from the airport, I called a Realtor about putting my house on the market. Dad is with Liz, and she'll be living with him until she's healed. And then...she's on her own."

Stunned at this gesture to show her commitment to him, to *them,* he smiled. His heart ached from sheer pleasure. "No maybes about it. This time we're gonna make it work."

"You think you're up for it?"

"You bet I am." Grinning, he pulled her with him down the hallway and into his bedroom.

He opened his closet. One side was empty.

She turned, questions in her eyes.

He moved to his six-drawer dresser and opened the three drawers on the right. All empty. He turned. "I wanted you to know you have a place here with me. Whenever you want."

A smile curved her gorgeous lips. Her eyes glowed at him. How had he ever lived without that? "Are you sure?"

"You bet your life."

"Oh, I was hoping you'd say that," she breathed.

He took her in his arms. "I trust you, Kit. I want you to know that. I was coming in to call you when you gave me that little surprise outside."

"I love you, Rafe Blackstock. And I'm never leaving again."

His chest swelling with love, Rafe took the one step he'd sworn never to take again. "Wanna prove it?"

"What do you mean?"

"Marry me."

She stared at him, disbelief in her eyes. For an instant, his heart stopped.

Then she threw her arms around his neck and pulled his

head down for a kiss. "There's no getting out of it now, Blackstock. I'm here to stay."

"It's about time," he said before covering her mouth with his.

* * * * *

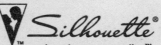

The unforgettable sequel to *Iron Lace*

RISING TIDES

Aurore Gerritsen left clear instructions: Her will is to be read over a four-day period at her summer cottage on a small Louisiana island. Those who don't stay will forfeit their inheritance. With a vast fortune at stake, no one will take that risk. Suspicions rise as Aurore's lawyer dispenses small bequests, each designed to expose the matriarch's well-kept secrets. Family loyalties are jeopardized and shocking new alliances are formed. But with a savage hurricane approaching, tensions reach a dangerous climax. And the very survival of Aurore's heirs is threatened.

EMILIE RICHARDS

"...a multi-layered plot, vivid descriptions, and a keen sense of time and place."
—*Library Journal*

Available the first week of January 2002 wherever paperbacks are sold!

MIRA®

Silhouette®

INTIMATE MOMENTS™

In February 2002

MERLINE LOVELACE

brings back
the men—and women—of

CODE NAME: DANGER

Beginning with
HOT AS ICE, IM #1129
He was frozen in time! And she was
just the woman to thaw him out....

Follow the adventures and loves of the
members of the Omega Agency.
Because love is a risky business.

Also look for

DANGEROUS TO HOLD in February 2002
DANGEROUS TO KNOW in July 2002

to see where **CODE NAME: DANGER** began

Available at your favorite retail outlet.

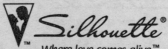
Silhouette®
Where love comes alive™

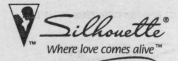

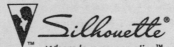